The burning of Arbor, and the hat Evangeline Clarion, but the fiery ar survived the flames of fanaticism a ..... gallery of her dreams with the help of her familiar and coven. As Eva wades into life as the director of the Manor Arts and high priestess of the Witches of Arbor coven, her conflicted heart struggles to choose between two loves—the dashing mercurial Alexander and the alluring ethereal beauty Celeste.

When Arbor's affable new mayor hires an architecture firm run by a dangerously stunning mother-daughter duo with their own unique magic and an old score to settle to oversee the downtown's reconstruction, chaos descends upon the vulnerable community, and the Witches of Arbor are once again called upon to protect those who spurn them. Yet jealousy, vengeance, and an unforeseen foe with a ravenous hunger for power brings Eva to her knees. With the aid of her familiar, coven, a few unexpected allies, and the magic within her, Eva must reconcile her heart and summon the power to rise again.

Arbor's Descent

The Witches of Arbor, Book Two

J.L Brown

A NineStar Press Publication

www.ninestarpress.com

Arbor's Descent

Printed in the USA

ISBN: 978-1-64890-381-6

First Edition, September, 2021

Also available in eBook, ISBN: 978-1-64890-380-9

CONTENT WARNING:

This book contains sexually explicit content, which may only be suitable for mature readers. Depictions of violence, alcohol and drug use, animal cruelty (inferred), and sexual assault (fade to black, recounted).

To all those who embrace their inner WITCH.

Chapter One

SAMHAIN

Most women would have felt like a queen. All the trappings were there—
the castle on a hill, the regal gown, the morbid curiosity of the general
populace. Not to mention the dashing gentleman of the castle wrapped
around one arm, and my ethereal companion curled around the other.
But I wasn't "most women," and I was no queen. I was a witch, a witch
who had triumphed despite my Arbor neighbors' best efforts to kill me.

They said we were evil. They tried to burn me. They killed my
friends. But I survived. And though I grieved for those who did not, I
refused to defile their memories by enacting revenge, however tempting.

*Because I'm not evil, despite the prevailing notion in Arbor. A little
wicked, possibly. Naughty, most definitely. But not evil.*

Instead of seeking vengeance, my coven and I chose a more
diplomatic path and invited the residents of Arbor to the Samhain grand
opening of the Manor Arts, our new gallery within Morgan Manor. This
magnificent walled estate sat high atop Red Hill and overlooked the once
bucolic village. I'd taken up residence due to my late nights in the gallery
and the manor's inordinate number of empty bedrooms. And of course,
proximity to the master of the house. The estate belonged to Alexander
Morgan, the man—the witch—whose fury and anguish had leveled half of
downtown. Not that his involvement in the fire was common knowledge.
The newspapers attributed the burning of Arbor to a severe summer
lightning storm. They weren't wrong.

Ignorant of Alexander's guilt, and relentlessly nosy, the people of
Arbor accepted our invitation. My small-town neighbors arrived in jewels

and formalwear, costumes and masks, on the most magical of nights when the veil between worlds thinned and the spirits of the dead laced the breeze. The very people who tried to stop me from opening a gallery in their town, joined the avant-garde and the elite of the arts community to celebrate the Manor Arts grand opening. They gathered for an event hosted by a witch they'd strapped to an elder tree pyre and set aflame only four months before. The witch who lived through it. The witch who saved them from Alexander's magical retribution.

Our newly enshrined coven, the Witches of Arbor, orchestrated every nuance of the evening to evoke wonder and trepidation. We had the perfect backdrop. The manor's rough, gray stone battlements and turrets and bell tower loomed haunted and menacing. Torch-light and jack-o'-lanterns, carved with ancient Samhain symbols, cast the shadows of those assembled across the sprawling lawn.

No matter where the eye landed, it fell upon the frightening, the seductive, the wildly unique. An army of black-clad servers, each with raven hair and candy apple lips, wove through the crowd with hors d'oeuvres and champagne. Jugglers with ghoulishly painted faces launched onyx orbs and flaming swords into the air. A buxom steampunk illusionist levitated six inches from the ground, beckoning the curious and brave to witness her other-worldly feats. Tattooed and pierced contortionists twisted themselves into impossible positions. A lone violinist conjured an eerily enthralling melody; her instrument tuned in nature's pristine pitch. Like the pied piper, she lured our awed visitors through the manor's gaping entrance. With nervous steps, they shuffled toward the alabaster hearth blazing beyond the iron doors.

Many of our guests, particularly the artists and their ilk, appreciated our theatrical welcome. It was Halloween, after all. But the Arbor residents were terrified. Their anxious hearts beat against their chests as if they were passing through the gates of hell itself.

Their dread swelled like static on my skin, and despite my repudiations of evil, I reveled in their fear.

The entire town would have burnt if I hadn't stepped in. Calling down the rain hadn't been enough to extinguish Alexander's flames. I drew water from the fucking Ausable River to put out the fire. These lemmings would have been scorched to the earth if I hadn't summoned the water. I saved them, even after they tried to kill me. Even after they stoned Celeste and burned Adelaide. They should fall to their knees, thank me for sparing them, and beg my forgiveness!

A strong, calming hand settled on my shoulder and halted my mental rant. I gazed up into dark eyes veiled by cascading chestnut waves. Clad in an impeccably cut tuxedo, Alexander towered over my left side, a mischievous twinge of humor playing on his lips.

He leaned down close to my ear. "You're right, *streghetta mia*—high priestess. The Arbor mundane should bow before you. You saved them from me, and in the process, you saved me from myself. I, too, bow before you. Evangeline Clarion, you *are* my queen." He winked before bending deeply at the waist.

Celeste, my elegant companion entwined around my right arm, snorted, and rolled her eyes.

"Don't tease me." I pinched Alexander's arm. Hard. "And stay out of my head, you ass. If I want you to know something, I'll tell you myself." I glared up at him.

"I'll tell you this," I continued indignantly. "I wouldn't want to be a queen. Being a queen isn't any better than being a witch. We both have power and can influence matters great and small. Sure, queens bask in riches, but witches have ways of obtaining wealth too, and we aren't bound to conform to society's stringent rules. We're free."

Celeste gave my arm an encouraging squeeze.

"Queens get beheaded, but witches get burned," Alexander countered, his jaw clenched tight.

"Only the naughty ones." A memory of the wise and brazen Adelaide Good, my late high priestess and mentor, passed through my mind. "And thanks to the Goddess, I don't have to worry about their fire. While I may not be evil, I *am* the wickedest witch in town."

Celeste clapped her hand over her mouth to check her mirth. "Like you said, Alexander, she is the high priestess."

Ignoring Celeste, Alexander lifted himself up to his full height, pulled back his shoulders, and glowered down at me. "You're not getting too big for those tiny britches, are you, *Your Highness*?" He couldn't fully hide the smile that threatened his stern face.

"Look who's talking, Zeus," I needled. "Or is it Hades?"

"You're hilarious, Persephone." He teased me with his words, but there was nothing playful in the look he gave me as he brushed a stray lock of hair away from my cheek. "But are you sure you're okay? I know crowds make you anxious. It's understandable, especially after..." He averted his eyes.

"You mean, especially after a mob of my neighbors cheered for my death and set me and Adelaide on fire?" I snorted. "Yeh, I'm ok."

Alexander growled low in his throat and ran his thumb along my cheek. "I won't let anything happen to you ever again."

"Oh, please." I waved the notion aside. "If you don't let anything happen, nothing will ever happen. And that is fucking boring."

"I think I heard that in *Finding Dory*," Celeste noted dryly.

"I'm just saying I can cover for you if you want to duck out. Hell, I'll shut the whole thing down. Say the word."

I shook my head with an indulgent smile and sighed.

"Alexander, I'm fine. Great, actually." I raised my hand and ran it along his stubbled jaw. I locked my eyes with his. "This is the biggest night of my life. This is all I've ever wanted, and it's more spectacular than anything I ever imagined. I worked my ass off for this. We all have. And I'm glad Arbor is here to see it. I want them to know they didn't stop me. I have no intention of hiding."

"Damn right." Celeste nodded emphatically.

"Then I'll be right here to make sure you're safe." Alexander dropped a kiss on my head, then turned his attention to the festivities and their looming dangers.

He still hadn't learned. He didn't have to be my great protector. I didn't need that. I didn't want it.

What do I want? I asked myself the question for the millionth time. I turned instinctively to the other-worldly vision curled at my right side, the evening's Mistress of Ceremonies, Celeste Galehorn.

Dear Goddess, she is luminous.

Her white-blonde hair cascaded sleek as silk over her delicate, naked shoulders, flushed pink from adrenaline and the crisp autumn air. Her deep-blue dress sparkled as if the night sky draped across her skin. Bright starlight on the outside, Celeste had a darker center. Yet her darkness sprang from loving me.

And how she suffered for it! Oh, what that fanatical hoard did to Celeste, laughing and cheering as they stoned her.

I cringed at the memory of the pitiful, repentant Wiccan upon her knees with her arms spread wide. She'd welcomed the rocky onslaught as penance for her lies and manipulation. She'd thrown herself at Arbor's mercy for my sake, her sacrifice an act of atonement. And love.

And I loved her too. I couldn't deny it. She'd hurt me, to be sure. Though that wound no longer festered, it hadn't fully healed. Her deception, and the spell she never thought would work, had driven a wedge between me and Alexander. I hadn't completely forgiven her for it. Yet a profound connection existed between me and Celeste, and it went beyond our physical attraction. Since the burning of Arbor, after the loss of my high priestess and one of my familiars, throughout the creation of the Manor Arts and planning the grand opening, Celeste grounded me. She grieved with me. She comforted me. And when it was time to get down to business, Celeste worked beside me, ever encouraging. She kept me focused and organized, but her humor and easy-going banter ensured I never took things—especially myself—too seriously. Every day, she proved herself to be savvy, smart, and ever loyal in business, coven affairs, and the trials of daily life.

I rely on her. Too much.

Celeste had enchanted me with her soul *and* body. I was captivated by the capable elegance of her hands, her lustrous golden-spun hair, the sultry lines of her clavicle, her long royal neck, the tender, ticklish spot behind her ear, and the way her eyes crinkled when she thought of something mischievous. And her lips. Once upon a time, I tasted those lips. It had been months, yet I could almost feel her eager mouth on mine, and her hands greedily roaming my body.

I ache for her, and still, I keep her at arm's length. How much longer can I resist?

As if she sensed the pull of my heart, Celeste leveled me with a wicked grin that lit me like a match. Her very presence teased my senses, and the twinkle in her eyes told me she knew it.

Fuck it. I want them both. I don't want to choose. That was the truth of it. And shielding these thoughts seemed a fruitless endeavor. If Alexander insisted on snooping around in my head, he'd have to deal with hearing things he didn't like.

A shadow of grief crossed Alexander's face. He had, indeed, been listening.

"I won't apologize. I love you both," I said matter-of-factly.

"Well, we love you too, sweetheart." Celeste batted coquettish lashes, ignorant of my mental deliberations. "Now, if we're finished flirting, we need to mingle."

Alexander, Celeste, and I swept into the manor's grand foyer to schmooze and socialize with our guests. We took up residence at the landing of the wide sweeping marbled staircase, just below the ruby chandelier that hung from the intersection of vaulted archways above. The staircase had become a centralized location from which the crowd divided, heading either to the dining room, music room, library, or the grand gallery—the location of the Manor Arts. We nodded polite hellos and thank-you-for-comings like bobbleheads at a tennis match. We shook hands with the barista from the café that burned down and the bank lady who declined my business loan, both coincidentally wearing Queen of Hearts costumes. We made small talk with members of the town council and the planning board, all dressed to the nines. And we chatted with a tipsy gaggle of Arbor public school teachers, thrilled to simply be out amongst adults.

As the crowd flowed around us, a name found its way to my ears. Once it did, I heard it everywhere—Harcourt. The name leapt out at me from passing conversations and taunted me with indecipherable context. Who was this Harcourt? I couldn't catch a snippet of explanation. It was a mystery, and I found myself eager to learn more.

An elderly woman in a fraying black dinner dress approached Alexander. "Mr. Morgan," she began, taking his hand in her paper-thin, frail one. "I want to thank you for continuing your great-grandfather Cain's Halloween tradition. I used to help him organize the festivities every year, you know. Cain and I and a few of our other friends would brainstorm new themes and decoration ideas. We had a good time of things. It was a nice way for the townsfolk to satisfy their curiosity about the manor and for Cain to give back to the community he loved." She broke out of her memories and looked clearly at Alexander. "And your generous donation toward the rebuilding of our precious downtown is commendable. Your great-grandfather would be so proud." She patted his cheek kindly. "With you and the Harcourts at the helm, we'll have downtown ship-shape in no time, I'm sure."

That name!

"The Harcourts, ma'am?" Alexander's puzzled expression mimicked my own confusion. He hated being out of the loop with downtown issues. This was a defensive posture, given the events of four months prior, but Alexander also worried over the spending of his money.

"Yes, of course." The old woman squinted up at Alexander. "The architects Mayor Riddle hired to spearhead the rebuild efforts. I'm surprised you haven't heard. You'll be working closely with them, I'm sure. But you shouldn't worry. They are magnificent. Everybody says so."

Magnificent architects. That's what all the fuss is about? So much for mystery.

Alexander's features hardened. Despite the Morgan fortune bankrolling the rebuild, Mayor Riddle had made this decision without his input—a deliberate slight.

He and the mayor need to have a hell of a chat.

After the elderly woman moved along, Alexander grumbled. "I need some food and a goddamned drink."

Celeste glowed. "Bring it."

"Yes. Wine. Now. Please," I agreed.

Because alcohol never screwed anything up. Way to make good choices.

We entered the dining room. Rich, tantalizing aromas drew me to the long buffet tables overflowing with autumn delicacies. I salivated as I gazed enthralled at the decadent spread. From the butternut squash casserole with apples and raisins, and the squid ink striped linguine with kalamata olive pesto, to the baked pumpkin mousse and chocolate crepes with concord grape compote, the master was on his game in the kitchen.

The executive chef of Morgan Manor, Gregory Massey, hailed from an ancient line of Druids, belonged to the Witches of Arbor coven, and had been one of my closest friends since infancy. He also happened to be an absolute culinary master. His Samhain menu was a work of art. Each dish looked and smelled enticing. Based on Alexander's reactions, they tasted wonderful as well.

I marveled at the way Gregory's magic worked through him, in the manipulation of the senses. However, hiring Chef Massey to run our kitchen constituted a scandal in and of itself.

As if we don't revel in such things.

As renowned as Gregory was for his culinary ability, his notoriety laid elsewhere. An impressively built, imposing figure of a man, Gregory's fondness for sex magic and his reputation as an intensely satiating lover ensured his infamy far and wide. Although he and I had never done the deed, I'd seen Gregory sky-clad on more than one occasion, and his generous endowments led me to believe he'd have no trouble pleasuring the most demanding connoisseur.

"The man's outdone himself. After this, he'll be asking for a raise," Alexander mumbled between bites of food. "And I'm giving him one. The guy's a fucking pro." He licked pesto from his fingers.

Celeste shook her head and raised her eyes heavenward as if pleading the Goddess for patience. Then she led me by the hand to a small table near a cluster of jazz musicians taking a break between sets.

"Be a dear, Alexander, and get us drinks," she called over her shoulder. "Rest up. The night is young, and your heels are high." She smiled at me brightly and then headed off to mingle.

While Alexander busied himself at the wine table and Celeste made friends with the entertainers, I closed my eyes. A heavy sadness settled over me. The festivities and celebration felt bittersweet without my Goddess-mother Maggie there to share it with me. I missed her terribly. We'd texted earlier that afternoon, and I knew she and her partner Ayo were with me in spirit. As were my mother, my high priestess, and my familiar. At least Maggie and Ayo would be coming home. A cascading parade of images rushed before my mind's eye of all the Goddess's blessings, making me feel like a spoiled brat for lingering over so much grief on such a celebratory evening.

Alexander jolted me from my meditations with a lingering kiss perilously close to being inappropriate for polite company. Left tingling and off-kilter, I shot a furtive glance at Celeste to gauge her reaction. She pointedly ignored us. A quiet defiance lifted her chin, and her boldness inflamed me. I imagined taking her in my arms and kissing her until her knees buckled. But Alexander recalled my attention with a devilish smile—the smile he saved just for me.

I think I heard my ovaries orgasm. What the fuck am I supposed to do with the two of them? I groaned. *I can think of so many intriguing possibilities, but what am I actually supposed to do?*

A twinge of guilt squeezed my heart. I squashed the feeling as soon as it wriggled into my brain. Guilt, in this instance, was a waste of an emotion. We were all adults. I loved them both. Our situation was that simple and that complicated.

Alexander handed me a heavily etched goblet of Barolo. "For the lady." He offered an exaggerated bow.

"Many thanks, kind sir." I took a sip, savoring the refined mouthful, and sighed with pleasure.

At the sound of my contentment, Celeste whipped around and leveled me with predatory eyes. She was a cat, and I was the tasty morsel of a mouse.

Unlike the mouse, I wouldn't mind being devoured by this particular kitty. I could almost hear her purr.

Alexander stepped between us, interrupting Celeste's silent seduction. "A Pinot Gris for the *Wiccan*."

He spat "Wiccan" like a dirty word, as if practicing the craft without the benefit of innate magic was frivolous or ineffective. He, of all people, should have known better. It was an ugly way to behave, considering Alexander had only recently come into his powers. And he hadn't practiced the craft before that either. His nasty side pissed me off.

But Celeste lifted an artless grin and accepted the wine with grace. She waited until Alexander turned to hiss.

When the musicians ended a song a minute later, Celeste raised her glass high.

"I'd like to propose a toast." Her voice rung out clear as crystal. "To this evening's hostess – artist, classical musician, fashion designer, proud director of the Manor Arts, and *the* Witch of Arbor – Evangeline Clarion! To Eva!"

I could kill her.

"To Evangeline!" Alexander cheered. The crowd around us chimed in, lifting their glasses high.

I could kill them all...if I don't die of embarrassment first.

"You're lucky I love you," I muttered through gritted teeth.

"Back at ya." Celeste winked.

My cheeks flamed red hot. Sweat broke out along my forehead and the nape of my neck. I dipped into a quick, awkward curtsey.

"Thank you. Thanks," I muttered. Avoiding eye contact, I trained my gaze on the intricacies of the marble pattern on the floor.

While I appreciated Celeste's gesture, the crowd's praise turned my stomach. Their adulation seemed too good to be true. I didn't trust it. The image of Stephen King's *Carrie* doused in blood popped into my head. It seemed like a warning.

Chapter Two

As the musicians struck up another tune, an enthusiastic male voice let out a final cheer. I turned with Alexander and Celeste to find a mousy-brown haired man of average height dressed as the Phantom of the Opera, flanked by two heart-stopping brunettes—neither costumed as the Phantom's Christine Daae. They couldn't have pulled off her sweetness if they'd tried. They hadn't a demure bone in their bodies. These two wore black. Swathes of supple fabric poured like inky midnight over the lush, hourglass figure of the older woman, flowing around her feet like ripples in a stream. Rubies dripped from her ears and neck. With her dark hair and eyes, and cherry lips, she resembled a red carpet Morticia Adams. The younger woman wore black leather—from her corseted bustier and metal-studded jacket to her sleek, ass-hugging pants and fuck-me pumps. Her dark eyes glared behind heavy liner and thick black lashes. She had a blood-red mouth with small, silver hoops piercing her bottom lip. Tattoos covered her neck and clavicle and wrists.

And more beneath the leather, I'm sure.

Were they in costume or did they dress like this on a regular basis? Either way, they were both smoking hot. And dangerous.

Are they sisters, maybe? Mother and daughter, probably. Witches, yes. And no.

Their magic radiated a distinctive vibration I couldn't identify. As I racked my brain, this vibration, like a magical signature, bloomed into an icy chill around the women. It wafted and spread like cheap air freshener, so potent, I gagged. It dissipated, leaving behind the faintest scent of a riverside in winter.

Alexander and Celeste didn't seem to notice a thing.

What the hell is that? Did these women direct that sickly icy bloom at me, or does it follow them around naturally? Are they saying hello? Or identifying themselves as witches? Are they showing off? Trying to intimidate me? What do they want? Who the hell are these women? Questions, questions...

The Phantom of the Opera bowed and removed his mask to reveal Arbor's newly elected mayor, Jonathan Riddle.

"Hi everybody! This is incredible." He spoke like a kid at his first trip to an amusement park, wide-eyed and a wee bit nauseous. "Thanks for the invite. This place is spectacular."

From our brief acquaintance, I'd found Mayor Riddle to be a good man, although more than a little milk-toast. Yet he seemed smart, kind, and eager to work with everyone, even witches, to heal and rebuild Arbor. The fact that he appeared so harmless and easy-going got folks on board with his agenda.

"Thank you so much for coming tonight, Mayor. Welcome to the Manor Arts." I did my best to appear a gracious hostess. "I hope you're enjoying yourself."

"I sure am. The music, the art... I'm beyond excited about what a space like this means for our town. The Manor Arts enhances the culture of the Arbor community. And it's so much fun!" He spoke with lively charm. "I mean, there's a girl levitating outside. And those contortionists!"

"Things are just getting warmed up, Mayor," Celeste chimed in. "Stick around. The real debauchery begins after midnight." She shimmied her shoulders and raised her glass aloft as Adelaide had been known to do. "Cheers."

Celeste's cheek took the hokey mayor by surprise. "Yes, well, ah, you should all be extraordinarily proud." He stammered, cleared his throat, and turned to address Alexander. "*Your* altruism in particular, Mr. Morgan, is to be commended. Your generosity and stewardship are truly benevolent. Would you mind if we took a selfie over here by the—"

The mayor's words stalled in his throat as the women flanking him stepped forward in unison. Neither spoke but stood stoic.

Blood rushed to Riddle's cheeks. "Please, excuse my rudeness. Allow me to introduce Vivian Harcourt and her daughter Eris."

These are the magnificent architects? Vivian and Eris. Energetic chaos. Just what we need.

Riddle avoided Alexander's eyes. "Harcourt Architecture is spearheading the downtown rebuild."

"Is it now?" Alexander cocked an eyebrow.

"Ladies,"—Riddle ignored the comment and addressed the imposing women— "these are our hosts, Evangeline Clarion, Celeste Galehorn, and of course, Alexander Morgan, Arbor's generous benefactor."

Eris gave Alexander a cursory once-over, and ignored me altogether, choosing to eyeball Celeste.

Vivian offered me a quick sharp nod. "Charmed." Replacing her icy expression with a warm one, she greeted my companions with enthusiasm. "Celeste, dear, pleasure to make your acquaintance. And Alexander, our new colleague! How lovely to *finally* meet you." Vivian batted her lashes at Alexander.

"Finally?" Amusement lit Alexander's eyes, and he folded his powerful arms across his chest.

"Well, yes. Mayor Riddle sings your praises. I've been imagining you as quite the hero." Vivian swooned like a Southern belle, fanning herself.

After a lightning-quick glance at me, Alexander leveled Vivian with a come-hither stare, and ran his hand through his long thick hair. "You've been imagining me, have you?"

I almost spat out my wine. *What the fuck! Is he flirting?*

"I have," Vivian replied without hesitation. "And I've been impatient to make the acquaintance of the formidable creature the mayor's been describing. His compliments haven't been exaggerated. Not a fault to be had." She swept covetous eyes over Alexander's impressive physique.

It's official. I hate Vivian Harcourt.

"I have faults enough, Ms. Harcourt. According to Evangeline, I'm the devil." Alexander flashed me a roguish grin.

"I have no doubt your dark side and I would get along well." Vivian struck a casually seductive pose.

"If only I hadn't already found my Persephone." Alexander pulled me in close, wrapped his powerful arms tightly around me, and claimed me with a deep passionate kiss that left no doubt of his affections.

Sweet Goddess! I don't think I can feel my toes.

"Well, all righty then." Mayor Riddle fumbled his words. "Ms. Clarion is extraordinary, of course." He addressed me directly. "I read on your handy event program that you've got a number of exhibitions tonight."

Still recovering from Alexander's knee-weakening kiss, I took a moment to collect my wits. "I do, yes. My sketches and paintings are on display in the gallery, and I've launched my first fashion design collection. I'll be performing in the back gardens at eleven to cap off the evening—cello and violin. My designs will accompany the music."

"Evangeline also made the costume our friend Ethan Massey, the program director, is wearing tonight," Alexander bragged.

"How...marvelous." An undercurrent of loathing poisoned Vivian's words. "Don't you agree, Eris? Isn't Ms. Clarion simply marvelous?"

"A modern-day Renaissance woman." Eris made it sound like an insult.

What's with these women? Why the hostility?

"But what about Ms. Galehorn?" Eris leveled Celeste with a come-hither look. "Surely a woman of such beauty hides a myriad of talents."

I sensed Eris's pheromones wafting out and enveloping Celeste. It made me nauseous. And murderous.

I officially hate Eris Harcourt too.

"Celeste makes jewelry and works with stones and crystals," I said, keen to do my own bragging, which had the added benefit of diverting my rage. "Her creations are nearly as stunning as she is. And we couldn't have opened the Manor Arts without her—certainly not so efficiently or with so much style. She is invaluable."

"It's true. This whole place would crumble without me." Celeste deadpanned.

"I don't doubt it." Eris leered. "You seem like a woman who can get the job done. We value that in my line of work."

Once again, I caught the distinct note of Eris's pheromones in the air. I clenched my fists tight to keep from throwing out my hands and incinerating the leather-clad tramp.

"How...kind." The corners of Celeste's mouth quivered, and she stepped closer to my side.

It wasn't like her to be skittish, and that raised my ire as much as anything else.

Who do these hags think they are?

I gritted my teeth. The grand opening of my art gallery seemed a poor time to tell off Arbor's new celebrities. But this insult wouldn't go unanswered. After a few calming breaths, my equilibrium returned.

"Yes, well, yes," Mayor Riddle stuttered again. "The Manor Arts is an impressive artistic and philanthropic undertaking, and you three should be commended."

"Thank you, Mayor. It's a team effort," I said, relieved the conversation had turned in a safer direction. "The manor staff, the crew in the kitchen, the artists and entertainers—"

"And eight witches," Celeste added with a cheeky grin, sounding more like herself. "Druid and fae and Romani..."

"Oh my!" I laughed. But the laugh died in my throat. The mayor and the Harcourts' expressions teetered somewhere between bewilderment and disgust.

"We've got a hell of a team," Alexander jumped in. "But the coven is its core with Eva as its high priestess, of course. The manor's executive chef, Gregory Massey, is a wizard in the kitchen. Do not leave here without tasting his food. His brother Ethan, the program director I mentioned, put together an unparalleled collection of entertainment. He's also an exceptional dancer in a renowned New York City ensemble. Then there's the remarkable Loveridge brothers. Nicolae is our eminently persuasive marketing and ad man. We stole him from his swanky position on the West Coast. His brother Luca handles tech and security when he's not moonlighting as a model down in the city. Apparently, he's huge on Instagram."

"Even my great aunt Mia, who's visiting from Italy, lent her talents. She creates the most delicate bobbin lace, in the Milanese style, with elegant open designs and elaborately braided patterns. She turns her lace into shawls and table runners and curtains. I set her display up in the library. I thought the quiet reverence of the space would encourage guests to appreciate the detail involved in fashioning such refinement. We couldn't have done this without each one of them."

Riddle looked at Alexander with a slack jaw and quizzical eye. Vivian was positively enamored.

"It isn't every day you hear a man speak so passionately about lace." The she-devil inched closer to Alexander, fawning over him shamelessly.

"You're lucky to have such talented friends." Eris leered greedily at Celeste.

"I am." *Damn right, bitch, and they're mine. And I've had enough of you two.*

Alexander hid a grin, once again reading my thoughts when he shouldn't be. With a knowing look, he attempted to adjust the trajectory of the conversation. "Any news on Chief Harrison?" he asked Riddle. "I heard he took a turn for the worst last night."

"If you would excuse us," Vivian interrupted. "It's been a pleasure. We'll see each other soon, but for now, I think my daughter and I are going to do some exploring."

Eris stepped forward and brazenly took Celeste's hand. "Show us the best haunts?"

Celeste cringed and withdrew from Eris's grasp. "Sorry, no. It's a big night, and I'm celebrating with friends."

Eris flinched, clearly unaccustomed to rejection. A piercing, vengeful look crossed her face for the briefest moment, but she maintained her cool detached appearance.

"Plus," Celeste continued, "Alexander knows the place *almost* as well as I do." She looked up at Alexander with impish mischief.

Alexander had visited the manor rarely as a child and had spent even less time there as an adult. Celeste had lived and worked at Morgan Manor as a maid long before Alexander took possession of the estate, back when Old Man Cain was still alive. And Celeste's family had been employees of the manor for years before her. She knew every nook and cranny of the sprawling estate.

"I'm sure he'd love to show you ladies around," Celeste said sweetly.

She does enjoy provoking him. I shook my head at her disapprovingly.

"What a luscious suggestion." Vivian practically salivated.

Oh, hell no.

"Another time, it would be an honor to give you and your daughter a tour of the manor, but as Celeste said, this is a big night for us." He looked down at me with pride.

"Yes, of course. You're a busy man," Vivian replied coolly. "But I will take you up on the offer another time." She swept her billowing gown around her, deigning to nod at me as she turned to leave. "Ms. Clarion. It's been a pleasure."

Unable to engage in any more pleasantries with the woman, I only nodded.

Eris didn't bother with polite farewells but turned on her heel and followed her mother.

As the mayor and Alexander turned their attention toward each other, I pulled Celeste in close. "I don't trust them," I blurted in a whisper, hoping Riddle couldn't hear.

"Me either. They're shady. I'll find out what I can," Celeste answered in a hushed tone. Her lips lingered an inch away until she brushed them across my cheek ever so faintly. Her breath feathered against my skin, and I shuddered. "I'll see you in a bit, sweetheart."

The moment I thought she'd pull away, Celeste lowered her mouth to mine and kissed me. Then she said a quick goodbye to the gentlemen and sauntered off to play detective.

She kissed me! And she tastes the same, like magic and honey. I touched my lips to savor the memory.

Just as Celeste had done earlier, Alexander ignored my affectionate interaction with a proud, raised chin and meaningful silence. He kept his focus on the mayor.

"So...Harrison?" Alexander asked Mayor Riddle.

"I'm sorry, what's that?" Riddle said, foggy. His focus had been on my kiss with Celeste, and he clearly needed time to adjust to this change in topic.

Alexander planted his hands on his hips in frustration. I couldn't help but chuckle.

He looks like a superhero.

"The chief. How's he doing?" Irritation laced his words. Alexander expected to be kept abreast on matters of importance in town.

"Right, of course." The mayor heaved an overdramatic sigh and slumped his shoulders. "He's not looking good." He shook a dejected head. "He's a fighter, but that was his third heart attack this year. I'm going to have to bring on new brass. I don't have a choice. Not really. Even if Harrison recovers, God willing, he'll be in no shape to keep up with the workload. He's going to hate me for it, but it's the right thing to do."

"Any thoughts on a replacement?" Alexander asked.

"We need a fresh face. Pulling up someone from the ranks is a bad idea. Too much of the old-school mentality lingering that I'd like to keep out of the leadership position."

"You have any leads?" Alexander pressed.

"Nothing solid. I'm looking for someone competent who can also shake this place up a bit. You know, drag the Arbor PD into the twenty-first century."

Good luck with that.

"Please, send Chief Harrison my good wishes," I said. "He's always been kind to me and mine, and I hate that he's struggling."

"If only Maggie was around," Alexander said offhanded.

"You know my Goddess-mother, Magdalena Maramma, don't you, Mayor?" I asked. When he nodded, I went on. "She's a skilled healer. She'd know if anything could be done. At least she could ease his suffering. I'll call her in the morning and give her an update on the chief's condition."

"I don't think—" Riddle began.

"Maggie's a miracle worker. I've seen her in action." Alexander persisted, a warm glow brightening his dark features. "And she's as humble as she is gifted. If anyone could help, it would be Maggie."

The blood rushed from the mayor's face, leaving his skin gray and ashen. "Maggie, yes, I..." He wiped his mouth with the back of his hand. "She's extraordinary. The fact that her reputation as a good and kind woman remains intact, despite being a known witch, does her credit given the prejudices in town."

"We know all about Arbor's prejudices, Mayor," I said with a steel spine.

"Yes, of course you do." Riddle cleared his throat. "Maggie's away for a while, doing some extensive travelling. I understand she's on the West Coast these days. And I heard she planned on being out of town for at least another year or more. It's not necessary to call and trouble her with things she can't control. I'm sure the chief's doctors have things well in hand."

"I suppose." The mayor's knowledge of Maggie and her whereabouts disconcerted me. "I mean, yes, she is travelling. Busy as a bee as always. Maggie and her partner are involved in charity work of sorts, bringing comfort and aid to witches across the country." Dancing around the truth seemed easier than explaining that my Goddess-mother was fulfilling the prophecy of Aradia, the foundress of Italian Stregheria witchcraft.

"Honorable work, I'm sure. You say she's got a partner?" Riddle fidgeted with the Phantom of the Opera mask in his hands. "I hadn't heard that. Well, it's a relief, I guess, that she's not travelling alone. Much safer."

"Without a doubt. Maggie's in good hands. Ayo Kehinde is a successful and...*electrifying* African American lawyer. She commands a crowd and takes no crap. Maggie's perfectly safe with Ayo around."

"How...reassuring. Yes, well, I uh, that's good. But, as I said, no need to bother her. Chief Harrison's being well looked after. His sister is by his side, and the nuns from Saint Francis have been tending to him. But I will tell him you said hello. Now I, uh, shouldn't take up any more of your time. I'll let you two return to your evening."

But Alexander grabbed Riddle's arm before he could walk away. "Excuse me, Mayor. I believe you and I need to discuss the rebuild," he snapped.

"Meet me in my office tomorrow morning then. Tonight's a time for celebrating. Enjoy it while you can." Mayor Riddle raised his Phantom mask to his face and melted away into the crowd.

There is something peculiar about that man, but he's a hell of a lot better than the last mayor. I curled my arm around Alexander's.

He squeezed me tight and kissed the top of my head. "That's not a high bar, streghetta mia. The last mayor was a despotic murderous psychopath."

I turned and looked up into Alexander's dark eyes. "Darling."

"Yes." He smiled wickedly.

"Stay the fuck out of my head." I stormed out of the dining room.

Chapter Three

Alexander followed.

"I can't believe you were flirting with her."

"What?" he yelled over the din of the crowd around us.

"Never mind," I sighed, frustrated. "You think we'll make it in time for the concert?" I hollered up to him as we squeezed through the bottleneck of humanity converging in the foyer. The music room was only fifty feet away, but wading through the density of flesh to get there strained my patience. My agitation grew as the crowds thickened, and their scrutinizing faces pressed in closer and closer.

"We better. Ethan's been raving about this singer from Ireland for weeks," Alexander called over the clamor of voices. "He'll hex us with fae flu if we don't make it."

Despite my anxiety, I chuckled. "No, fae flu's not his style. He'd steal the *toradh* from our food—all the nutritional properties. That way he could watch us starve to death." I shook my head with a grin. "He can be a twisted fucker sometimes. And I love him for it."

By the time I realized that I'd shouted all of that in the middle of the foyer, it was too late. Everyone around us stopped and stared.

Alexander barked out a laugh. "That's one way to cut through the crowd." He grabbed my hand and used his dazzling smile and a modicum of brute force to maneuver a path through the gawking throng.

Sweet relief washed over me as we made it into the cavernous marble music room. Orderly rows of gold, cane-back chairs filled the space. Eager music lovers occupied every chair but the three nearest the stage beside Ethan. The fae flaunted his magic with his silver hair, gently pointed ears, and gossamer wings. The hair and ears were his; the wings were mine.

Alexander and I made our way down the center aisle, the symbolism not lost on either of us. Muttered whispers rolled through the crowd as we passed, and we bobbed our heads and smiled politely. We shook hands with the ensemble musicians before taking our seats.

I leaned in close to the winged fae beside me and whispered in his ear, "You do look marvelous."

"Yes. I know," he said pointedly. "Where's Celeste? I saved her a seat too."

"She's trailing a couple new witches in town."

"New witches? Let me guess...the Harcourts? They're all the boys are talking about. They're all *anyone* is talking about, besides you, of course. I need details." He scanned the stage. "Later. Shit, I almost forgot. Celia Bartoli can't sing with you tonight. She backed out five minutes ago. But no worries." He cut me off before I could fly off the handle. "Siobhan Quinn says she can fill in. She knows the piece. She'll be perfect. You'll see."

Before I could respond, Ethan stepped lithely to the microphone, his elaborate costume eliciting an excited murmur from the crowd. He raised his hands above his head and snapped. At his signal, the lights dimmed low. As the room darkened, hundreds of tiny white candles appeared, hovering overhead. Gasps reverberated through the room.

"Welcome, ladies and gentlemen. My name is Ethan Massey. I am the program director here at the Manor Arts, and I'd like to welcome you to Concerts at the Manor. This concert series will regularly feature premiere talent in a variety of genres.

"For our inaugural performance, I'd like to invite you on a journey to the land of my birth, Ireland." Ethan's voice grew softer. "Imagine with me, if you will, tranquil lakes and winding rivers, storm-swept coastlines, rugged mountain cliffs, rolling hills in forty shades of green, and enchanted forests where fairies dance and magic lives most freely. Tonight, you will hear the magical music of this land. We begin with an ancient Celtic folk song: music performed by the Clover Ensemble and sung by the incomparable Siobhan Quinn."

Ethan lifted onto the tips of his toes, pinpoint straight and without a wobble. Then he swept a dramatic hand toward the ensemble before going into a spin. He spun faster and faster until he stopped on a dime, no longer dressed in tights and wings but in a tuxedo and white tie.

"Enjoy!" he said.

The crowd went wild.

After taking a bow and blowing a few kisses, Ethan took his seat beside me. "I like to keep things dignified."

The room fell to a hush with the entrance of the striking Siobhan Quinn. Like the rest of the crowd, I was instantly enchanted.

She wore a graceful sheer white tea length with crystalline embroidery that glittered in all the right places. Reflecting magically in her icy dress, Siobhan's ears, neck, and wrists sparkled with emeralds. Even her eyes glittered green in the candlelight. Flaming red hair framed her elegantly freckled face. And when she leveled me with her brilliance, I thought *I* might burst into flame.

Apparently, Alexander thought I might too because he nudged me with his elbow.

I snickered and muttered, "Sorry," but my focus never wavered from the sparkler on the stage.

That is, until the music room disappeared. In its place, a fantastical forest sprang up around us, green and verdant. In the distance, through a break in the trees, lush fields and rolling hills were visible.

Ethan brought us to Ireland. Or rather, he brought Ireland to us.

The illusion, a glamour of Ethan's creation, was detectable if you knew what to look for—a slight shimmer along the edges of the trees— but it confused and frightened the crowd. They gasped and clutched their chests as they searched for the music room in the forest around them. But Siobhan calmly raised her arms and offered a reassuring smile. The crowd's anxiety eased.

Siobhan cupped her hands together at her diaphragm, and her song lilted soft and dreamy as if filtered through a great misty expanse. Siobhan sang with an easy, gentle passion, so delicately complex that it bordered on supernatural. She led us along, her voice like a leash of finely spun golden filament. A harmonium, cello, guitar, and violin joined in her mesmerizing Celtic journey. Throughout the performance, panoramic Irish landscapes surrounded the stunned audience.

Siobhan turned toward me and captured my eyes as she sang the last few bars. And the music room returned.

I wiped a tear from my cheek and joined the audience in their thunderous ovation.

Alexander leaned down close. "It's time to go," he said in a clipped monotone.

"Just a minute." I turned to congratulate Ethan.

Yet as I hugged the daring fae and we promised to talk later about the Harcourts, it became clear that Alexander remained on high alert. His body stiff, his eyes darted around the room and shot to me every few seconds. He glared as I approached Siobhan Quinn. Given Alexander's obvious concern, I planned to say a quick thanks and be on my way, but Siobhan took my hands and kissed me on both cheeks.

"I'm tickled pink to sing for you, Eva Clarion. You and your gallery are all anyone is talking about, and I see why." She beamed down at me.

"You—were—" I tried to speak but found myself struck dumb.

She let loose a deep, hearty laugh that surprised me given the lightness of her song.

"Thank you. I'm thrilled to be here. It's exciting to see women succeeding in small town America."

"Yes—you're..." *What are words?*

"You're very welcome here. We're happy you've joined us," Alexander said, stepping in. "Now, I hate to rush things along, but we really must go. We'll let you return to the show."

"Yes, of course. I look forward to our performance tonight, Eva Clarion." Siobhan said my name with a sparkle in her emerald eyes. She brushed her warm lips against the back of my hands before rejoining the musicians.

Alexander took my elbow and hurried us down the center aisle and out into the grand foyer. His eyes darted, frantic as he scanned for dangers. Although a scowl contorted his handsome face, I couldn't help but smile, elated. Whether due to his unfailing over-protection, or my supreme confidence in my powers, I didn't dwell on threats to my safety.

How could I when such agreeable thoughts as that of Siobhan Quinn occupied my mind?

Ethan was right. She's going to be perfect for Bach's Erbarme dich. *So striking and emotive. How can anyone not be enraptured? I can't wait to play with her!*

Anticipation and something approaching real joy bubbled up inside me. But I was a damned fool. I'd allowed myself to become distracted, and this lapse in judgement immediately caught up with me.

Alexander and I had just passed in front of the blazing alabaster fireplace on our way to the gallery when my blood turned to ice. My joints and muscles locked up. My eyes became fixed in their sockets. My body froze from within, completely paralyzing me. My immobilization lasted no more than five seconds. The fire inside me thawed the hex, and the protection spell I'd cast over myself that morning shielded me from the full force of it. But I'd gotten a taste of the magic. As the hex's residual energy faded, I recognized it. Recalling Ethan's Irish folktales, I realized what we were dealing with.

Before I could explain anything to Alexander, however, he *rescued* me. Incapable of restraining his heroism, Alexander swept me into his arms. He dropped his lips to my forehead.

"I've got you." He rushed me out the front doors and down the manor steps. He charged across the lawn, in the opposite direction of the crowds, to the edge of a thick forest rimmed in orange-tipped sugar maple trees. He set me gently on my feet.

"Are you ok? Fuck, it's got to be fifteen degrees colder under these trees." Alexander feverishly inspected me for injury. Finding me unharmed, he shrugged off his tuxedo jacket and wrapped it around my shoulders. "Take this."

"I'm fine." I swatted his hands away. "You didn't have to go all he-man on me. At least a dozen people watched you carry me out of the manor. They're going to think something's wrong."

Alexander glowered. "Well, isn't it? Why'd you freeze up? You scared the shit out of me."

"Magic."

"The air's thick with it; it's Samhain." He shrugged.

"No, it's more than that. I wonder, what do you think of our new acquaintances, Vivian and Eris Harcourt? Did you sense anything from them? Hear anything?"

"I didn't dip into their thoughts if that's what you're asking. What I sensed from them, more than anything, was predatory desperation. But I'm used to mothers flinging themselves and their daughters at me. I'm rich. It goes with the territory."

"Lovely," I groaned. "Anything else?"

"Yeh, they don't like you. That's obvious enough. Am I missing something?"

"They're witches with true power, but not like us. I sensed a unique essence to their magic. They're something *more*."

"Like the boys?"

"Not like Gregory or the Loveridge brothers. They're Druid and Romani—human. I suspect the Harcourts are more like Ethan. The fae are a different species altogether. I believe these Harcourt witches share their bloodline with a creature similar to the fae, what myth and legend call naiads."

Alexander stared blankly. "Ethan's not human?"

"Come on, you know he's part fae." I laughed.

"Well, yeh, I guess I know that in theory, but he's—I don't know, a normal guy to me. As normal as any of us are around here."

"It's pretty straight-forward. At some point in Ethan's ancestral past, a human and a fairy got busy. The couplings are rare, and a child from the affair is rarer. So, yes, there is a part of Ethan—who knows how large—that is not human. He's part fae with all the magic that goes along with it. Although, Ethan's special among the fairy folk because he's immune to iron."

"Wow, okay." Alexander shook his shaggy head as if to shuffle his jumbled thoughts into place. "So, what the hell's a naiad?"

"They're freshwater enchantresses who haunt rivers and lakes and streams. Like in Greek myth and Ethan's Irish folktales, only...real. The lore is all over the place though," I rubbed my temples, trying to recall what I'd learned of these creatures. "Some naiads are thought to have the power of prophesy, some enchant with their song, while others have the ability to heal. There are few universal traits, one being their penchant for stunning or stupefying. Not unlike the fae."

"What makes you think the Harcourts are naiads?"

"I felt their magic. Even before Riddle introduced us in the dining room, their energy engulfed me, heady and pungent. They were stretching their magical legs, testing the waters, I guess. Anyway, I caught a distinct essence in their magic I couldn't identify at the time. And then, I caught this same magical signature a few minutes ago in the foyer when I was hexed."

Alexander didn't speak at first. He locked his jaw tight, knitted his brows together, and the veins in his temple pulsed. It seemed to take every ounce of his self-control not to freak the hell out.

"They fucking hexed you? That's why you froze up?" he growled.

"At least one of them did, yes."

"What did the hex do exactly?" Alexander asked, although we both knew he didn't want to hear the answer. It would only fuel his desire to avenge me.

"It froze me from the inside out. Or, I should say, it froze the seventy percent of my body made of water. A being who controls water—like a naiad—can control the water within someone's body, therefore controlling them. If they're twisted enough to try it."

Alexander slumped. "Fuck. We've got a serious case of naiads. Sounds like a venereal disease." He cringed, but when his face lit with a suspicious expression, I drew back.

"Evangeline..." Alexander spoke my name like a teacher about to scold me for missing assignments or showing up late again to class.

"Yes?" I asked hesitantly.

"Can't you control water?"

"Yes, of course. Why?"

The veins in Alexander's temples pulsed, and his face reddened. "What makes them more dangerous, more of a threat, than you are?" He raked his hands through his hair.

"Do you think I'm that twisted? I never said the Harcourts were more powerful than I am, or that I couldn't best them should the need arise.

Lucky for them, I'm in no mood to fight. Yet, they are a very real threat. These women are part naiad and part witch, making them even more formidable. My fire melted the ice hex, but that was by no means the extent of their powers. We have no clue how strong these two are. One thing I do know is they take their magic dark."

"How can you tell?" Alexander raised an eyebrow.

"You mean, besides their goth queen getups? They reek of wickedness."

Alexander leveled me with a *you-must-be-kidding* look. "There are more than a few who'd say the same about you—who have said it."

"True, but theirs is a misconception derived from intolerance and willful ignorance. My observation comes from study, intuition, and my own Goddess-blessed magic."

"Mm hmm..." Alexander fell into brooding-mode. He paced along the tree line with his head low and his hands clasped at the small of his back. But he halted midstride, and his head sprang up. "You're right. Vivian hexed you. She was at the concert."

"What?"

"While you and Siobhan Quinn were eye-fucking each other, I caught sight of Vivian glaring at you from across the room. Eris wasn't with her. I looked around for Vivian when we left, but she was gone." He rubbed his temples. "And that's when you were hexed, right after we walked out of the music room."

"First of all, don't be crude. We were not *eye-fucking* each other. And second, why didn't you mention this before?"

Alexander shrugged. "I got caught up with your story about fairies and naiads."

I stared at him for a beat but looked away. *Men.* I shook my head, exasperated.

"So, you didn't see Eris or Celeste at the concert?"

"No, but it doesn't surprise me that Eris took her first opportunity to ditch her mother. I'm sure Celeste is tailing her for you, ever loyal," he said with reluctant approval in his voice. Alexander scuffed his foot absentmindedly against a tree trunk and stared deep into the woods behind us. "The Harcourts are definitely up to something. There's no way it's coincidental that the architecture firm Riddle hired under my nose just happens to be run by two witches—naiads—whatever. Does he know what they are? Is that why he kept it from me? And why did the Harcourts come to Arbor in the first place? We have to figure out what they're up to and keep you safe in the process."

"Alexander—"

"I won't allow you to get hurt. We need to get to the bottom of this."

"Alexander—"

"I said *we. We* will figure this out, together."

"Well, you will have plenty of opportunity to investigate the Harcourts. You'll be working closely with them, after all, and Vivian seemed taken with you." I knew I was being snitty, but these women irked me to no end.

Alexander lifted my hands, pressed them against his lips, and closed his eyes tight. When they opened, a bolt of lightning flashed within them.

"I only flirted earlier to get a rise out of you. You look sexy when you're fierce." He leveled me with a searing gaze. "But I didn't expect things to take this kind of turn. Don't you know how much I love you? I'm going to have to work with the Harcourts, but I don't have the smallest interest in them. If they, or anyone else, tries to hurt you, I will end them. I'll destroy the entire town this time if it means keeping you safe. I'll raze Arbor to dust," he raged in a whisper.

I slowly retrieved my hands and spoke with a calm and level tone. "Sweetheart, you're not Zeus. You're not the Green Man or Odin or Jesus Christ. You're not a god. You are a witch and relatively new to your magic. You are not invincible." I took a breath to center my thoughts. "Embrace your power, yes. But you've got to show restraint. Remember, what one projects into the Universe will return threefold." *A lesson I learned with dire consequences.*

"Maybe, but I'd incur the wrath of every force of the Universe to protect you. I will keep you safe." He spoke his words as a solemn vow.

"Damn it, Alexander, you forget who you're fucking dealing with," I snapped. I whipped his tuxedo jacket off my shoulders and flung it at him. Drawing myself up as tall as my four-foot-eleven-inch frame would allow, I fumed. "You still don't grasp the extent of my power. I am not the same girl you saved from Stuart Cudlow. I'm not the same witch you kissed on that bench under the weeping cherry tree. I don't simply create anymore—paint pictures, play music, and sew pretty dresses. Thanks to the Goddess, not only am I impervious to fire, but I burn from the inside out. Do you think I need your jacket to keep me warm?"

I allowed the fire under my skin to surge, lighting me up from within like a jack-o'-lantern. Pulling my magic back took only a thought. "Not only do I manipulate the elements"—with a snap, I turned the crispy leaves above us a lush, brilliant green, as fresh as springtime. And with another snap, I returned them—"but now, I create elements at will. With the exception of spirit, of course."

I lifted my palms. From the left, sprang a fountain of water. From the right, crackled a lively flame. I flung them at each other, and they dissipated. I knelt and waved my hands over a spot of dirt. A moment later, a green shoot sprouted from the earth. As I coaxed the plant upward, it bloomed into a thorny, blood-red rose bush. Waving my hands above the roses, I created a concentrated cyclone with winds so strong, the rose buds ripped off their stems, and the petals rained down like droplets of blood. I allowed the winds to cease as my thrumming pulse regulated.

When I spoke next, I attempted a measured tone. Yet the passion of my convictions poured out as I tried to make him understand.

"Thanks to Rocky, and my disquieting ability to micromanage my suffering and release all that weighs me down, I can fly. Think of the implications, Alexander. A flaming, flying witch who can create and manipulate all four elements." I took his hands and held them close to my heart. "Don't you understand the horror I could inflict? Yet, I show restraint and command over my magic. I am not evil like they say I am. But if I'm attacked again, or those I care for are threatened, I can and will defend me and mine." I lowered his hands and stepped back. "I don't need you to fight my battles for me. I don't need a savior, Alexander. I'm not a Christian."

Chapter Four

We glared at each other until Alexander blinked. He hung his head, clasped his hands at the small of his back, and returned to his pacing.

"Oh, enough already! I need some time alone, in the elements, to... reboot from the hex. I'll meet you in the gallery."

Desperate for a chance to clear my head, I left Alexander standing at the tree line and ventured into the dense woods. Despite the darkness, I navigated the gnarled paths and thick undergrowth with ease. The forests around Morgan Manor had become as familiar to me as those that edged my cottage home. Red Hill's elevation meant woods filled with red spruce, eastern hemlock, sugar maple, yellow birch, and American beech trees. The heady scent of evergreen blended with the damp richness of the carpet of decaying leaves. With my dress hiked up and my heels in my hand, my bare feet crunched over fallen branches and skipped over muddy puddles. At first, the noise from the Samhain festivities followed me. But the deeper I traveled, the quieter the woods became until the only sounds were that of my footsteps.

When I'd wandered far enough, I made use of a fallen log and sat down gingerly, careful not to damage the elegant crimson couture. My heaving breath hung like smoke in the chill of the forest.

"Fuss and cuss if you must, but don't mess the dress" was one of many lessons Shasta instilled in me. She'd been curiously attuned to modern life for a black bear, even for a familiar. She certainly kept me in line. Shasta had been my rock. She'd arrived in my life after my mother's death when I was eight years old. My heart and soul and fragile young psyche had shattered, and Shasta mourned with me. She wrapped her warm girth around me and comforted me in my grief. Then she lifted me up again and gave me the strength to move forward. Fourteen years later,

Arbor's hate and ignorance and fear, coupled with a best friend's betrayal, stole Shasta from the world—from me.

Familiars impart a blessing upon their witch, and Shasta brought me strength. Since her death, I'd become physically weaker. I tired much more easily. My muscles ached from the strain of a long day. Mundane tribulations never bothered me so acutely—thanks to Shasta. Her absence, and the absence of her magic, left a barren chasm in my chest. I told myself that over time, the void would fill with a myriad of life's inevitable blessings. I told myself it would get easier to live without her. So far, it hadn't.

What sage wisdom would the shrewd and formidable high priestess Adelaide Good have imparted—about the Harcourts, about Alexander and Celeste, about running this gallery and dealing with the folks from Arbor, about mourning and grief—had she lived? Adelaide would have told me to put on my big girl boots and show them what a witch is capable of. She'd have wanted me to follow my heart and trust my gut, and to use these challenges to grind myself into a sharper, more resilient witch. She'd have reminded me not to look to the past, but to savor the sweet bitterness of each new day. But Adelaide wasn't around to guide me. Arbor killed her too. Still, I could abide by her counsel. And I would.

A piercing "Keeee-aaar" sounded from high above me in the trees, interrupting my reflections. A red-tailed hawk landed on a sturdy branch amid thinning red leaves. He skipped across his perch with agitated steps and ruffled feathers. I knew the telltale signs of a bird with something to say. And I understood the behavior of this particular bird well.

Not all witches have animal familiars, and even fewer have two. Yet, like my mother before me, the Goddess blessed me with a second familiar. Habrock the red-tailed hawk, my Rocky, came to me as I entered high school. Good judgement being a trait most teenage witches lack, Rocky was never shy about imparting his wisdom in his tireless struggle to keep me on the straight and narrow. In addition to his boundless and verbose sagacity, Rocky granted me the ability to fly—when he was in close enough proximity for me to feed off his magic.

As the idea of flight entered my thoughts, Rocky took wing, swooping down and landing deftly on the boney, low-hanging branch of a gnarled beech tree.

His stately tenor sounded within my mind. *Cowering doesn't become you, Evangeline.*

I am not cowering. I'm taking a breather.

As long as that's all it is. You've got matters to attend to.

Can't a witch take a minute? You didn't need to trek all the way out here to scold me for shirking my hostess duties.

Pardon me, but I am a hawk. I do not trek. And my intention in seeking you out was not to scold but to warn you.

Warn me? Of what?

While patrolling the estate, Archie and I identified almost a half dozen unknown familiars on the grounds. Archie is out there right now, using his German shepherd tracking skills to determine to which witch these familiars belong. Two of them are ravens, one black and the other an albino.

An albino raven? They're rare. And I've never heard of one as a familiar. Its witch must be extraordinary. An image of the Harcourt women stormed through my mind. *I bet it belongs to one of the naiads.*

Naiads! Oh dear, they are a terrible bother. Clever, cunning... devious creatures. And alluring. You know the tales. Oh no, no, Evangeline, this is no good. What are the identities of these vile beasts?

These particular fiends would be the salacious mother-daughter duo of Vivian and Eris Harcourt. Vivian hexed me just a bit ago.

Impossible. Simply preposterous.

Excuse me?

If you had been hexed, I would have known. I don't feel your pain as intensely as you feel mine, but a hex would have at least sent shivers down my feathers. Not so much as a quiver ran through me.

And yet, I was hexed. It penetrated my protection spell. I froze up, every inch of me; my blood turned to ice. Thankfully, my fire thawed the hex in seconds, but it was a doozy nonetheless.

Confounding. He fluffed his feathers and paced along his branch. *What kind of magic is this that can manipulate the bond between witch and familiar? And she hexed you at your own party! The audacity! Oh, Evangeline, my dearest witch, no wonder you needed time to recover yourself among the elements. Are you quite alright?*

Yes, of course.

Good, good. Now tell me, how did you stumble upon these Harcourt naiads?

Mayor Riddle introduced us earlier tonight. They run Harcourt Architecture, the firm he hired to oversee Arbor's downtown rebuild. And with Alexander dumping all his money into said rebuild, he's going to be working closely with them, which I'm less than thrilled about. What I'd really like to know is why they came to Arbor in the first place. Why would these talented, sophisticated women want to spend their time in a burnt-out, backwoods, hole-in-the wall town like Arbor? What's their real agenda? I have so many questions. And all I know for sure is they are going to be trouble.

Do not doubt it. He fidgeted on his branch. *And trouble not merely for you or Arbor in general. Alexander and the boys are good men, but they're susceptible to a naiads' wiles. However...* Rocky drifted off into his thoughts.

My thoughts turned to Celeste. *Rocky, is it only men who succumb to a naiad's enchantments? Can women fall victim?* My heart thumped heavy in my chest, anxious for his reply.

Certainly, naiads prey on women too. I suppose men are simply easier targets for their magic. It's all about manipulating attraction.

Fabulous. Not the answer I hoped for.

The hawk cocked his head to the side. *There is one creature I am confident is immune to a naiad's allurements.* Rocky paused for dramatic effect.

Are you going to make me guess?

The fae.

Ethan is immune?

He is, yes. As you know, naiads are creatures not unlike the fairy folk. The magic of both naiad and fae is ancient and similar in its manifestation. Like naiads, Ethan is a beguiler of sorts. He befuddles, confuses, distracts.

Something else to bring up with our resident fae. But speaking of distraction, I believe we were discussing unknown familiars on the grounds. You mentioned the two ravens. What about the others?

Oh! Yes, well, it's all quite strange, you see. Rocky smoothed out his ruffled feathers, rustling around until he settled into a comfortable position. *There's a horse, of all things, white with no saddle, reins, or rider. And some pesky black cat—yet another of our mysterious familiars—has taken to swatting her claws at the horse's hooves for fun. The horse is in a bit of a tizzy, and I worry it could inadvertently ruin an exhibit or hurt someone.*

For Goddess sakes. We've got to—

And there's the octopus to contend with.

I'm sorry, the what?

Octopus. It's like a squid, you see, and—

Yes, I know what an octopus is. Why the hell is there an octopus here, and why do I have to contend with it?

Well, I assume it's here for the party. And you must contend with it because it currently resides in the fountain of the formal gardens, not far from the cat and horse. Guests assume he's a part of the festivities. The creature has been slithering out with his gelatinous tentacles and grabbing at people as they pass. He attacked a dumpy, middle-aged couple from town.

Oh no! We—

The octopus sort of...squeezed them around the middle. It's a good thing they had a healthy bit of padding there, or I dare say, their spines might have snapped.

For the love of the Goddess, Rocky! Why didn't you lead with this? We need to—

It was that pencil pusher from the bank and her husband. You remember, the nasty piece of work from the Arbor Savings and Loan who wouldn't give you the money to open up the gallery?

Oh, I hope they're okay! I have to—

The boys arrived. They took up positions surrounding the fountain and warded the area to keep any others from harm.

We really ought to—

The boys are doing their utmost, but I don't know how long they can contain the situation. Something must be done about these blasted familiars.

My dearest hawk, you and I must discuss the importance of brevity and prioritization, but now is not the time.

I sent Rocky off with a message for the boys that I was on my way and messages for Celeste and Alexander to meet me by the fountain. Once again, I grabbed my heels and hoisted up my skirt. Then I set off out of the forest to confront a black cat, a horse, a couple of ravens, and a damned squid.

*

The formal garden's fifteen-foot-tall trellis walls, thick with blood-red, late-blooming roses, concealed half a football field's worth of black lilies, dark-purple heather, flame-like plumes of burgundy celosia, and precisely pruned shrubbery. This garden sanctuary showcased the excellence of Morgan Manor's new groundskeeper, Mr. Blomgren. Alexander had tasked the gardener extraordinaire with reining in the wildly overgrown estate. Mr. Blomgren had not only completed the daunting task Alexander set before him but exceeded expectations to a staggering degree. I could almost believe he worked magic on the land.

However, it wasn't Mr. Blomgren's floral prowess that captured my attention, but the curious collection of magical beings inhabiting his garden. Just inside the arched entrance, Nicolae and Ethan stood beside each other with their arms raised high, each invoking his own protection over the space. Nicolae's ward kept guests at bay with his power of persuasion. If anyone ventured too close, they'd get the sudden urge to visit the gallery and turn right around. Ethan cloaked the area in an illusion—a glamour that shielded the entrance to the garden and everyone inside it from view. Toward the back corner of the hidden garden, Gregory soothed a magnificent, white stallion by feeding him carrots, stroking the horse's dripping wet mane, and muttering ancient Druid incantations in his ear. Gregory had already appeased the sleek black cat, with eyes as wide and orange as a harvest moon, with a healthy dose of catnip. As an extra layer of precaution, Gregory wrapped the garden in a muffling spell to keep the goings-on from prying ears.

The main problem was the octopus. The imposing, gelatinous creature commandeered the basin of the large stone fountain occupying the center of the garden. Its tentacles rippled like ocean waves and then whipped outward aggressively. Standing valiantly before the fountain,

Luca clutched a flaming torch and swung it from side to side to control the beast. At Luca's feet laid the lifeless figures of a man dressed as the Mad Hatter and a woman as the Queen of Hearts.

Dear Goddess, Rocky was right. That's the loan officer and her husband.

I ran to them and fell to my knees beside the bodies. Their skin was mottled blue. Their mouths hung open, and their eyes popped wide. My hands shook as I fumbled with their wrists in a desperate search for a pulse. I found none. They were dead.

"Fuck, fuck, fuck, fuck. No, no, no, this isn't happening," I muttered feverishly.

Luca looked down at me, angry desolation twisting his angular features. "It killed them, Eva. The fucking thing killed them." He groaned. "When we showed up, the thing was just letting go of them. We sent Rocky off to find you, but since they were already dead, we haven't called 911 yet. What the hell are we going to do?"

Luca shared his big brother Nicolae's Romani features—the strong lean build, olive skin, and onyx hair and eyes—but the similarities didn't spill over into their magic. Unlike Nicolae, Luca had no active powers. His magic rested in finding the truth of a person or situation. Luca uncovered secrets and hidden intentions. These powers were useless when squaring off against the kraken.

He doesn't have active powers, but I do.

"I don't know what we're going to do about them yet," I said, staring down at the Hatter and the Queen, "but we've got to get that thing under control first."

I thrust out my arms and willed the magic within me into action. I drew the water from the fountain, and rolled it into an undulating sphere that swallowed up the octopus. Before the creature could escape, I froze the circumference of the sphere, trapping it inside.

"Gotcha!" I shouted.

The octopus lunged, but the frozen orb held firm, constraining him. This realization clearly infuriated the creature. It inked in fear, filling the inside of his icy cage with a slick, black liquid cloud. The creature quieted for a heartbeat before lunging out again against the orb.

What the hell do I do with him now?

"What in the name of Hecate are you doing to Octavius?" Eris Harcourt said as she stormed toward me. Her leather glistened and her piercings glinted in the torchlight. She walked straight through the boys' magical shields without a passing glance at the dead couple on the ground and charged up to within inches of my face. "Get him out of there. Now!"

Momentarily stunned, I fought to maintain control over the octopus in the orb. "No. That thing's dangerous. He's killed two people tonight. There's going to be hell to pay."

Just then, I noticed Celeste over Eris's shoulder. She'd tucked herself in the corner amid the trellis roses. I didn't know how long she'd been standing there, barefoot with her dress dragging in the grass and her sapphire stilettos dangling from her hand. She played it casual, but I could practically hear her frantic heart rate and the blood that raced through her veins. I thought her hair seemed mussed and her cheeks a brighter rose.

"If you kill Octavius, I vow to Hecate, it'll be *you* who pays," Eris said in a deadly whisper, interrupting my distractions.

"Wait, what?" I took a step backward. "I have no intention of killing him. I only put him on ice until we can decide what to do with him."

"You idiot, you're killing him now," she snarled. "You scared him, so he inked. Now he's suffocating in his own poison."

Fuck. I lowered my arms and released the octopus into the fountain with a shattering splash. The creature shlopped around, and I released a sigh of relief.

"There. He's alive. Guess who's not. Those two people your *familiar* squeezed the life out of," I said, making sure she knew I understood her nature.

Eris's lips twisted in devious amusement. "Octavius isn't my familiar." She tapped her shoulder, and an albino raven with a proud raised head and sleek, creamy-white wings landed gracefully upon it. "*This* is my familiar, Abramelin. *That* creature," she said, motioning to the octopus, "belongs to—"

"Cease and desist! Octavius, mind your manners," Vivian Harcourt interrupted as she emerged like a dark goddess from a dense, creeping fog that billowed in her wake. A black raven perched on her shoulder. Somewhat smaller than her daughter's albino familiar, this bird was a tad on the gangly side with ruffled feathers and a scar on his wing. Despite this, I sensed great power emanating from him.

Alexander followed coolly after Vivian with his tuxedo jacket slung over his shoulder and his familiar Archie at his feet. He looked every bit the dashing leading man, his swashbuckling interpretation of Cary Grant to Vivian's malevolent Liz Taylor.

I think I'm going to be sick.

I closed my eyes a moment before turning to Vivian. "This...*beast* is dangerous."

"Yes. He is," Vivian said matter-of-factly. "Octavius, we are guests. Show some respect," Vivian chastised the creature in her oil slick voice. She pointed a red manicured finger at a spot on the ground beside her. "Here. Now!"

The creature slurped and undulated to her side, leaving a sloppy trail of ink staining the ground behind him.

Vivian swept her attention my way. "We're minding Octavius for a friend," she said by way of explanation.

"And that friend would be..." I prompted.

"Momentarily indisposed," she answered, clearly with no intention of elaborating.

"If you're not going to divulge the name of this creature's witch, I'm holding you responsible for him. He killed two people tonight."

"Oh dear. That is inconvenient," Vivian said with faux concern. "Although"—she took a closer look at the couple on the ground, a crooked sneer slipping onto her lips—"I would have thought you'd be pleased to see this particular woman find her end. Isn't she the banker who refused to loan you the money to open an art gallery here in the quiet, wholesome community of Arbor? Thought you'd corrupt the place, didn't she? Well, look at you now. It's poetic justice for her to die at your grand opening, don't you think? You can tell me. Deep down, you wished it. In some dark place, you hoped she'd see your success and choke on it. Didn't you?"

"Are you out of your mind?" I cried out in disgusted awe. "I didn't want her dead!"

How does Vivian know my history with this woman?

"Oh, don't fret." She waved off my concern. "I wouldn't think of allowing such a tragic turn of events to mar your special evening. Eris and I will handle it."

"And how exactly do you plan on doing that?"

Vivian slinked closer. "Magic. Not unlike your own." She patted my head as if I were a small child. "It's a shame you didn't have a mother to teach you how to use your talents. But not to worry, dear. I'll clean up this mess."

What the hell does she know about my mother or my powers? Twisted, condescending bitch. I wanted to speak these words aloud, but her reference to my mother struck me dumb.

"Eris, come," Vivian snapped. Eris followed reluctantly behind.

They approached the dead couple and knelt on either side of them. They raised their arms, and water poured out over the couple from their outstretched hands.

Vivian and Eris chanted, *"Aquas ab aquilone, et veniet ad me. Aquas ab austro veniet ad me. Aquas orientalem, veniunt ad me. Occidens aquas, venerunt ad me."*

A thick fog rolled in. A great gale caught up the water with the fog and whipped them together around the cluster huddled on the ground. The spinning grew faster until it swirled into a cyclone, shielding the Harcourts and the lifeless couple from view.

While the boys remained at their posts, Alexander and Celeste made their way to my side. A minute, two, five passed. We stared transfixed at the swirling vortex. The whole coven was there, except for Mia, and she would surely hear of it all before the night's end.

Some high priestess I am. I have no clue what to do. We are true and righteously fucked. Not even open a day, and we've got dead bodies.

"Relax. I'll figure it out," Alexander commented.

"Did you seriously dip into my head again and tell me to relax? And please, explain how you're going to 'figure out' two dead bodies?" I hissed.

"Rich, white male privilege." He shrugged.

The bluntness of his reply threw me. As I unwrapped his words, the Harcourts' cyclone slowed down. The fog dissipated, revealing the bank lady and her husband, sitting up, embracing each other. Unsteady, they got to their feet and brushed themselves off as if they'd simply tripped and bumped their heads.

Dear sweet Goddess. How is this possible? What is this darkness?

I was thrilled they were alive, but the fact that they'd been stone dead five minutes before seriously freaked me the hell out.

"I suspected the Harcourts went dark, but this is worse than I imagined. This is necromancy," I whispered to Alexander and Celeste.

"Well, either necromancy or resurrection. Necromancy only re-animates the dead. Resurrection brings someone back to life," Alexander whispered.

Celeste snickered, and I popped an eyebrow.

He looked down at his shoes and blushed. "I played World of Warcraft as a kid. Let's not make a thing out of it. And I thought there was no such thing as dark magic, only dark intentions."

"This is life and death we're talking about. The Harcourts aren't healing like Maggie does. Those two had no pulse. And they were dead for how long? What's that do to a person's brain? It can't be good." I closed my eyes and took a breath to clear my thoughts. "I can create and manipulate four of the five elements—earth, air, fire, and water. Clearly the Harcourts can manifest and control water. If they brought these two back from the dead, and they aren't just mind-controlled zombies, it means Vivian and Eris can control the fifth element—spirit. We don't know their intentions, and I sincerely doubt they're noble."

"Well, fuck. At least nobody's dead?" Alexander said.

I tipped my head to the side, considering whether he was in shock or trying to lighten the mood.

The Harcourt women stood coolly, somehow not a hair out of place. And after spending some time speaking to the bank lady and her husband, they approached the three of us.

"Mr. and Mrs. Bowers are fine," Vivian said. "Merely feeling a tad foggy from having one too many cocktails and taking a tumble. They've decided to pop by the hospital for a check-up to be on the safe side."

Eris leaned toward me and spoke conspiratorially. "We've dolled up their memories a bit. You may want to have your henchmen escort them out to avoid any further embarrassment."

I looked over at the boys. Their absence would leave the remaining familiars and the gardens unguarded, but it couldn't be helped. I needed the couple escorted out discreetly and expeditiously but with respect and care; they'd just died, after all. I trusted the boys would handle the situation. I nodded to them, and reluctantly they abandoned their positions; Ethan and Gregory leading the Queen of Hearts out of the gardens, followed by Nicolae and Luca guiding The Mad Hatter.

When they were gone, I turned to Vivian.

"I suppose you expect me to thank you for that." I motioned to the spot where the couple had been lying.

"Not at all. Consider it a friendly gesture to our new neighbors."

Her blasé attitude threw me. As if bringing the dead back to life was an everyday occurrence; as if their actions bore no great significance.

"You go around raising folks from the dead then? That's your thing? Necromancy? Or do you consider it resurrection? Either way, it's not something one typically sees flung around willy-nilly at a party."

"Oh, my dear little witch." Vivian tipped her head to the side, squinting as she looked at me with something akin to pity. "I'm not explaining my powers to you. Call it whatever you'd like. At the end of the day, magic is merely a tool, a means to an end. You needed those two people alive. My daughter and I had the power to make that happen. So, we did. It's as simple as that."

Her nonchalance floored me. "Is the mayor aware that the architecture firm he hired is run by a couple of witches?"

"Of course he is." Vivian waved dismissively.

Okay, not the answer I expected. "What about the town council or the planning board? They're here tonight, as I'm sure you know. Are they aware of your...abilities?"

"No," Vivian snapped. "And they have no reason to know. Our private lives are irrelevant to our work. I'd kindly request that you keep that information hidden under your own pointy black hat."

"That's out of the question," I said emphatically.

A collective gasp rang out, my comment producing as sharp a reaction from Alexander and Celeste as from the Harcourts. With strained expressions, my companions closed ranks around me, clearly prepared to leap to my defense should my big mouth get me into trouble.

"Excuse me?" Eris snapped.

"They deserve to know who they're working with," I said with a definitive nod.

Eris flinched, and her mouth dropped open. "You would out us? You would subject us to ridicule and speculation and gossip when we simply want to do the job the mayor hired us to do? Riddle's a good enough guy, but I don't trust a single one of those puritanical fools on the council or the board. And neither do you. They simper and smirk, but there isn't a genuine bone in their bodies. If they found out... You know more than anyone what these people are capable of. You've experienced their hatred firsthand."

I was unmoved. "That's exactly why I need to make it clear that you and your mother have no connection to our coven. We can't be painted with the same brush. The Witches of Arbor have a delicate truce with this town. You two roll in here, unleash a murderous octopus, and then raise its dead. I mean, kudos for cleaning up your mess and all, but we don't need that kind of trouble. And I suspect trouble follows you. Not only does the town need to know you're witches, they need to know you're not associated with the Witches of Arbor." We'd all worked too hard to maintain our tenuous peace with Arbor, and we couldn't afford to have the Harcourts' bad behavior ruin things. "You never know," I said, trying to mimic Vivian's blasé demeanor. "They might surprise you. Four months ago, they burned me at the stake, yet here they are, drinking my champagne."

Vivian looked down her pointed nose at me. "I believe you have an overinflated sense of your own power and influence, little witch. You certainly underestimate ours. Go ahead and run your mouth. No one will believe you. No one trusts you. This town looks at you and sees the evil slut responsible for the loss of their mayor, reverend, and church." She sneered. "They're not here tonight out of some new-found respect for you. They're here to pry."

However true her words, I wanted to punch her in the mouth. I imagined the way her jaw would crunch under my fist. But I remained impassive.

"We've been in town a week"—Vivian gave a smoldering look—"and they're already in love with us. We're going to give them what they want. We're returning their cherished downtown, better than before."

"Good for you," I said, hiding my revulsion at Vivian's admission that they were manipulating Arbor. "Like you said, I took down Arbor's corrupt, despotic mayor and the depraved reverend, along with their deviant spawn and their hate-filled excuse for a place of worship. I don't scare easily. And, by the way, along with 'evil slut,' the town also enjoys the terms: harlot, heathen, Jezebel, and Satan spawn."

"Why are you such a bitch? We just saved your ass. We're not hurting anyone." Eris sounded almost sincere.

"What a joke! You two are part blooded witch and part naiad with all the power that implies, but you have no intention of using any of those powers?" I pressed.

"Oh, you are astute." Vivian's mouth lifted deviously. "Naiad blood flows within our veins, yes. That doesn't make us evil." She arched her brow sharply in a challenge.

"No. It makes you dangerous," I said.

"The silver-haired Massey is part fae," Eris said. "He doesn't go around messing with the locals' heads, does he? And aren't you powerful? You manipulate the elements. Yet you aren't a danger to the community, are you?" She heaved a great, exasperated sigh. "We'd never hurt anyone."

I blurted out a laugh. "Your mother hexed me an hour ago. She wasn't trying to hurt me?"

Eris lost her tongue, and she leveled her mother with a venomous glare.

Looks like Eris was clueless about that particular incident.

Vivian smirked. "A witch who cannot hex cannot heal."

"And you hexed me because...?" I was astonished at her reply and reluctantly impressed that she didn't deny it.

"A simple test of your powers," Vivian answered, unconcerned. "Nothing to twist your knickers over. No harm done. And more to the point, there's no evidence of harm." Her eyes were alight with a sly glimmer. "But what do the downtrodden townsfolk really know about the

Witches of Arbor, hmm? How would they respond if they realized how much power you actually possess? Would they be all right if they knew Nicolae could persuade them to *do* just about anything, or that Gregory could make them *feel* anything, that Ethan can make them *see* anything, or that Luca can uncover their deepest, darkest truths?" Her eyes darkened and narrowed. "They'd be okay with that? Please." She brushed away the notion with a derisive snort and a wave of her hand. "You're making us out to be the bad guys here, and what did we do? We saved two lives."

Fucking bitch.

As much as it pissed me off to admit, Vivian was right. I had no evidence that she hexed me, no proof of any wrongdoing whatsoever. And they *had* done me a service by resurrecting the bank lady and her husband. Despite knowing in my gut that the Harcourts were dangerous, I had no choice but to let the farce play out.

"Fine. I'll agree to keep your secret from the council, planning board, and general public...for now. But the moment I suspect you've used magic to harm a soul in this town, all bets are off."

"It's a deal," Vivian smirked triumphantly.

A cold shiver ran down my spine. "Great. Now please, get that damned octopus out of here."

"Of course, of course, very good, by all means. Octavius's social ineptitude *is* tedious. He's certainly not as well-bred as my Reginald." She stroked the bird perched upon her shoulder. "Please accept my sincerest apologies for Octavius's bad manners. He'll inconvenience you no further. I assure you."

"Good. We can't have familiars going rogue. I don't want any more blood spilt." Her proper demeanor irritated the hell out of me, and at that point, I wanted to be rid of her—and her daughter.

"Wouldn't that be a sin. Well, we won't detain you a moment longer. Enjoy your party. My daughter and I will get out of your hair. Eris, come," she directed over her shoulder as she traipsed away.

With an unmistakable pout, Eris followed her mother along with Octavius the octopus, the ravens Reginald and Abramelin, and the white stallion with the wet mane.

"What? Where the hell is the horse going? They never mentioned the horse belonged to them! Who does he belong to?"

Before I could get answers to my queries, all hell broke loose. Growling, snarling, screeching, hissing rang out, and I turned to find Archie, Alexander's German shepherd familiar, in a battle royal scrum with the black cat that had been tormenting the horse.

Celeste and Alexander fell to their knees, pain contorting their faces.

The connection between a familiar and their witch transcends that of pet and owner. In exchange for the unique power the familiar imparts upon their witch, any pain or distress felt by the familiar is felt by their witch. It is a symbiotic exchange of energy from one to the other. Alexander and Archie shared this deep bond, so I understood why he struggled. But that would mean...

"Eva"—Celeste peered up at me with pain and wonder—"I think I'm a witch."

Chapter Five

Of course, Celeste was right. And since she and Alexander were in such agony from their familiars' fight, neither would be any help controlling the animals.

I had to act. Once again, I lifted the water from the fountain, only this time, I dumped it onto the cat and dog. The effect was immediate. The animals launched themselves away from each other and feverishly shook themselves dry.

The pain slid from Celeste and Alexander's faces, and they carefully rose to their feet. Archie raced to his witch and steadied him. With his familiar's connection, Alexander recovered himself within moments.

Celeste, on the other hand, looked like she might puke, and she slumped back to her knees. The cat sprinted over and curled up on her lap. It nuzzled its head against her breasts and purred. Celeste jolted, and stared down at the feline as if seeing it for the first time. Through her pale-gold veil of hair, I watched her cheeks regain their color and joy spread across her face. With gentle hands, she embraced the animal and held it close to her heart. Nestling in the soft fur, Celeste breathed in her new familiar's scent. When she raised her eyes to me, they shone with awe.

"Allow me to introduce you to Luna...my familiar." She kissed the cat on the head. "Luna, this is the high priestess of our coven, Evangeline Clarion. My Eva."

The cat lazily lifted her head, offered me an indifferent glance, and returned to nuzzling in Celeste's lap.

The Goddess had blessed Celeste for her years of devotion. She'd been a practicing Wiccan all her life. The appearance of Luna revealed the breath of the Goddess within her—magic. And a familiar and their witch must acquaint themselves with each other. They would need time to connect. With this Awakening would come new powers; both innate and those imparted by her familiar.

"Luna, it's a pleasure and an honor to meet you." I spoke to the familiar's back. "Welcome to the Witches of Arbor family. You and Celeste will need to spend time together to complete your Awakening. I'll understand if you need to steal her away."

When I didn't get a reply, I assumed Luna was taking a cat nap. But the looks on Celeste and Alexander's faces told me we had a bigger problem than a sleepy kitty.

"The fucking cat's got an attitude," Alexander snarled. "She doesn't want to connect, converse, or interact in any way with anyone but Celeste. She's pissed I can read her thoughts. She's not a fan of you or Archie either. And for some reason, she hates that horse. Funny, she's surprisingly tight-lipped on why."

"You're reading the thoughts of animals now?" I said, impressed that his abilities had grown so strong, although baffled that I hadn't realized it. "You can hear that broadly?"

"Not all animals, only familiars. And not broadly but specifically. I target. Without intention, there's usually silence, but Luna won't shut up. I hear her loud and clear. And that cat is a damn menace."

"Hey! Be nice." Celeste gently scooted the cat off her lap and sprang to her feet; Luna's magic clearly aiding her recovery. She faced off against Alexander, feisty and indignant. "That menace is my familiar."

"You should hear that hellcat, Evangeline. She's...vicious." Alexander gritted his teeth as he spoke, like he battled a desire to skin the cat alive.

"Vicious? I'll show you vicious," Celeste hissed.

"Okay, that's enough!" I hollered much too loudly, considering the ward had dropped that shielded my big mouth from prying ears.

I continued with a measured tone and carefully chosen words. "Luna, I know you can hear me. I'm sorry if I've offended you in any way. Please know that I understand the bond between witch and familiar. I know you and Celeste need time to form that bond. Celeste—" I wished I could take her hand but didn't dare for fear of the cat curled at her feet. "You and Luna need to be alone. That is not a suggestion. Go wherever you'd like and take your time. Get to know each other. Get to know your new self and your new powers. Enjoy your Awakening. But first—" I took a deep breath as I wondered whether or not I wanted to hear the answers I sought. "—first, please, tell me what happened when you followed the Harcourts."

Celeste took a few minutes to compose herself, whispering softly in her familiar's ear.

"I ended up following Eris mostly." She knitted her brow in thought.

Amusement lit Alexander's face. "Come on, let's hear details."

"Don't go getting all snarky, mister." I cocked an eyebrow at him. "I want to hear about your tête-à-tête with Vivian, too."

Alexander smirked. "Yes ma'am.

"So, you followed Eris. What did you find out?" I asked Celeste, temporarily taking Alexander off the hot seat.

Celeste shook her head, confounded. "Eris is a piece of work. She puts on a hard front, but she's not as tough as she lets on. She's a lot like you, if I'm being honest."

I chose to ignore her last comment and pressed for more. "But where did she go? What did she do? Did you talk to her? What did you talk about?" I asked, anxious to hear her tale.

Celeste shook her head and grinned. "Don't work yourself into a tizzy. Yes, I spoke to Eris. And to answer your unspoken question, yes, she hit on me. But I did not succumb to her wiles, though she laid them on thick." She shivered. "I followed both Vivian and Eris to the gallery first, but Vivian snuck away. Eris couldn't have been happier about it. That is one woman with mommy issues. I approached her by the modern sculpture collections. She didn't seem surprised to see me. We chatted a bit, and after a second glass of champagne, Eris vented her frustrations about her mother. She cast Vivian as merely the face of their company and portrayed herself as the real architect in the family. She tore into her mom pretty savagely. It's hard to imagine them working together. It can't be a pleasant office environment. Anyway, after the gallery, we headed to the library. Eris wanted to see Mia's lace and my jewelry, of course."

"Of course," I said calmly, despite the sour bile of jealousy that rose in my throat. It tormented me, the way Eris leered at Celeste, like her conquest was inevitable.

Celeste went on. "A handful of people lingered in the library, but they cleared out not long after we arrived. The instant the last person left, Eris...came on to me."

Celeste paused to gauge my reaction, which I endeavored to maintain steady. I nodded for her to continue.

"I anticipated her advances. I could feel her pheromones in the air. But she was more assertive than I'd expected."

"Did she hurt you?" Alexander asked with a deep, protective growl and balled fists.

I was surprised Alexander felt so protective over Celeste.

"No, she didn't hurt me." Celeste gave him a quizzical look. "But her aura was highly intoxicating. She lured me closer and closer to her even though I fought her pull, even though every inch of me cried out, 'No!' But when she backed me into a corner, my what-the-fuck meter finally went off, and I snapped out of her spell. That's when Rocky showed up. He has excellent timing, by the way. I'd never wanted to kiss a bird before." She laughed softly. "Rocky gave me your message, and here we are."

No commitment existed between us, yet despite the supernatural temptation, Celeste remained loyal. I swelled with gratitude for such a rare gift.

"Are you sure you're all right?" Alexander asked.

"Yes, I'm fine." She brushed off his concern with a puzzled expression and sounded none the worse for wear.

"Why don't you head off with Luna now? You've got an Awakening to attend to, and I don't want to hold you up any longer than I already have," I said, hoping to curry favor with the cat.

"Are you kidding?" Celeste blurted out a laugh. "There's no way I'm missing what went down with Alexander and Vivian. Luna can wait." Celeste recoiled as Luna hissed her reply.

"If you insist." I folded my arms across my chest and turned to Alexander. "So, what have you got to say?"

Alexander grinned with roguish charm. He ran his hands through his hair and planted them on his hips. "Well, I didn't fall prey to Vivian." He tried to sound flippant, but I caught a nervous edge to his voice. "After you took off into the woods, I headed to the dining room to grab a drink and a quick bite. I was hitting up the buffet when I spotted Vivian and Riddle huddled together, whispering at a small table tucked in the corner of the dining room. I honed into Vivian's thoughts, but I couldn't read a thing. It seemed like she had a shield around her mind."

"Great. More powers," I groaned.

"It gets weirder. I tried listening to Riddle. I figured at least I could get the conversation from his perspective."

"And?" Celeste prodded.

"And I heard nothing. Again. But Riddle was different. No shield blocked my way. Instead, his mind was a great, empty chasm, dark and desolate. No thoughts, no images. Just...blank." He shook his head in frustration. "I don't fucking get it."

"You think Vivian hexed him?" Celeste asked.

"Your guess is as good as mine. But when Riddle left, I approached Vivian. I made with the pleasantries and asked what brought her and Eris to Arbor. She brushed it off as a simple business decision, the job was too tempting to pass up. But she mentioned that she had a history with folks here in Arbor."

"History in Arbor?" I said, taken aback. "I've never heard of the Harcourts before tonight, and I've lived here for fourteen years. Unless she's referring to my mother again. She's mentioned her twice now. Or maybe she knew Maggie? What else did she say?"

"Well, that was about the time Vivian—how did Celeste put it?— came on to me. That just sounds fucking weird. Anyway, she hit on me. I didn't feel any of the pheromones or intoxicating aura bullshit Celeste did. But yes, Vivian was...assertive. However, I rebuffed her advances like the fucking gentleman that I am. And serendipity hastened Rocky's approach with your missive."

"Celeste was right. Rocky has excellent timing." I planted my hands on my hips and hung my head as I shuffled through the reams of new information. "The two of you uncovered a mountain of info, but most of it leads to more questions. But one thing is clear. Vivian and Eris have huge balls."

Celeste and Alexander grinned at me wryly.

"What? They have to have huge balls to waltz into my grand opening and brazenly hit on you two. Who do they think they are? They're shameless. And fucking nuts. I mean, they brought an octopus to a party. Who does that?"

I grew more agitated by the second. But Celeste and Alexander took my hands, and my anxiety subsided.

"Thanks." I took a calming breath. "Okay, speaking of familiars, going forward, you are each responsible for minding yours. Keep them under control and keep them away from each other. Whatever you do, play nice." I turned to the newly anointed witch. "Celeste, I think it's time for your Awakening. Are you ready?"

"I am." She kissed me on the cheek. After scooping up Luna, Celeste headed out of the garden to the woods.

I stood on tiptoe, wrapped my arms around Alexander's neck, and looked up into his dark eyes. "Thank you for looking out for me... and Celeste. I'm grateful. You are infinitely overprotective, but your apprehension isn't always unfounded." I placed a kiss on the neatly manscaped stubble of his cheek. "You looked dapper beside Vivian, you know. You'd make a handsome couple."

"Now why in hell would I want Morticia, when I have Persephone by my side?" He pulled me tight against him. And when he kissed me, I felt it in my toes. "Now"—Alexander rested his forehead against mine for a moment before reluctantly retreating and offering me his arm—"how about we check out some art? This is a gallery opening, after all. May I escort you?"

I curled my arm around his. "My dear Hades, I'd follow you anywhere."

*

The grand gallery hosted three quarters of the evening's exhibits and would be the focal point of the Manor Arts after opening night. A mass of intricate paper chandeliers and hanging art installations fell from the gallery's vaulted ceilings. Blown glass, woodwork, metalwork, and sculpture filled the space. Collections of photography, sketches, and paintings lined the walls.

This is where I belong. The truth of this sang in my blood. The magic in my veins sizzled with the power emanating from the creativity in the room.

With Alexander flanking me, I wove through the crowd and soaked in the energy. The initial terror of the evening had abated, and the folks from Arbor meandered through the exhibits with polite curiosity. Artists mingled with the throng of costumed guests as well as could be expected. Some artists brooded. Others bragged. Some oozed sleek sophistication smacked with a dash of superiority complex.

Alexander and I chatted up the artists and admired their mastery as we made our way over to my collection. Crowds clustered around my pieces; some faces bright and joyful, some contemplative, others full of awe.

This. This is what I dreamed of all my life.

My collection began with a group of oil paintings, most depicting the elements at their wildest and most fantastical. Among these, hung the painting of the stream and forest surrounding my cottage home; the painting I'd created the afternoon of my first date with Alexander. The fan favorite was clearly the portrait of Celeste. Hair like lemon chiffon framed her sharp blue eyes, milky skin, and strawberry lips begging to be nibbled. She clasped a yellow sheet loosely around her bare shoulders. *My* yellow sheet. And just as she captivated me that afternoon in my bedroom, the ethereal vision of Celeste that shone from my painting captivated all who gazed upon it.

A dozen drawings hung next, as detailed as any black-and-white photographs. My favorite was the illustration of a stone bench and weeping cherry tree. I'd confided my deepest secrets to Alexander beneath that tree. We shared our first passionate embrace on that bench. One drawing sent shivers down my spine. As striking as it was, the piece depicting downtown Arbor unnerved me. It portrayed the view of town from my window at the manor before the burning. The bucolic scenery, quaint shops, town clock, church steeple. So charming. So inviting. So misleading. And now, gone.

"They're all here for you," Alexander whispered in my ear.

So caught up was I in the moment, that his voice jolted me. I squealed and slapped my hands over my mouth with an uncharacteristic giggle. "This is crazy. I can't believe we pulled it off."

"I'm so proud of you." His dark eyes charged with admiration.

I marveled at the enraptured faces around my work. "I'm going to say a few words," I said with a burst of courage and left Alexander with a kiss.

I lost track of time as I gabbed away with the diverse group of art lovers who crowded around me. They peppered me with questions about individual pieces and the techniques I used in creating them. They asked about the Manor Arts itself and listened intently as I described my lifelong dream of opening a gallery and the incredible collaboration that brought that dream to fruition. Their authenticity made it all so special. They genuinely enjoyed my work and wanted to know more. Unfamiliar with this type of recognition, I reveled in it.

I deserve this.

I could have stayed there all night. And I would have if Alexander hadn't tapped me lightly on the shoulder, and whispered, "It's time to go."

I pouted, and he laughed.

"We should return to the festivities, streghetta mia." He tucked a rogue wisp of hair behind my ear. "We still haven't visited the three footpath exhibits, and we need to finish up in the back garden for your performance."

A strength of purpose surged through me in that moment. The positive response to my collection gave me new energy. I could tackle anything.

"I'm ready."

Chapter Six

Three winding footpaths with high, thickly vined, trellised walls led from the front of the estate to the back gardens. On any other evening, they were a lovely stroll. Tonight, each path displayed a spectacle of obscurity. An avant-garde fashion collection by an intriguing young designer out of New Orleans dominated the first path. Ghostly models paraded in their daring creations as a Cajun-fusion band performed a frighteningly thrilling rendition of "Bottom of the River," complete with black eyes and masks.

Alexander and I reached the end of the path when his executive assistant, Deidre O'Shae, barged up to us out of nowhere. Typically cool as a cucumber, Deirdre was visibly shaken. "There you are," she addressed Alexander as she fought to catch her breath. "There's a...situation. I think you're going to want to deal with this personally."

Fantastic. What now?

"All right." I bucked myself up to tackle the next obstacle. "Let's go."

"No. I'll handle it." Alexander kissed my cheek. "You check out the other paths, and I'll meet you in the gardens. It's getting late, and you can't miss your performance."

"Fair enough," I said, resigned.

Alexander and Deirdre hustled off, and I strolled on toward the second footpath. As I turned the corner to enter, I let loose a scream, clutched my chest, and scampered backward like a frightened child. This seemed a rational reaction when one had a run-in with a grotesque, bat-winged demon with his fangs a hair's breadth away from piercing the bared neck of a lusciously nude victim. I slowly reached out my hand and grazed my finger along a fang.

Clay. The realism is remarkable.

Every few yards along the path stood another life-sized statue of a human in varying degrees of undress on the brink of being consumed by an otherworldly creature. Wendigo, centaur, ogre, werewolf, the likenesses of each creature captured a moment before they devoured their victims. Portrayed in vivid detail, the statues were disturbingly beautiful and highly seductive.

Besides the gasps and squeals of horror from my fellow travelers along the second path, all seemed well. I debated whether I should bother checking the third footpath at all or head straight to the gardens. The evening grew late, and I needed to be on stage soon to wrap up. But I wasn't ready just yet to put on a performance. A little liquid courage might ease my nerves. Thankfully, I knew I could find some bubbly along the last path.

Before I could enter, however, three young men hustled by me, all dressed in the black uniforms of the Morgan Manor staff. They offered quick nods and muttered greetings of, "Ma'am," as they lugged busted hunks of an ice sculpture.

I cringed at the aged moniker. *I'm only twenty-two, for the love of the Goddess!*

A fourth staff member trailed behind, hauling trash bags.

"Excuse me." I stopped the tall, broad-chested redhead who I recognized as Killian O'Shae, one of Deidre's sons, who worked as the manor's footman on a typical day. "What happened?"

"Evening, Miss Clarion." Killian gave a quick bob of the head and lowered his bags to the ground. "A couple ladies got wasted and crashed into the champagne ice fountain. My mom and Mr. Morgan are taking care of them. We cleaned and set up another champagne station."

This is what had Deidre all flustered? I wonder who the women were.

"There were bound to be a few lushes tonight. I appreciate your help."

"Not a problem, Miss Clarion. It's my pleasure." He bowed debonairly.

Alexander had hired the entire O'Shae family. The manor was lucky to have such valuable employees.

I grinned. "Working for Elliot—excuse me, *Mr. Parker*—as a footman in the main house is a huge responsibility. And Mr. Blomgren referred to your brother as his right-hand man when I spoke to him today. High praise, indeed. I saw Keegan setting up an elaborate pumpkin display earlier tonight. With such hardworking sons, your mom must be proud."

Killian smirked, his eyes shimmering with boyish charm. "It's an honor to work at Morgan Manor. Mr. Parker's a great guy. And yes, Keegan's wandering around, keeping the jack-o'-lanterns lit. I told him they're lit by magic and not likely to burn out, but he insists on keeping watch. He's not the brightest bulb. He does have a green thumb though, I'll give him that. Knows these woods and grounds like the back of his hand. And we don't make our ma proud half as often as we drive her mad." He laughed.

Remembering himself, Killian straightened up. "Is there anything you needed?"

"No, thank you. I'm sorry to take up your time."

"No worries. Have a good night, Miss Clarion." He hoisted the trash bags like Santa sacks. But before he hustled off, he looked over his shoulder. "And if you don't mind me saying, you look amazing tonight. Killer dress."

Well, that was sweet and unexpected. I blushed.

I headed over to the newly arranged beverage station, even more desperate for a drink. The intricately carved scorpion ice sculpture flowed with champagne, and the table beside it held garnish bowls of strawberries, black berries, and pomegranate seeds as well as crystal champagne flutes in precise rows.

Killian and the others did a nice job. I snagged a glass, filled it from the scorpion's tail, and took a long sip. *Veuve Cliquot. I've been spoiled here at the manor of late, because I'd know these bubbles anywhere.*

However excellent the drink, the food was the real star of the show along this footpath. Table upon table displayed some of the world's most exotic and dangerous delicacies: cassava roots, carambola star fruit, Jamaican ackee fruit, Mexican escamoles, scorpionfish, and more. Warning signs were posted with every dish, and medics waited on call.

As I sipped champagne and sampled my way along the hazardous fare, I recognized a familiar face at the end of the path. A nun in her full regalia—black robes, white bib, long silver cross, and black habit trimmed in white—would have stood out in a party on any other night. On Halloween, the habited sister appeared as nothing more than a woman in costume. But this nun wasn't playing dress-up. Mother Hildegard was the Mother Superior of Saint Francis Roman Catholic Convent located in the valley of Red Hill. And although we shared little by way of our belief systems, she and her sisters were allies.

I held out my hand in greeting, and she gave it a firm shake.

"You've outdone yourself, Evangeline. You've used your talents to the fullest while shining a spotlight on the talents of others. This is an impressive accomplishment."

"You aren't offended then?"

She grinned good-naturedly. "Offended by what? The frightening sculpture or provocative fashion? Of course not. Artistic expression is the manifestation of the divine spark within each of us. Should I be offended by the extravagance of the celebration? Simply because I take a vow of poverty doesn't mean I should thrust those parameters on others. As Pope Francis says, 'Who am I to judge?'"

Her speech was far more progressive than one might imagine a nun capable, but this particular nun cavorted with witches.

"You're quite a woman, Mother Hildegard."

"I could easily say the same about you. And have." She offered a crooked, wrinkled smile. "Speaking of remarkable women, please pass along my hello to your Goddess-mother the next time you speak with her. Maggie is sorely missed—by the sisters, the elderly neighbors we visited together, as well as at the food pantry. We're approaching our busy season, and it's getting harder to keep the shelves stocked and deliver the food we do have to the needy and infirmed. With winter approaching... I worry. Not like I am trying to lay on a guilt trip or anything, but..." She knew that was exactly what she was doing. "I miss my sidekick, truth be told."

It saddened me to think that Maggie's absence meant so many in the community would suffer, the local pantry especially. She'd provided hefty donations, both of money and food, to the pantry and convent before setting off on her travels. But her time, compassion, and healing touch were irreplaceable. However, a bit of elbow grease from the coven ought to hold down the fort over the holidays. And what better way to prove our good will to the community than volunteering alongside the Catholic nuns at the local food pantry?

"I promise to pass on your message to Maggie. You two were a powerhouse team. You helped a lot of people."

"And we're both still helping people. Your Goddess-mother is an extraordinarily caring and empathetic person. She has a gentle soul and a fierce heart, and she follows her own path. I've always understood that. Our callings are different, and yet both are rooted in love and service."

The way she spoke of Maggie nearly brought me to tears, and it spurred me to make the offer. "On behalf of myself, my Goddess-mother, the staff of the Manor Arts, and the Witches of Arbor, I vow to do all I can to help you and the Sisters of Saint Francis take care of the food pantry over the holidays."

"You're a newly minted high priestess, if I'm not mistaken. Your words carry weight. So, I will hold you to your vow."

The starched nun looked around at the tables overflowing with perilous fare, the alcohol flowing over ice, and the costumed guests. "You don't play it safe, Evangeline. I admire that. And I admire your integrity. I'm sure Maggie is prestigiously proud."

Her mirth did not last long, and worry crept into her eyes. "I feel I must warn you, however." She looked surreptitiously over her shoulders and lowered her voice. "These architects the mayor brought in, the Harcourt women, they don't sit well with me. I feel their evil intent."

I heaved a sigh, stepped closer, and whispered conspiratorially. "It's a relief to hear you say that. I'm not a fan. I think they're dangerous."

"That's a rare sentiment, it seems. The Harcourts are universally admired in town. Still, I trust my instincts, and it's good to see you're trusting yours. You are powerful, which is why so many were—are— frightened of you. Yet there's light within you. Anyone with open eyes and an open heart can see it. But the Harcourts bring a darkness with them. They must be kept in check."

"And you think I'm in a position to do that? You think anyone in this town is going to listen to a witch? Listen to *me*?"

"Well, they're not going to listen to a Catholic nun, that's for sure. And you have a few more tricks up your sleeve than I do. But be cautious. The Harcourts are up to no good. I can feel it in my bones." The old nun looked around again nervously. "Listen, with Reverend Cudlow gone, the town is without a spiritual leader. And their new political leader, Mayor Riddle, is untested. Arbor is vulnerable. I'm not suggesting you lead folks. Let's be honest, that would never work. But maybe keep an eye on things. I know you've got...abilities. Please, do whatever you can."

"I'm an artist, and I am a witch. What I am not is a damned superhero...excuse the language."

"You saved this town once already whether they realize it or not. You can do it again." It was clear Mother Hildegard felt strongly. I appreciated both her concern for the community and her belief in my ability to protect them.

"First, however"—she checked her watch—"I understand you're presenting a piece from Bach's Matthäus-Passion this evening, Erbarme Dich. It's considered a masterpiece of classical sacred music. '*Erbarme dich, mein Gott, um meiner Zähren willen.* Have mercy, my God, for the sake of my tears.'"

"It is an odd selection for a witch, a song so connected to the passion of Jesus Christ. But the rawness and the depth of emotion drew me to this particular sonata. It *is* a masterpiece. I was supposed to perform it with Celia Bartoli, but she couldn't make it. Siobhan Quinn's singing with me instead. I heard her perform earlier tonight, and she's magical."

"I wouldn't miss it for the world." She tapped her watch. "But if you don't hurry, you'll miss it yourself."

"Excuse me?"

"It's time for the show," she said matter-of-factly.

A jolt of adrenaline coursed through my veins. *It's time!*

"Thank you, Mother Hildegard! I'll talk to you soon about the pantry, okay?" I took off toward the back gardens.

I made a beeline for the stage but tucked myself behind a stack of hay bales, cornstalks, pumpkins, and mums on stage left so I could check out the scene. It was a packed house except the two empty seats I'd reserved at center stage for Alexander and Celeste.

Damn.

I scanned the faces in the crowd. I found Mia, each of the boys, Mayor Riddle, and Mother Hildegard settling into her spot, but there was no sign of Alexander or Celeste. No sign of the Harcourt women either, which unnerved me. As I cast an eye over the orchestra, I noticed the absence of Siobhan Quinn.

First Celia Bartoli bales on me, and now this? If Siobhan doesn't show, I'm screwed.

A lump settled in my throat. I couldn't put it off any longer. It was time. The grand finale. I stepped onto the stage and took the mic.

"Good evening, everyone." My voice sounded remarkably steady given the agitated state of my nerves. I kept my shoulders back and swept my eyes across the crowd, everywhere but at the two empty seats before me. "On behalf of Alexander Morgan, Celeste Galehorn, and the entire Manor Arts team, I'd like to thank you for joining us this evening. I hope you've enjoyed the wonders and the frights. And I hope you've all had fun."

The audience offered polite applause.

I lifted a proud chin and went on. "In this, the last of the evening's entertainment, I have the honor of performing two classical pieces for you. The first is Bach's Suite Number One in G Major, a solo on the cello. Dancers will accompany the music, costumed in gowns of my own creation. These garments make up my debut fashion collection which uses sustainably sourced materials and celebrates diverse body types.

"In the second piece, Bach's German opera, Erbarme Dich, I will be performing on violin, accompanied by..." I cast a glance around for Siobhan but in vain. I offered up a silent supplication to the Goddess that I wouldn't have to pull off the piece without a singer. "...by the New York chamber orchestra." I gestured to the twenty or so tuxedoed musicians posing with their instruments. "Enjoy."

Again, they politely clapped.

I took my seat in the center of the stage, spread my legs, and positioned the cello between them. I drew my bow across the strings, creating sound waves that resonated through the wood and straight to the soul. The vibrational energy of the music enveloped me, and I surrendered to it. I allowed it to transfix and transport me. So enraptured was I with the drawing of my bow, I almost missed the models, draped in my garments, who danced through each movement. Tall and short women, curvy and waiflike women, Black and brown and white women in charmeuse and satin and lace, moved as specters in misty shadows.

When the song ended, the audience was stunned silent for a heartbeat before erupting in applause. Their unexpected accolades drew me to my feet and lifted my heart into my throat. After a quick bow, I took the mic.

"Thank you. Thank you, everyone. Please give a warm round of applause for the models!"

The models did a turn around the stage to the crowd's raucous delight.

I again addressed the audience. "And now, Erbarme Dich by Bach. Enjoy."

This time, I took my violin and bow in hand. It was a superb instrument, and as I raised it to my shoulder and rested my chin upon it, echoes of concertos past washed over me. The spirits of the instrument filled me. Anticipation prickled my fingers. But before I began, I chanced a glimpse at the seats before me. Still unoccupied. I peeked over to the spot where Siobhan should be. Still empty.

Damn. Okay then.

After a deep, steadying breath, I cued the orchestra.

My violin led the haunting strings, sweeping and dipping and swelling. I closed my eyes, and once again, the vibrations flowed through me. And when the aria would have normally joined in the song, I kept them closed.

This accounted for my shock as a rich contralto entered right on cue. My eyes popped open and widened further when I discovered the source of the lush and soulful voice.

Eris Harcourt strolled amid the crowd as she mesmerized us with her song, her hands clasped together lightly over her leather-clad diaphragm. Her voice flowed like liquid magic, and it danced with my violin in rippling waves. We locked eyes, and our intertwining melodies swelled. The song swept onward until Eris's voice and my violin brought the song gently to a close. When the final notes ceased to reverberate, I lowered my instrument.

The ovation floored me. It erupted with such force, it rattled the windows and sliding doors of the manor behind me.

Eris smiled as if she had a secret. I smiled because I knew it. She'd replaced the word *Gott*—God—in the song with *Gotten*—Goddess. It was perfect. I wished I'd thought of it. Eris's mischievous eyes never left mine as she ascended the stage and took my hand. We bowed together, waved, and murmured our thank-yous.

I slipped my hand from her grasp and stepped to the microphone. "Miss Eris Harcourt, everyone." I waited while they cheered. "Thank you once again for coming. We hope to see you all often at the Manor Arts. A blessed Samhain and happy Halloween. Safe travels. Good night!"

I dropped into one last bow and hustled off the stage, concluding the Samhain Grand Opening of the Manor Arts. The staff would usher out the guests and engage in hours of cleanup, but my role in the evening's festivities had blessedly come to an end. My night, however, was far from over. I had a Samhain ritual to lead at midnight with the coven and little time to prepare.

I hurried toward the sliding glass patio doors, but before I could make it inside, Eris headed me off. She leered down at me, and the most extraordinary sense of déjà vu engulfed me. I searched her face and shuddered to recognize so much of my own reflected back at me, like Eris was a faraway memory of myself.

What does it mean? Who is Eris Harcourt?

"I saved your ass twice now," she sneered. "Remember that the next time you consider telling anyone about the brooms in the Harcourt closet."

Eris Harcourt is a bitch.

Chapter Seven

Alexander and Celeste gushed penitent for missing my performance, but they escaped my wrath when I heard their contrite tales. Celeste had lost Luna immediately after venturing into the forest for their Awakening. She'd spent forever looking for her familiar and longer trying to make her way out of the woods while wrangling the cat in her arms. Celeste hinted there was more to her Awakening with Luna that she'd like to share at the Samhain ritual, and I was eager to hear her story.

Alexander's escapades proved as daunting as herding cats. He, Deidre, and the paramedics had to deal with Vivian Harcourt and Siobhan Quinn—my missing singer. Apparently, the two had struck up a spontaneous friendship while strolling along the third footpath. *Hmm... I wonder how that happened?* They caused a ruckus as they gorged on exotic food from the dangerous cuisine buffet, downed untold gallons of champagne in a relatively brief period, and crashed into an ice sculpture, shattering it and the champagne glasses beside it. Both women sustained minor injuries. After the paramedics patched them up, Alexander offered them rooms at the manor for the night. Siobhan declined, so Alexander sent his chauffeur, Jasper, to drive her to her hotel. Apparently still green around the gills, Vivian took Alexander up on his offer. So, the manor staff settled her into one of the guest rooms with a room beside her for Eris.

Peachy. Trouble is staying the night. It's like Alexander welcomed vampires into his house, and they brought toothbrushes. Fang brushes.

The Harcourts were the last people I wanted under the same roof. Regardless of what they claimed to be—architects, businesswomen, witches, naiads, whatever—they were a couple of diabolical shrews. But Vivian and I had reached a truce of sorts, and Eris's otherworldly voice had spectacularly saved my ass. And at the end of the day, Morgan Manor was not my house. I was as much a guest as anyone. Alexander could welcome whomever he wished. I had no right to complain.

I prepared for my first Samhain ritual as high priestess of our new coven by running around my room gathering everything I'd need into my bag of magical sundries. I flung off my dress and practically squealed with delight to be free of the confining and irritating garment, as stunning as it was. I stood naked before the scarlet high priestess's ceremonial robe that Celeste had laid out for me. I'd once worn the silver robe belonging to Adelaide, but when the new Witches of Arbor coven formed, my fellow witches gifted me with a ceremonial robe, representing the fire and blood that preceded our coven's formation. Foregoing a shift, I reverently draped the blood-red robe over my bare skin. Then I grabbed my besom broom and bag of magical tools and headed outside into the woods.

Gusts of stinging autumn air rustled through the trees. Leaves, crisped and reddened, descended in surrender from spindly branches. On their downward spiral, they met their brethren in a waltz with the breeze. Barefoot, I trekked over the leaves deep into the woods and headed for the clearing where, months ago, I'd found Alexander and Archie on their own Awakening Day. The ground was frigid and damp, but the cold didn't bother me. I cherished the connection of my soles on the earth. The grounding kept my energy balanced.

As I walked, I reflected on my first coven, the one I'd been born into. It was a community of witches and workers of magic who supported and cared for one another. Until my eighth birthday, my mother and I lived among the Loveridges and the Masseys, the Finnegans and ancient Wiccans, and the great magician, Alastair Gant. Since Adelaide had chosen me as her successor prior to her death, I became their high priestess. But the distance between Arbor and the original coveners became an ever-greater burden. And with the addition of Alexander, Celeste, and Mia, and with the boys back in town, the coven had grown large. So, we decided to form a new coven here in Arbor, an offshoot, and I would be its high priestess. The original coven chose Mr. George Massey as my successor.

An excellent choice.

Mr. Massey was a badass. Besides being Gregory and Ethan's father—in the first case, by blood, in the second case, by choice—George Massey was descended from an ancient line of Druids. He was a decorated military veteran and a true gray witch of the highest order. He was a strong and steady choice to lead the coven in these turbulent times.

And like Massey, I need to be prepared. I must be worthy of the coven's trust.

When I reached the clearing, I set up shop. First, I built a small bonfire. Then I prepared an altar facing east and laid out the tools I'd need for the Samhain ritual—fat white candle, athame – a ceremonial knife used in rituals, bell, earthen bowl of consecrated water, white sage, and a large jar of salt. With my besom broom, I swept the area clean of negative energy. Finally, I purified with white sage.

I lowered the robe from my shoulders and draped it across the bag at my feet, leaving myself exposed. Yet I felt no fear or hesitation. I wielded the power of the elements, and the fires of the universe burned beneath my skin. I sought wisdom and the Goddess's blessing and knew the best way to receive it was skyclad.

Taking the athame, I sliced the tip of my finger and let the blood drip onto the earth. I raised my arms to the heavens and spoke in a strong, clear voice.

"I am maiden, yet priestess high,

Of fire, water, earth, and sky.

I call on mother and on crone

So I mightn't stand alone.

Lavinia and Adelaide

Mentors from beyond the fade.

With guiding hands, do lift me high

From dusty earth to cloudless sky,

From sweltering flames to ocean tide,

Be my rock and be my guide.

Great Goddess, bless this lowly soul.

Fill me up so I am whole.

Through blood and magic, I call to thee.

As I will it, so mote it be."

A mighty wind swirled around me, gaining warmth as it sped into a whistling gale. My hair lifted from my shoulders, twisted around my neck, and whipped against my face. The air grew hotter and more humid. The intensifying heat drew the sweat from my pores until it dripped down my legs and into the soil beneath my feet. When the first drop of sweat hit the dirt, the wind subsided, and with it, the warmth. The swift return of the crisp midnight air froze the sweat that coated my skin.

I saw a flash of memory, the green apple slushy incident that had kicked off the vicious vendetta of former mayor Doreen Crandall and Arbor's Most Moral.

A screeching "Keeee-aaar" resounded above me, and the familiar call jolted me from my memories.

You haven't a stitch to cover you! You'll catch your death in this chill. Rocky admonished me as he hopped impatiently from one spindly leg to the other on the altar. Noticing my robe on my bag, Rocky swooped down and lifted it into his beak. Then he flew up and dropped it on my head.

It's too cold to go skyclad.

I flung the robe aside with a scowl. I got the feeling Rocky cared more about my modesty than my health, and that pissed me off. I looked down at my bare feet scarred with mud, the wide curve of my hips, my soft belly, and my proud, heavy breasts.

I do not need the robe. The temperature doesn't affect me. And I am not ashamed of my flesh.

But respect caused me to pick up the robe, shake it out, and lay it neatly aside.

At that moment, the members of the coven emerged from the forest into the clearing. They gawked in awkward silence as I stood there naked, dirty, and wild-haired. Each member of the coven had witnessed me bare to the world on one occasion or another. However, given the surprise on their faces, no one expected to find me skyclad on such a frigid Samhain evening.

It's good to know I can still shock them.

Celeste offered a wry, approving smirk. Alexander scowled but knew me too well to publicly criticize.

Never one to be put off by the sight of a naked body, Gregory strode forward and greeted me in a boisterous voice. "Samhain greetings, priestess." He lifted his scruffy, blond cheeks wide as he brazenly checked me out. "No better way to be close to the Goddess than skyclad. You're an inspiration to us all."

"Blessed Samhain," I said in a solemn voice. I approached the altar where Rocky perched stoically. "We're all here, and it's midnight, so let's gather up." I lifted the bell and rang it three times.

*

SATURDAY

Celeste hustled over to her regular position at my right hand, and Alexander stood to my left. Their familiars acted as well-behaved sentries behind them. Mia and the four boys—Nicolae, Luca, Gregory, and Ethan—completed our coven circle.

"We gather to celebrate Samhain and the turning of the Wheel of the Year." I lit the large white candle in the center of the altar.

I am worthy. So do I will it. So mote it be.

"Let's cast our circle."

Each witch used their besoms to sweep away any negative energy they'd dragged along with them. From the large jar, I spilled salt in a thick, protective line around the circle. Back before the altar, I took my athame, this time slicing it across my palm. The pain hurt worse than expected, but I refused to flinch. The glinting silver dagger dripped with my blood, and I dipped it into the bowl of water.

"As I consecrate this athame with water and with blood, so too do I consecrate this coven circle." I drew the dagger's edge in the air around the circle. Returning to my place before the altar, I again rang the bell three times. "The circle is cast. None can leave it but with good reason. So do I will it, so mote it be."

"So mote it be," the coven replied.

"Come forward, Witches of Arbor, and declare yourselves."

Each member filed deosil, or clockwise, around to the altar and received a blessing with white sage smoke. They called their names aloud and dropped a stone or crystal that corresponded to their own personal magic into the bowl of water and blood on the altar.

"Celeste Galehorn," she said and dropped in a moonstone.

Unknown/unidentified powers.

"Nicolae Loveridge," he said, leaving turquoise.

Power of persuasion.

"Luca Loveridge." Lapis lazuli.

Finding truth.

"Ethan Massey." Staurolite.

Glamours and illusions.

"Gregory Massey." Clear quartz.

Manipulation of the senses.

"Mia Aradia." Blue lace agate.

Green thumb and precognition.

"Alexander Morgan." Diamond.

Show off. Lightning and telepathy.

With this complete, they returned to their positions in the circle.

"Evangeline Clarion," I said, completing the circle. I placed a moss agate for earth, aquamarine for water, opal for air, amber for fire, and apophyllite for spirit into the bowl.

Creative arts. Creation and manipulation of the elements. Internal fire/impervious to flame. Flight.

I lifted my hands high and called for the others to do the same.

"We are the elements of the universe—the fire that sanctifies, the water that purifies, the air that uplifts, the earth that enriches, the spirit that inspires. As we wield the power of the elements within us, let our magic bind us to one another and to the coven. So do we will it, so mote it be."

"So mote it be," the coven replied.

I lowered my arms, and the others followed.

"As the Wheel of the Year turns on and ever on, we leave behind the light and enter the darkness. We leave behind the long summer days and welcome the chill of winter. We leave one year behind, and enter a new one, with all its mysteries. On this Samhain night, when the gateway between our world and the next plane is thinnest, we honor our ancestors. We honor the spirits of our fathers and mothers, our brothers and sisters, those who were persecuted and who suffered for their power. We honor those who taught us the old ways, those who guided us, and those who watch over us still. We remember them and honor them. Blessed be."

"Blessed be," the coven responded.

"The Goddess *has* truly blessed our coven." I turned to my right. "Celeste Galehorn, you've been a lifelong practitioner of the craft, but now we know that the Goddess's magic breathes within you. You've been joined by your feline familiar Luna and have gone through your Awakening. While every witch is different, you should expect two new powers—one innate, and one gifted by Luna. I encourage you to identify these powers quickly. Once you do, the coven will guide you and help you develop them. You strengthen the coven, and the coven strengthens you."

"Thank you, priestess. Yes, I've been blessed," Celeste said. "It's going to take time to develop my new powers, but you'll be happy to hear I've already identified them."

"That's fantastic," I said, surprised. "What are they?"

"Broadly speaking, the Goddess granted me sight. Technically, divination through lithomancy and crystal gazing—that's casting stones and peering into a crystal ball. How cool is that?" She laughed lightly. "Oh, and killer night vision."

"Badass," Gregory said approvingly.

Dear Goddess, my girl's going to be strong. I grinned. "How did you figure it out?"

Celeste closed her eyes for a moment and clasped anxious hands at her diaphragm as she settled into her tale.

"My Awakening. Things didn't exactly go the way a new witch might hope. I didn't receive any wise counsel or secret truths. Instead, I traipsed around the woods, trying to find Luna. She vanished altogether. During my frantic search for my errant familiar, Luna gifted me with the night vision I needed to find her. I didn't realize it at first, of course. I was too distraught and distracted. Once I stopped, calmed the hell down, and focused on the magic I knew was inside me, my eyes adjusted.

"That's when I noticed, half-buried beneath a pile of leaves at my feet, a polished pink stone, rose quartz. I picked it up, brushed it off, and looked on down the path. A few yards ahead, a green aventurine sat conspicuously on a fallen log. Beyond that, a silvery hunk of pyrite wedged in the V of a sapling. I followed the path, collecting stones as I went along, until I eventually found Luna, curled around a large crystal ball. I knelt, placed my hands on the crystal, and saw my powers within it."

Celeste picked up Luna and held her close. "I need to cultivate my magic, but one thing I see clearly is this—Luna will help in the troubles ahead."

"Wonderful, more trouble," I grumbled.

Mia raised her viper cane to summon our attention and spoke with a voice thick with accent and wisdom. "I will help Celeste. I have the sight, too, don't forget. I will teach her how to navigate the visions. And this trouble she foresees, I know its source. And so do you, Evangeline. *Le naiade streghe*," she said with a wrinkled scowl and a shiver. The bent old woman pulled her black shawl tighter around her shoulders and white-knuckled her viper cane. "They're no good. No good!"

"I assume you're referring to the Harcourt women," Nicolae interjected. "I'm of the opinion we're making Vivian and Eris out to be much worse than they are. They brought that couple back to life, didn't they? And I thought Eris sang beautifully."

"Ah, you speak so because Eris plied her wiles thick with you tonight," Mia cackled.

Celeste, Luca, and Gregory all popped their heads up.

Mia let lose a riotous, grizzled laugh and slapped her knee. "It seems Eris plied her wiles liberally," she rasped.

"And Vivian was all over Alexander and Siobhan Quinn. I've never been so glad to be left out," Ethan teased.

"Don't you all see?" I said, frustrated. "Naiads are seductresses. They manipulate and corrupt. Of course, they're going to appear harmless, make you feel comfortable with them, enjoy their company, crave it, desire them. But then you'll allow them to consume you. They don't give their time and affections away for nothing. Magic always has a cost. They're here for a reason. Mia is right. These women are dangerous."

I explained everything that went on with the Harcourts throughout the grand opening and all the revelations that Alexander and Celeste found out about them to catch Mia and the boys up on what they'd missed.

"We'd be fools to underestimate them. Even Mother Hildegard came to me with a warning. They're going to be trouble. And I, for one, have no intention of allowing them to wreak havoc."

"Look, while I know they're trouble, and I'd never let them hurt you, remember, I do have to work with them," Alexander said, aggravated.

"I know," I groaned.

"There's too much at stake downtown. I can't jeopardize it. But I may as well use it to our advantage. I can keep an eye on them." Alexander paced within the circle as he spoke.

As long as that's all you're keeping on them. I knew he'd hear me.

"Your motives are pure," Mia said to her nephew, "but le naiade seduce their prey. And you are a handsome man. You are not safe around them, Alessandro. None of you are safe."

"How do you suggest we deal with the Harcourts?" I asked the wise old la strega.

"Get rid of them," Mia answered with hard eyes. "Presto." She snapped her knobby fingers.

"Get rid of them! And how do you propose we do that?" Alexander asked with genuine shock in his voice.

"Magic, of course," I answered.

Mia cackled hard. "Si, yes, there's that too."

"We need to know more." I reviewed a mental laundry list of Harcourt facts but was unable to come up with a clear narrative of their story. "Luca—while you are susceptible to the naiad's seductions, your powers could prove invaluable." I stopped in front of him and placed a hand on the stiff shoulder of the vintage leather jacket he'd changed into.

He looked like a greaser from the fifties who'd sauntered through the pages of *GQ*, all polished, snarling angst. "What do I need to do?"

"Do what is in your nature to do. Find the truth. Find out all you can of the Harcourt women. Do they have a hidden agenda, and what is it? Recon, Luca, you need to do recon."

"I'm all over it." His sharp brow arched upward. "But that means I'm going to have to get close to them. I shouldn't go alone."

"I'll go with you." Ethan stepped forward. "I understand naiads and am blissfully immune to their temptations."

"Thank you, Ethan. Yes, team up with Luca, look out for him, learn the truth. And you know, I've been waiting to hear what you have to say about naiads. What can you tell us that might help?"

Ethan thought a moment before answering. "First of all, never trust their compliments, but don't disregard them either. Naiads don't compliment without good reason. Don't talk about money or things of value around them; they are greedy and jealous. Unless you have a death wish, ask no favors of a naiad. And for the love of the Goddess, don't make deals with them."

"Awesome," I grumbled.

"What are their weaknesses? We've got to be able to go after them, right?" Gregory asked.

"Sure, you can try." Ethan already sounded defeated. "Figure out a way to turn their vanity, greed, and jealousy against them." He turned to address me. "When it gets bad, Eva, and it will get bad, separate them from their element—their water source. That is where their magic lies."

"Thank you. Your knowledge is invaluable."

I turned to the coven. "I warn you all against engaging with the Harcourt women beyond surveillance, reconnaissance, and the downtown rebuild efforts. Take no offensive actions—for now. Let's see how they play their hand, and then we will proceed with caution."

I opened the circle, and the coven dispersed to their beds in weary contemplation. Celeste and Alexander took turns tempting me to their rooms before reluctantly returning to the manor alone. Relishing the bit of solitude, I took my time, clearing off the altar and packing up my bag of magical sundries. When all was neat and tidy, I draped myself in my scarlet high priestess's robe and trekked up to the manor where my own bed beckoned.

Chapter Eight

T'was the night after Samhain, and all through the manor, there were ghosties a 'stirring and causing a clamor. I hid in my room, in my bed, nice and snug, sheltered from the shenanigans on the hall's emerald rug.

A sharp knocking jolted me awake. I clung to my pillow, desperate for rest. I peeked my eyes open a sliver. The clock read three a.m., the witching hour. I waited, listened. At all hours of the day and night, Morgan Manor reverberated with knocks, footsteps, and muffled voices. But not all the sounds in these hallways came from the living. The manor teemed with ghosts causing a ruckus in some form or fashion. And this was Samhain, after all, when the veil was thinnest.

I held the covers tight under my chin as I listened for sounds of distress—of the corporal or unearthly persuasion. I'd just decided it was safe to close my eyes again when I noticed the rustling of sheets. Celeste rolled over in her sleep, curling around my legs.

The tricky vixen snuck into my bed after I fell asleep.

I brushed her white-blonde hair away from her face and skimmed my hand across her cheek, down her neck, and along her shoulder. Her skin flowed like rose petals beneath my fingers. Her presence in my bed intoxicated me, a rush of anticipation shivered along my body, but exhaustion overcame my intense craving for her. My eyes drooped, and I snuggled back down under the blankets.

On the edge of REM sleep, a sharp knocking awakened me once more. Muddleheaded and groggy, I assumed a pesky spirit, taking advantage of the thinly veiled night, decided to act up. I slipped out of bed, careful not to wake Celeste, and lit the white sage that sat on my nightstand. The knocking sounded again.

"You don't have to go home, but you can't stay here," I muttered drowsily as I opened the door with my smoldering sage held high.

"Oh! Shit." A bare-chested Alexander dodged the burning herbs.

I sputtered a laugh. "Sorry, I thought you were a ghost."

"Understandable. I'm sure I look—" he raised his arm and sniffed "— and *smell* like death. But I hoped you'd let me in anyway." He gave me an uncharacteristically silly pouty face. "I only want to sleep next to you. I'm fucking beat."

"Even rumpled, you look tasty, although you do reek." I wrinkled my nose. "But"—I stood aside so he could see behind me—"Celeste had the same idea. I woke up, and she was there."

He cringed at the sight of Celeste in my bed, but his tortured look passed with shocking quickness. "Like I said, I only want to sleep next to you. I'm tired, Evangeline." Alexander kissed the top of my head and maneuvered around me into my room. He unleashed a mighty, wide-mouthed yawn, scratched his beautiful backside, and flopped down on the far-left side of my bed, opposite Celeste, leaving a me-sized, empty space between them.

"Well, okay then." I shook my head.

They're both in my bed. At once. Oh, the possibilities.

I whimpered to myself, worn out and sexually frustrated. If only I weren't so tired, and it wasn't so late—or early. Why did it have to be such a terrible idea to mingle with these two intensely seductive individuals in one bed? It wasn't fair that being with them both came with an ocean of repercussions. I wished I didn't have to choose. I wished...

Before joining them in bed, I saged the bedroom doorway and the hall outside it. Then I poured a thick line of black salt across the threshold of the door. I needed a restful sleep, and I wasn't taking any chances.

The space between Celeste and Alexander beckoned. I could no longer resist.

"Move over and make room. Here I come," I said softly. I crawled onto the bed, all the way up to the pillows, and shimmied down under the covers between my two loves. Laying on my back, I allowed my eyes to close, and breathed deep, calming breaths.

Half-asleep, Alexander rolled over and draped a heavy arm under my breasts. He nuzzled his scratchy face into my neck. The commotion on the bed caused Celeste to roll over in her sleep too. She curled herself around my legs once more and rested her head low on my belly, under Alexander's arm.

"Naughty Eva, leaving me alone." She squeezed me tight.

And I smiled, wide and wild as a Cheshire cat, because in that moment, I was so much more than a queen. I was blessed with mighty riches, but they were made of flesh and blood and magic.

"My angel and my devil. But which witch is which?" I whispered.

There is light hidden in his darkness and darkness shielded by her light.

Their hands moved at the same moment, each evidently vying for the position of devil. His hand skimmed up my arm and over my shoulder. Hers ran up along the inside of my leg. My breathing hitched at their touch. Alexander's nose grazed my jaw, and I shuddered. With her cheek rested against my soft belly, Celeste exhaled a moan, and I felt the reverberations in the cleft between my legs.

"You two are gonna be the death of me," I whimpered.

Alexander grinned against my cheek. Their movements stilled. Before long, Alexander and Celeste matched their breathing patterns to mine, and we drifted off together.

*

The dream folded seamlessly into my present, and as often occurs in dreams, everyone was naked. Encased in a twist of arms and legs, I couldn't move without stirring my luscious, slumbering captors; his taut, muscled arms and chest, her long neck and plump, soft breasts, all bared to me.

I reached down, and with the lightest touch, drew Celeste up from where she curled at my hip to lay beside me. I lowered my lips to hers, and we melted together.

"You taste like honey and magic," I whispered and kissed my way down toward her breasts.

Before I arrived at my destination, Celeste pinned me to the bed. "I want you," she purred.

Damn, she's strong for someone so slender.

Celeste shimmied her way down between my legs and lifted wide, voracious blue eyes. "I want to taste you," she pleaded, hungry.

"Yes," Alexander said, now clenching his raging, hard cock.

Holy shit. This is a dream, right? So it's okay if I do this. If we do this. Are we doing this?

"Yes," I answered Celeste.

Without hesitation, she lowered her mouth onto my glistening center. I fisted her hair and held her against me.

"Fuck," Alexander groaned as he stroked his raging erection. "Spread your legs wider. Let her devour you."

I let my legs fall open wider, and Celeste feasted.

"Do I taste good?"

"Mmm, yes," she said, nodding into me.

"Yes," Alexander echoed.

She licked and sucked with voracious abandon. I was at her mercy, luxuriating in every pass and plunge of her tongue.

Alexander growled low. "Slow down. Use your hands," he instructed Celeste.

The obstinate woman ignored him.

"Slow down," I ordered her. "Use your hands."

She plunged two fingers into me and suckled my throbbing bud.

I threw back my head and moaned.

"You're still going too fast. Slow down," Alexander snapped.

"Shut the fuck up, Alexander." Celeste snapped her head up. "I'm not yours to command."

Fuck. They even fight in my dreams.

Alexander grabbed a handful of Celeste's hair, eliciting a hiss from her glistening lips.

"No, you're hers." He pressed Celeste's mouth against my eager pussy. "Please your priestess," he snarled and lowered his own mouth to mine.

There was nothing gentle about Alexander's kiss or the way he kneaded my heavy breasts. There was nothing sweet in the way Celeste consumed me as she pumped two, three, four fingers inside me.

They feasted upon me for what seemed ages when a pinch from him and a nibble from her threw me over the edge at last. I belted out a scream and rode wave after wave of pleasure.

*

I woke up natural from my deep sleep with drool and mascara staining my pillow. Despite the stresses and late hour of the previous night, I was bright-eyed and lighthearted, no doubt as a result of my nocturnal fantasies. I craved a shower and a toothbrush, but thanks to Celeste and Alexander, getting out of bed was my first challenge of the day. They remained in the same positions in which they'd fallen asleep—wrapped around me. I struggled to get up without waking them. They grumbled and groused but remained asleep as I slipped out of the bed between their arms and legs.

When I stepped out of the bathroom a half hour later, I found the bed empty, Celeste at my desk, tapping away on her tablet. Somehow, she'd already showered and had dressed smart in a sleek, black pencil skirt, silk blouse, and black pumps. Wisps of fair hair fell softly out of the knot atop her head, and she capped off the look with thick, black-rimmed reading glasses. How she accomplished this at such breakneck speed was magic, pure and simple.

"There's a pinup girl in my bedroom," I teased as I toweled off my hair.

"Morning, sweetheart." Celeste lifted her lips coyly. "Maggie texted her love and luck on the gallery's opening day, and Ayo sends her best wishes. Maggie asked you to text her tonight to let her know how things go."

"I wish they were here for this," I lamented. "Ok, I'll text her later. What else?"

"We've got the board meeting in forty-five. I laid out your clothes. Oh, and Gregory brought up breakfast and coffee. Personally." She snickered and lowered her eyes. "He hoped to wish you good luck and was disappointed he missed you. But he got a kick out of finding me and Alexander *both* in your bed. Gregory's the one who woke us up."

"Oh, great," I bemoaned with a laugh, "I'm sure Alexander was thrilled."

"Yeh, it wasn't pretty."

"And where is the lord of the manor now?"

"He's in his room getting ready. And you need to do the same. Let's kick things into high gear," Celeste said firmly. "Eat. Be quick. I'll help you dress when you're finished."

After devouring Gregory's breakfast and a damn fine cup of coffee, I stood before the full-length mirror in a chic gray pants suit with a ruby blouse and houndstooth Mary Jane pumps. Celeste had pinned my hair up into a bun on the back of my head. I looked nice. Nice and boring.

I am not boring. I may run a business now, but I'm still an artist, for Goddess' sake.

Celeste crouched in front of me, her head at bosom height. Unfortunately, there was no intimacy in her actions. All of her focus went to affixing an oversized, flouncy red bow to my lapel.

I wriggled and fidgeted, uncomfortable in the stiff suit jacket. Grunge, boho chic, and couture attracted me equally, but *these* clothes were not me. They weren't freeing or empowering. They were stiff and fussy.

"I really don't think I—"

"Shh! Hold still," Celeste hissed around the two-inch-long needle she held clenched in her teeth.

"But I—"

"Give. Me. A. Minute." She lifted a brow and glared.

"No, that's enough!" I snapped and swatted her fiddling hands. "This is ridiculous. I don't need this monkey suit."

Celeste removed the needle from her mouth and stood. She had a few inches on me, and she took advantage of them as she glowered down at me, simultaneously intimidating and alluring. "Eva Clarion, you are the director of the Manor Arts. You must look the part."

"I'm not playing a part. I *am* Eva Clarion." I heaved an exasperated sigh as I scrutinized the clothes. "I'm an artist—a designer with a new collection, a brand. And *this* is not *on brand*. Look, the gallery's first full day is going to be stressful enough. I've got to be myself."

Celeste frowned. "You need to make a good impression. These clothes may be a bit...*stuffy* for your taste, but you should look competent and professional."

I conceded the necessity of making a good impression, but I had no intention of changing myself to please or placate anyone. And I was tired of arguing about fucking clothes. "I appreciate your help, I do, but I will wear whatever strikes my fancy, thank you very much."

I studied the mirror. I ditched the suit jacket first, next, the chic gray pants and red blouse. Stripped down to my undergarments, the only things that remained of the ensemble Celeste selected were my updo and Mary Jane heels. I pulled on a snug pair of jeans that showed off my ass with a fat, black braided belt that cinched my waist and my Nine Inch Nails T-shirt. And for good measure, I pinned the floppy red bow onto my shirt.

"Little bit business. Little bit rock and roll." I smiled proudly.

Celeste rolled her eyes and grabbed our briefcases. "Yes, yes, you're lovely. But now we're late for the board meeting, so we gotta locomote."

*

Ethan noticed our arrival in the conference room first and had mimosas in our hands before we could say, "Good morning."

"We were desperate without you." He kissed us each on the cheek.

"You look like you've survived in my absence," I teased, and sipped the fizzy citrus jolt.

"It's about time you showed up. You left us sitting here with our cocktails in our hands," Gregory said playfully. "Then again, you had a fatiguing evening." He wiggled his eyebrows at Celeste and Alexander.

She laughed. He didn't.

"Our Eva's late as always, but as always, she's arrived looking stylish. Very editorial," Nicolae added from the far corner of the room where he leaned, casually dapper like Dean Martin. Forgoing mimosas for the hard stuff, Nicolae sipped his whiskey and dangled an unlit cigarette from his fingers.

"What was it Adelaide once said?" Luca asked and answered himself. "'There's an art to arriving in style, and our Evangeline is nothing if not an artist.' And we all know Adelaide had style."

"I'm just relieved you're not wearing some Goddess-forsaken pants suit. Your ass is too fucking fine to hide in a pair of slacks," Gregory joked.

No one laughed.

This kind of talk from Gregory didn't shock me. As with all the boys, we'd grown up thick as thieves. We held nothing back. Gregory had never been shy about his appreciation for the human figure, or his ravenous sexual appetite. These were critical components of his personal magic, what made him the magnificent witch he was. But commenting on my ass was not exactly appropriate for an office environment. And it pissed off more than one person at that conference table.

My head swiveled between Celeste—who'd had her fashion sense questioned for the second time that morning—and Alexander—whose machismo threatened to boil over. His face reddening and his self-control thread-thin, I worried Alexander might knock Gregory out, not only for checking out my ass, but because he appeared perfectly comfortable remarking on it. I suspected Alexander was still pissed that Gregory had found him and Celeste in my bed that morning.

Before I could decide what to say that wouldn't escalate the precarious situation, a chair scraped across the floor. All eyes trained themselves on Alexander; on his imposing figure shown off in a perfectly tailored Brooks Brothers suit, his dark eyes shadowed by darker waves of hair that skimmed his cheekbones, and his chiseled, demanding jaw covered in well-tended stubble. Alexander coolly checked his platinum and diamond cufflinks and straightened his tie before clearing his throat.

Talk about style. Damn.

"Those at this table represent the Manor Arts Board of Directors. Outside of the Manor Arts sphere, we are all friendly, however, we are running a business here. Gregory—" He paused as if to collect his thoughts—or his patience, "—please refrain from commenting on a coworker's physical body while at a board meeting. That kind of talk is not appropriate in an office setting. Or in the kitchen, for that matter. As an employee, you must adhere to company policy. As the head of the Culinary Department, you must be a model of good behavior for your team. Evangeline and Celeste" —Alexander turned to face us like a scolding father, not allowing Gregory a chance to reply—"out of respect for the valuable time of everyone here, please be prompt to our meetings.

Your fashion sense should not outweigh your common sense. Now, we have business to attend to. Please everyone, have a seat."

Stop being an asshole, would ya? I know you can hear me. I don't know what crawled up your ass and died this morning, but fucking deal with it, and don't take it out on everyone else.

I sensed a softening of Alexander's features, but other than that, he gave no indication he'd been listening to my thoughts.

Alexander waited until we all had settled down around the conference table before continuing. "Last night was a success. You should all be proud. I know my great grandfather would have loved the show we put on, despite the hiccups."

"You mean, hiccups like the two dead people?" Luca blurted. Watching them die had taken a serious toll on him.

"Yes, besides the dead people." Alexander cleared his throat again. "Who, by the way, are now resting comfortably at their home this morning after a thorough exam at the hospital last night." He capped off this declaration with a definitive nod.

"The fact that you can make the statement with a straight face is a testament to the bizarre nature of the evening," Nicolae added without humor.

"Yes." Alexander stared at him blankly for a beat before continuing. "Despite all that, the grand opening ended with nothing but rave reviews from one and all. But now the real work begins—the day-to-day operational collaboration between the Manor Arts and Morgan Manor. The people who showered us with praise yesterday won't think twice about damning us tomorrow. We need to make a good impression on every guest, every interaction, every day. And we've got to do it while maintaining the standards and integrity of Morgan Manor itself."

Alexander spoke with easy poise and a sharp command of the boardroom. He discussed the finances, the mission of the Manor Arts, and the strategies essential to achieve these desired ends.

When he wrapped up, Alexander handed the reins of the meeting off to the boys. Nicolae, our marketing director, delivered an ambitious report on our advertising campaign. Luca related the latest on tech and security and explained how his efforts merged with Nicolae's to tackle social media. Ethan reviewed the special events, art classes, and entertainment schedules. Gregory gave the culinary department rundown and reminded us that he'd given most of the kitchen staff the day off.

"I've got a small crew tackling some prep work and deep cleaning, but nobody's doing any cooking. My team killed it last night, and they deserve a break. So, if you're hungry, you've got to fend for yourselves." Gregory reclined in his chair to indicate he'd said the final word on the matter.

Elliot Parker rose to speak next. Originally hired as a footman, the sandy-haired young man with the apple-pie smile arrived at Morgan Manor looking better suited to farmhand work. After a shaky start, he acclimated quickly and threw himself into his work. He'd been promoted to butler after Alexander fired his grizzled predecessor, Franklin, for plotting to kill me. After the burning of Arbor, Elliot worked closely with Alexander, who eventually named him estate manager on top of his duties as butler. And poor Elliot tried his damnedest to tackle it all.

He reviewed a few general notices and reminders, then spoke about the staff. "Now, I think you all know the manor staff by now, but it's important you show them some appreciation. They're the ones cleaning up after you. So please, give them a bit of gratitude, okay? As for the inside crew, besides myself, we've got Mrs. Fletcher, our housekeeper, Nora Mormont, the house maid, and our footman, Killian O'Shae, who's been indispensable to me. This, by the way, is a skeleton crew on an average day for a manor this size. And we don't have average days here at Morgan Manor." He sighed wearily and then bucked himself up. "Our outside crew consists of Mr. Blomgren, our groundskeeper, who looks after the maintenance and landscaping of the property along with Keegan O'Shae. He's Killian's brother. Their mother, Deidre, is Alexander's assistant."

"Killian and Keegan are good people." Alexander cut in. "Just like their mother, they're hardworking with a low tolerance for bull—" He caught himself. "—drivel."

"Couldn't agree more. I'm proud to say Morgan Manor is staffed by an impeccable group of diligent, tenacious individuals," Elliot said with a seriousness that aged him. "But they are stretched thin, sir." He directed his words to Alexander. "This is a large estate to care for, and with our current number of residents and the Manor Arts responsibilities...this workload is unsustainable. We need to hire at least another maid and footman and one more in maintenance to work with Mr. Blomgren. What do you think?"

Thanks to his efficiency, professionalism, and down-home manner, the staff respected Elliot. He'd managed to keep the ever-increasing number of residents of the manor comfortable and accommodated; no small task, as this group boasted singular tastes. So when Elliot made a request, I paid attention.

Alexander stared down at the conference table for a beat. "I'll take it under advisement."

"Fair enough, boss." Elliot returned to his seat with far less enthusiasm than he rose.

"I'm sorry, what?" I blurted.

Every face at the table turned to me.

"Is there a problem, Evangeline?" Alexander scowled.

Heads turned to Alexander and back to me.

"'You'll take it under advisement?' What's that? You heard him. Their workload is unsustainable, and it's only going to get busier around here. Elliot has been as competent and loyal as an employee can possibly be. And he's coming to you for help not to ease his own burden, but in order to maintain standards."

When no one spoke, I added, "I think you need to listen to him."

Every face turned to Alexander with a collective inhale.

He sat back in his leather armchair at the head of the table and appraised me with a critical eye. His face impassive, his steepled fingers tapped against his chin. I held his attention and didn't flinch from his penetrating gaze.

Breaking eye contact, Alexander turned to Elliot.

"Hire whoever you need." Alexander kept his expression blank. "What's next?"

Elliot looked at me and mouthed, "Thank you," with shock freezing his features.

Strike while the iron's hot. I got to my feet.

"I believe I'm up next." I cleared my throat. I reviewed the feedback I received from the exhibiting artists the night before and went over the gallery's staffing schedule for the coming week. Then I took the plunge.

"So, I spoke with Mother Hildegard from Saint Francis Convent, and she has a concern. Maggie used to help her and the sisters down at the food pantry, and they delivered food to the elderly and infirmed. Since Maggie's been gone, they've been struggling. Now, with the holidays coming and colder weather rolling in... I mean, it's their busiest time of year. I think we should help them, in the spirit of goodwill. And I think Thanksgiving would be a great time for all of us to volunteer at the pantry together. What do you guys think?"

Heads nodded around the room, but Alexander remained unreadable.

"Hell yeh," Gregory chimed in. "My crew will roast some turkeys and whip up some sides, and I'll put you all to work serving it up down at the pantry."

More nodding from the table.

More of nothing from Alexander.

"I understand, volunteering is another responsibility added to everyone's already busy schedules. Between our personal projects, work for the Manor Arts, and of course, Yule, we have our work cut out for us. If Yule is going to be as successful as Samhain, we need to start planning now. But helping at the pantry will be a good way to play nice with the community. And remember, Mother Hildegard and the sisters stood by us in our time of need. I think we should reciprocate."

"I'm sorry? Did you say Yule?" Alexander leaned forward in his chair. Disgust marred his handsome face and cracked his controlled façade.

"Yes, of course. The Wheel of the Year turns on and ever on. The Winter Solstice is one of the most important sabbats on the calendar. And the holiday season will hopefully be a major source of revenue. The Manor Arts is a gallery that celebrates art in all its forms. We'll need to put on a great show."

"You're extraordinarily liberal with my money, ya know that?" Alexander ran his hands through his hair in frustration.

I felt like he'd slapped me in the face. "Excuse me?"

Liberal with his money? Using Morgan Manor as the location for my gallery had been his fucking idea. And I sank twenty grand of my hard-earned money into this business. That might not seem like a lot to a bazillionaire, but it was a hell of a lot to me. How could he speak to me like that? I didn't care if he listened in.

"Look Evangeline, we can't go throwing parties every month for everyone in New York. Last night was all about the grand opening. The fact that it fell on Halloween was a bonus for marketing and budgetary reasons. But no one ever said anything about Morgan Manor celebrating every holiday."

"What did you expect? The Manor Arts is a business, and the winter holiday season equals shopping and merry making. Celebrating Yule, with all its bells and whistles, means foot traffic, which leads to revenue, which leads to a successful business."

"There will be no Christmas at Morgan Manor, and that's final!" Alexander pounded the table, thundered to his feet, and clenched his fists at his sides.

Unlike the rest of the table, I didn't flinch at his rage. He and I stared each other down, and not a soul—not even Celeste—seemed interested in taking sides on this one. I didn't blame them. Who in hell would want to grapple with either of us? We were both stubborn. And deadly.

I breathed deep and summoned my power to strengthen my resolve. "As much as I'm loathed to admit it, the Manor Arts must be an active part of this community if we're going to succeed. You said yourself, the people of Arbor will support us if we make them look good, and they'll damn us if we don't. That's the beginning and end of it at this point. They've lost their religious and political leadership to scandal, and the town's reputation is tarnished. The town council has spent the last few months on damage control and PR. Arbor uses the holidays to show off the community as sparkly and bucolic. The businesses in town go all-out for Christmas every year. If the Manor Arts skipped Yule, skipped *Christmas*...it would be a mistake."

"Businesses *would* go all-out this year if there were any left in town," Celeste snipped with a raised brow to Alexander.

Ouch. Here we go.

"Too bad there isn't some huge, luxurious mansion on a hilltop to host a bit of Yuletide merrymaking to lift spirits and bring folks together. Good will toward men, and all that," she said dryly.

Alexander grumbled.

"So, what is your vision for Yule, Eva?" Celeste asked with a notebook balanced on her crossed knee and a pen dangling from her fingers. The woman was prepared at all times, like she could see and anticipate the needs of others.

"I'm glad you asked," I said cheerfully. I loved this time of year and was excited to share my ideas. "I'm thinking traditional—as in old-school, Celtic-Druid traditional. Candles scattered around the manor like stars. Natural decorations everywhere, evergreen bows and holly strewn from every archway and column, mistletoe hung above every door, and a Yule log in every fireplace. I want carolers and wassail and dancing. And a feast! A fattened pig and a bull roasting on spits outside. All manner of festive dishes and desserts. The scent of cinnamon and clove filling the air."

As I spoke, I saw the scene; not in my mind's eye but surrounding me. I smelled the cinnamon and tasted the roasted pig on my tongue. The cheeky, knowing looks on Gregory and Ethan's faces betrayed the surreptitious glamor they whipped up around me.

"Sounds a hell of a lot like Christmas," Alexander grumbled. "Except for the animals on spits."

"It is." Gregory answered him with a hefty—and justified—chip on his shoulder. "The Church hijacked our ancestors' Yule traditions and offered them conversion or death."

"Good times," Ethan added with a sardonic nod.

"That's why we'll include a few traditions unique to the ancient ones—a bonfire and releasing ceremony, and a journey around the solstice spiral."

"As the resident Druid," Gregory piped up, "and the one who will have to deal with that pig and bull, and all the Yule fixings and trimmings, not to mention the catering for the Manor Arts, and a Thanksgiving feast for the pantry, I say *bring it*. What's the point of running a business like ours—in a fucking gothic mansion, no less—if we're not going to throw some kick ass parties? Especially when *I'm* cooking." He turned to me. "I like your vision. I'm all in."

Approval resounded from each member of the Manor Arts Board of Directors. All but Alexander.

He and I locked eyes. "It's your house."

He rested his forehead on his steepled fingers. When he eventually looked up, irritation creased his face. "Fine." Alexander gritted his teeth. "But leave me out of it. This is all you guys. And don't stress out Elliot and the manor staff too much. They already have their hands full."

"Now that Elliot's hiring more staff, that shouldn't be a problem." I couldn't suppress a self-congratulatory smile. "And does everyone agree to help Mother Hildegard at the pantry?"

The table agreed, and I looked to Alexander.

"Yes, of course! Why the hell not?" he said with sarcastic jubilation. "We'll all add volunteering at the food pantry *and* planning Christmas— excuse me, I mean *Yule*—to running a brand-new art gallery, and all the rest of our responsibilities. Like rebuilding a town."

"A town you destroyed," Celeste snapped.

I expected a sharp retort, but Alexander governed himself. "It looks like we've got work to do." He checked his watch and rose. "It's time to wrap this up. I've got a meeting with Mayor Riddle this morning. I'm going to remind him that communication and coordination are a requirement for spending my money. Does anyone have any other business to address? Evangeline, anything else to add to our to-do lists?"

Not for the first time that morning, the needling desire to hit him surged through me, but I reined in my roiling emotions. "No, I'm good. Let's do this thing."

"You heard the woman. Let's get to work."

The room emptied. Deidre commandeered Alexander the moment the meeting ended. But before she dragged him out of the room, he stepped in front of me.

"Have a great first day. I'll try to visit later when I get back from town," he said in a clipped manner and left me with a strained expression and a kiss on the head.

Celeste wove her arm around mine. "Come on, witch, we've got a gallery to open."

Chapter Nine

Celeste and I started for the gallery but only made it as far as the foyer before the appearance of Vivian and Eris Harcourt sidetracked us. Their arrival both awed and annoyed me. Their Samhain getups had obviously been costumes because, this morning, they epitomized the intersection of business and fashion. Eris sported a chic pair of charcoal cuffed, flair-bottom pants, a silver blouse belted tight around her waist, and suede Manolo Blahnick stilettos. She swept up her thick, black hair in a loose knot, and wore a large beaded necklace with an even larger pair of sunglasses perched on top of her head. Her tattoos and piercings added an edge to the posh look. As if Eris wasn't intimidating enough, there was Vivian to contend with. She wore her raven hair down, so it flowed over her crisp, white, button-down blouse with a sharp collar. A high-waisted, black pencil skirt and red-soled Christian Louboutin pumps underscored Vivian's sophisticated style.

Why do they have to look so fucking perfect?

I looked down at my T-shirt, jeans, and Mary Janes, almost threatened by a sense of inferiority. Almost.

"Ms. Clarion, Ms. Galehorn, how delightful to run into you." Vivian grinned wryly at us.

"Good morning, ladies." I forced the pleasantries. "Glad to see you looking so revived, Vivian."

"Yes, I'm quite recovered," she replied without a hint of embarrassment for her drunken behavior the night before. "Thank you for your gracious hospitality. The bed was comfortable and the shower hot." Vivian gave a slight shimmy of her shoulders, reminiscent of Adelaide.

"The Morgan Manor amenities are Alexander's domain. You should thank him." I tried to be polite.

"Oh, I plan on it." She had a devious glint in her eye. "As a matter of fact, we're all heading downtown together for a meeting with Mayor Riddle and the planning board. But don't wait up, dear. It's a breakfast meeting, but you never know how these things go. It could take all day."

"Oh...really," I stuttered. This information took me by surprise, and it no doubt showed on my face.

Alexander never mentioned the Harcourts were joining him for Riddle's meeting. Why?

"It's a massive reconstruction project, you understand. So much to do. There's bound to be long hours."

Vivian's insinuation maddened me, and I didn't want to take her bait. Still, I couldn't shake my curiosity. "And where are you staying during these long hours in Arbor?"

"Didn't you hear? We're moving the office of Harcourt Architecture from Ithaca down here to Arbor."

"Is that so?" *Beautiful, I'll never get rid of them.*

Vivian nodded. "Yes. You see, while other firms shied away from Arbor's blackened, skeletal destruction and scandalous reputation, we saw the charred rubble as an opportunity. When we're through, Harcourt blood, sweat, and tears will seep from the very pores of Arbor."

Cause that's not creepy. Or gross.

"That's an, ah, ambitious goal, but I'm still not clear on where you'll be staying."

"By the river, of course." Eris seemed to immediately regret speaking.

Vivian shot a menacing glance to her daughter and cleared her throat before elaborating.

"Yes, we purchased an old estate along the river. It will eventually become our home and the offices of Harcourt Architecture. At the moment, however, it's in a dreadful state. It'll require tremendous renovations before it's habitable. But when it's complete, it'll be the crowning jewel of Harcourt Architecture. We have an excellent team working on it, but it will take time." Passion filled her voice. She clearly cared about her work, regardless of her daughter's criticisms. "The magnitude of the downtown project, however, necessitates a daily, hands-on presence. So, for the time being, Eris and I rented out a vacated apartment on Parson Street, no more than half a block from the site. Eminently convenient, and a lucky find. It's the only apartment on the block without damage."

Oh fuck.

"Yeh, you know, it's kind of weird," Eris added. "Every structure around it burned, but this one apartment was spared. Funny, huh?"

Please, no. They can't be living in Adelaide's apartment!

I wanted to scream and curse them. I wanted to throw something. But Celeste squeezed my hand, and my roiling emotions simmered. "Hysterical."

"We settled in earlier this week, and already feel quite at home." Vivian said cavalierly.

"Drop by for a spell when you're in town." Eris smirked. "I'm sure you know the way."

What the hell? Do they know it belonged to Adelaide? Can they still feel her magic?

I had had no time to process this twisted revelation when Alexander arrived at the top of the staircase.

"Good morning, ladies!" He descended the stairs with such an exuberant swagger, I wondered if he'd gotten high with Gregory after the board meeting. He'd been such a grump.

Alexander headed straight to my side. Ignoring Celeste, he wound an arm around my waist and dropped a sweet kiss on my lips.

I didn't smell any pot.

"I hope I haven't kept you waiting too long," he addressed the Harcourts with his arm still firmly around me.

"Not at all, Alex dear," Vivian cooed. "We were merely chatting with the ladies of the manor. But—" She pursed her lips and scrunched her brow. "—we must get moving. The mayor is a patient man, but I can't say the same for the planning board."

"You're not wrong," Alexander groaned.

He called for Killian to retrieve their coats. As Alexander and the brawny footman helped the Harcourt women slip into them, I noticed

Killian's gray eyes lingering over me. I smiled at him, and Killian lit up, his cheeks blushing as red as the unruly, ginger mop on his head. This insecurity lasted only an instant before he squared himself and hit me with a toe-curling grin and a voracious look that told me this was no naïve novice. Schooling his features, Killian hustled off before his boss could catch him ogling his girl—something Celeste had not missed.

"You ladies head out. Jasper's waiting with the car. I'll only be a moment." Alexander motioned the Harcourts toward the door.

Once Vivian and Eris were out of sight, all joviality slipped from Alexander's face.

"Look, I'm sorry for being an asshole this morning. My stress level is through the roof—not that that's an excuse. And I'm, ah, obviously not a big fan of the holidays. But I love you, and I'm on board with whatever you decide. Just don't make me promise to be jolly about it." He grinned sadly. "Now, I do have to run. Have a great first day. And don't worry. I'll keep an eye on them." He followed the women outside.

"That's what I'm afraid of," I muttered.

"So, we've got a Scrooge on our hands. At least he's self-aware. And he did apologize," Celeste said thoughtfully. "But are the Harcourts seriously living in Adelaide's apartment?" She shivered.

"They have to be. Adelaide's place was the only one without fire or water damage after the burning." The thought of those women in my high priestess's space sickened me. "But is it coincidence? There have to be other offices somewhere in town to rent." I shook my head and slumped my shoulders. "And as for Alexander...it seems the holidays have opened old wounds. I'll talk to him, see what I can do to ease his wariness and include him in the festivities. I want *all* of us to enjoy this season and celebration."

"Eva, you need to consider that Alexander may be happier staying away from the holiday hubbub. Don't let him ruin the fun for you though." Celeste brushed her lips against my cheek. "But these are concerns for another time. Now, you get the hard-earned honor of opening the Manor Arts."

Standing at the doors to the gallery, I took a moment to appreciate the awesomeness of the achievement, and excitement shivered down my spine.

I pulled it off. I opened an art gallery!

I danced a little *I-did-it!* jig much to Celeste's delight. With a dramatic flourish, I flung the gallery doors open wide.

"Welcome to the Manor Arts."

*

Visitors arrived within minutes. A handful of curious locals were the first through the door, but there weren't many Arbor residents the rest of the day. I assumed most of the community stayed home to nurse their Samhain hangovers. Instead, high school and college students, a bus from a local retirement community, and folks from nearby towns streamed in. For many of our guests, the Witches of Arbor were as much of a draw as the gallery itself. Celeste and I were curiosities as much on display as the artwork. At least my clothes were cute and comfortable.

The gallery bustled, and I tried not to let anxiety take hold as I welcomed guest after guest, directed them through the exhibits, and answered questions. Everywhere I turned, people wanted to speak to me. Celeste's calming energy, and the hum of magic emanating from the art, helped me deal with the crowds, but my patience grew thinner with every "yoo-hoo" and tug of my sleeve.

I ducked my head and averted my eyes when Ms. Harrison, the rotund, eighty-some-year-old sister of Arbor's ailing police chief, flagged me over with a wave of her handkerchief. She was a sweet old woman, and like her brother, had shown me kindness when few in Arbor would. But she liked to prattle, and I wasn't in the mood for excessive idle chitchat. There was no escaping her, however.

"Oh, I'm glad I caught ya, Miss Eva." She grabbed ahold of my hand and held it to her voluminous bosom. "You've done such a marvelous job! My brother wanted to be here to see it for himself, but ya know, he's not well."

"Thank you." I extracted my hand as politely as possible. "And yes, I heard he's taken a bad turn. Please, send him my regards and wishes for a speedy recovery."

"Yes, well, you see, that's why I've come. Don't mistake me; I wanted to glimpse these wonders with my own eyes, of course. But...my brother's getting worse every day, Miss Eva." She looked about and tugged me closer to her. "We need your help. I know ya have powers, dearie. And I know you're a good girl who tries to use those powers to help folks, like Ms. Magdalena and poor, poor Adelaide. My brother's always known too, of course, and he's done his best to protect ya. Well, now he's calling in a favor, as it were."

"Ms. Harrison, please understand. I would help the chief in an instant if I could, but I can't. I have...gifts," I whispered, "but I'm not a healer. That's Maggie's gift. And unfortunately, she's out of town. Across the country, actually. The most I could do is make him comfortable."

The old woman recoiled. "Make him comfortable?"

"Oh, I didn't mean—"

"No, no, I know exactly what you meant. My brother looked out for you witches for years," she said without a hint of the kindness that had once filled her voice. "But now that you have all this"—she motioned to the splendor around us—"you can't be bothered to lift a finger to help him in return."

"No, that's not it at all. Please understand—"

"You've said enough. I'll leave you in peace. I'll pass along your *regards and best wishes* to my brother." She huffed away.

Despite all my anticipation for the day, when five o'clock rolled around, I eagerly left the gallery night shift in Ethan and Nicolae's capable hands. Alexander still hadn't returned from his meeting downtown. It hurt that he spent the day with the Harcourts instead of with me at the gallery. I moped as Celeste and I headed out to the foyer. I paused between the yawning fireplace and the curling marble staircase and considered whether to visit the wine cellar or hit the kitchen first. I was feeling a bit peckish, and with most of Gregory's crew off for the day, I had to fend for myself.

Before I could make up my mind, Celeste squealed, "Luna!" She lunged forward to snatch up her familiar, but the cat sprang up half a dozen steps and hissed. "I'm so sorry I neglected you, but I needed to be with the high priestess last night, and I had work to do in the gallery today," Celeste explained with a regret that stung my heart. "Please forgive me."

Luna lifted an arrogant head, paced, and swatted her sleek black tail against the steps, clearly still perturbed. Celeste knelt and opened her arms to her familiar. The pacing stopped, and Luna leapt into her witch's embrace. Celeste caught her as gracefully as one can catch a cat, wrapped her arms tightly around Luna's middle, and nuzzled her nose deep into the dark black fur. Luna snuggled and purred, all having been forgiven. The duo seemed blissfully content.

"You two do your thing." I peered down at the fledgling witch and her familiar. Although they appeared oblivious to my presence, I continued. "I'm going to grab a bite and turn in early."

"Mhm, okay sweetheart. See ya later," Celeste waved over her shoulder.

"Okay then." *Wine. I deserve it, dammit.* When my stomach growled in protest, the strangled gargling reverberated through the vaulted foyer. *Fine, food first.*

On an average day, the expansive commercial kitchen bustled with rubber soles thudding on a maze of mats and resounded with choruses of, "yes, chef" and "hot soup, watch your back!" Tonight, the kitchen was quiet. Eerily so.

I ducked into a walk-in fridge and rustled around for something to tempt my taste buds. I clasped my hand around a hefty stick of salami when Gregory barged into the fridge.

"What are you doing in here?" he thundered with the hard eyes of a head chef.

I flinched at his dominance. "Just getting a snack." I hid the salami behind my back.

He lifted his bushy beard wide, and a deep laugh rumbled through his barreled chest. "Aw, hey, no worries, priestess. My fridge is your fridge. But what do you got there?"

I raised the salami high and suppressed my laughter.

Gregory shook his head, grinning. "You could hurt yourself with that thing. Return the salami and let me feed you. I'll whip you up something tasty."

"No, I don't want to bother you. I'm perfectly capable of taking care of myself."

"I don't doubt it, but I've got a bit more experience satisfying folks." He winked.

Cheeky, but not wrong. "Okay, but just a snack."

"Sweet." Gregory filled his large arms with an assortment of items from the shelves, and motioned to the door. "Let's get cooking."

I trailed Gregory through the kitchen to his own spot at the back of the prep area. He dropped the armful of groceries onto the cutting board and got down to business.

Gregory made quick work of thinly slicing a Granny Smith apple, then went for the cheese. "Dubliner Irish Stout, Blarney Castle, Emmental," Gregory named them and their characteristics as he cut. His strong hands maneuvered with staggering deftness and precision. He arranged it all on a plate with some red grapes, walnuts, and wheat crackers. Then, grabbing a massive, serrated knife, he cut inch-thick slices of a crispy French baguette, drizzled them with olive oil, and threw them on the grill behind him. After flipping them over once to get them nice and toasty on both sides, he pulled the crusty bread off the grill. After rubbing them with garlic, he topped them with tomato and roasted red pepper bruschetta, microgreens, a fat sliver of parmesan, and a drizzle of balsamic reduction.

Bending over, showing off what had to be the greatest ass on the East Coast, Gregory grabbed a bottle out of a small fridge under the counter. "Paired with a fine Italian Prosecco, and this, priestess, is a proper snack."

He's going to make someone positively rapturous someday.

"It's a work of art. I'm sure it'll taste as wonderful as it looks. Thank you." Standing on my tiptoes, I wrapped my arms around his neck and kissed his fuzzy cheek.

"Well, isn't this a pretty picture." Vivian Harcourt simpered from the kitchen's back door.

Alexander stood beside her, clearly agitated, his jaw clenched and a vein bulging at his temple as he glared at me and Gregory.

"What's going on here?" Alexander snarled.

"Gregory whipped me up a snack."

Take it down a notch. I knew he could hear me. *Cut the jealousy bullshit, especially when you walk in here with that slimy naiad by your side.*

"Tales of Chef Gregory Massey's skill at whipping up some magic are legendary. And not only in the kitchen," Vivian said suggestively. "Word gets around, you understand."

She wasn't wrong. Gregory's reputation proceeded him.

"That's one hell of a spread for a snack," Alexander growled. "You're not trying to work your magic on Eva, are you, Druid?"

I flinched at his accusation.

Gregory squared his shoulders and lifted a noble chin, the accusation clearly insulting him as well. "It's a hell of a snack because I'm a hell of a chef. And I take special care when preparing food for Evangeline. She's one of my oldest friends and my high priestess."

"Your devotion to your priestess's palate is impressive," Vivian taunted.

"I have a knack for catering to the senses," Gregory replied breezily.

"I believe your catering prowess is misdirected at present, Chef. Now run along and find something else to occupy your time." Alexander gave a dismissive wave.

Shocking, ugly behavior!

Gregory didn't flinch. "We're in your house, *sir*, but this is my kitchen. Maybe you could take your guest on a tour of another part of the manor." Gregory glared pointedly at Vivian. "I don't allow anyone in the kitchen who isn't on the payroll or delivering me lobster. Insurance liability, you understand."

"Excuse me, but—" Alexander began.

"I think we all have other places we should be," I cut him off and shot a glaring eye to Vivian. "We should let the chef return to his work."

I took the lovingly prepared snack and the bottle of Prosecco and turned to Gregory. "Thank you. This is exactly what I need."

"My pleasure." Gregory ignored Alexander's glower. "Let me know what you think of the wine pairing."

"I will." Once more, I kissed Gregory's fuzzy cheek and walked out without another word to Alexander or the naiad wench.

The enormity of Morgan Manor turned the smallest errand into an epic journey. With the bubbly and a serving tray in my hands, and a tiring day behind me, the trek from the kitchen to my room felt particularly arduous. The muscles in my arms ached and trembled under the weight of my precariously balanced snack. When I reached my bedroom, I stared at the doorknob, wishing I possessed the telekinetic power to open it with my mind. At the thought, a hand reached out from behind me and turned the knob. Startled, I jostled the tray, but Killian grabbed ahold and steadied it.

"Whoa there, Miss Clarion," he said with his soft grey eyes crinkled with concern. "Are you ok? May I take this in for you?" He motioned to my room with a tip of his ginger head.

"What? Yes. No," I stammered.

Killian cocked a wicked brow.

I huffed. "I mean, yes, I'm fine, and no you don't need to take the tray in for me. I've got it. But thank you," I added, not wanting to appear rude or ungrateful.

"It's my pleasure to serve you, Miss Clarion." A playfully devious expression lit Killian's face, but an instant later, his features softened into kindness. "I brought this for you." On my tray, he placed a small, pale blue candle wrapped in lavender and carved with sigils for serenity. He rubbed the back of his neck nervously. "It's supposed to bring you peace. I figured you could use some."

"Wait, you made this?" I asked, pleasantly surprised.

Killian's cheeks reddened, and he smiled sheepishly. "Yeh. It's no big deal really. Google, ya know." He shrugged.

"It's very thoughtful, Killian, thank you."

He cleared his throat. "Well, you better get in before you drop your snack. Have a good night, Miss Clarion." He offered the ghost of a smile before heading off down the hall.

I entered my room, set my tray on the bed, and immediately popped open the Prosecco. I'd forgotten to grab a glass, so I went right for the bottle. After a few hearty swigs, I kicked off my heels, stripped to my T-shirt and panties, let my hair down, and burped.

Thank the Goddess, that feels better.

I lit Killian's serenity candle, and let the scent of lavender envelope me. Then I lounged in bed, nibbled on my snack, and washed it down with more Prosecco. My entire body relaxed. Gregory had produced the precise flavors to sate my soul and my appetite. His meal eased the stresses besieging me—the fragile truce with the Arbor residents threatened by a resurrected dead couple, the arrival and subsequent antagonism of the Harcourt women, my tenuous relationships with Alexander and Celeste, my responsibilities as high priestess of the coven, my work for the Manor Arts, and the brief time that remained to create. And that was before I added volunteering at the food pantry and planning the Yule celebration to my list.

What the hell was I thinking?

I fished my cell out of my pocket and shot Maggie the text I'd promised. Maybe she'd have some words of encouragement. There'd been a time, not too long ago, when I would spend hours hashing out my day with my goddess-mother. Maggie would've brought me in a cup of her magical tea. But before I could take a sip, she would listen as I unburdened myself. Only when I'd laid all the troubles of my heart before her would she have imparted her wisdom. Finally, she'd nod to the tea, giving me permission to drink. And the tea would wash over me in a warm healing wave.

But Maggie wasn't around. And she hadn't texted back.

So, I ate carbs, drank prosecco, and thought about the holidays.

Chapter Ten

THREE WEEKS LATER

Every commercial and TV special portrayed the holidays as a time of joy and family, giving thanks, giving back, and festive merrymaking. While I'd glimpsed what one might call "holiday spirit" over the years, more often than not, the period spanning October thirty-first through the New Year was marked by gluttony and debauchery. Roaming the streets for tricks and treats. Alcohol and flirtation-fueled office parties. Stolen kisses at midnight. All socially acceptable.

Who the hell was I to judge?

Yet, in the weeks that followed our Samhain gallery opening, as our holiday preparations kicked into gear, I watched in impotent horror as Vivian and Eris Harcourt preyed on my Arbor neighbors. I caught no trace of witchcraft or even naiad magic. Instead, the Harcourts wove their spells using the very human art of seduction. While the Witches of Arbor stocked pantry shelves with donated groceries and delivered food to the infirmed, and the Manor Arts hosted free music lessons and art classes for kindergarteners and retirees, the Harcourts, and their ever-increasing number of acolytes, partied on Parson Street. From their home base in Adelaide's apartment, Vivian and Eris whipped downtown into a depraved frenzy, night after night.

The Harcourts beguiled and buttered up everybody who was anybody in town. It began with a few members of the town council and the planning board but swelled to include a massive swath of the community. The fallen pious reveled in alcohol, drugs, gambling, and some genuinely pornographic public displays of affection. Previously genteel, prim-and-proper folks were cursing, fighting, stealing from one another, and generally causing a ruckus. Chief Harrison, still convalescing at home under the care of his sister, failed to stir a recalcitrant police force into action against this flagrant malfeasance.

Some of our intel came from Ethan and Luca's recon missions, although Luca could never get close enough to lay a hand on either woman to detect their truth. Some info came from Rocky's stealthy surveillance and some from Alexander's downtown rebuild work with Harcourt Architecture. But most of the Harcourts' exploitations of Arbor were out in the open for all to see. Vivian and Eris flaunted their bad behavior.

Generally speaking, I considered people's proclivities and extracurricular activities none of my fucking business. Technically, I couldn't have cared less if a handful of teachers were openly having a polyamorous affair with the elementary school principal or that half of the Arbor PD smoked pot and another quarter snorted coke, except for the fact that they were doing it in Adelaide's old apartment. I would have found it all pretty damn funny, truth be told. But the Harcourts were manipulating these people—seducing them into this behavior. With or without magic, that was downright wicked.

And yet, I could do nothing. The coven couldn't go on offense. No proof existed that the Harcourts had broken our truce; no proof they'd used magic to hurt anyone. They'd corrupted Arbor the old-fashioned way—temptation.

The rumors rumbling through the community further poisoned the well. In hushed whispers, people told stories of hearing others tell of dark gatherings down by the river, blood rituals and black eyed, mindless dancing on the banks of the AuSable River. Every story was told third or fourth hand, and we never glimpsed any gathering at the river. The ramshackle house the Harcourts purchased remained dark, despite their assertion that they had a crew working on the restoration of the place. We found no signs of construction, but nothing appeared out of the ordinary either.

Yet it was Maggie who filled my mind every waking hour and gripped my heart each night, not the Harcourts. She and Ayo were missing.

No one had heard from them since Maggie's good luck text to me on the morning of November first, the Manor Arts' opening day. At first, I attributed Maggie's neglectful correspondence to her occasional bouts of flightiness. When Nicolae grew concerned that Ayo hadn't checked in either, fear settled in. After some investigating, we traced them as far as LA. Since Nicolae and Ayo had worked together on the West Coast for years, he flew out and, together with their old connections, set up a search. But weeks of combing through the psychics, mediums, pagans, Wiccans, and witches of California produced nothing. One minute, Maggie and Ayo were buzzing from one coven to another, aiding witches with their magical, medical, and legal concerns, and then...poof!

I'd dealt with having my goddess-mother, the woman who raised me, on the other side of the country because I understood the importance of her work. But the incessant speculation of not knowing where she was, what had happened, if she and Ayo were hurt, if they were alive tortured me. Running the gallery and volunteering became mind-numbing distractions instead of soul enriching experiences. My heart, my chest cavity, my entire core hollowed out with Maggie's absence. I'd never be filled again until we found her.

*

THANKSGIVING

Jasper had the cars waiting out front to take us all down Red Hill to the food pantry, but it was still early, and I wasn't ready to leave the quiet calm of my room. Instead, I snuggled into my armchair with a steaming mug warming my hands, mulling over the chaos of the last few weeks. What I felt most thankful for in that moment was my incredible cup of coffee and the article on the front page of Arbor's daily newspaper *The Messenger*. I looked over the article—printed above the fold—and marveled at the large black-and-white photo of me and Mother Hildegard loading cases of food donations. I'd read the article three times already.

LOAVES & FISHES – NUNS & WITCHES

The coven and the convent, caring for their community.

In the spirit of the season, the nuns of Saint Francis Roman Catholic Convent have joined forces with the Witches of

Arbor coven to tackle hunger and poverty in Arbor. In the weeks leading up to Thanksgiving, the nuns and the self-described witches have collected food, clothing, blankets, and monetary donations for the Arbor Community Pantry, and distributed care packages to the elderly. The nuns and witches have also collaborated on today's Thanksgiving feast serving Arbor's less fortunate. They promise turkey, stuffing, and all the trimmings.

"Mother Hildegard and Ms. Clarion are leading by example," Mayor Jonathan Riddle told The Messenger *as he left his office late Wednesday afternoon. "They're showing us that we can find common ground with others of good will, and we can work together toward accomplishing a common goal."*

The article went on to provide details on where to donate food and money, and how to volunteer at the pantry. It was as good as it gets as far as publicity was concerned. And we were in a public relations war of sorts. While the Harcourts targeted desires, the Witches of Arbor went after hearts.

I put down *The Messenger* and drank the last of my coffee.

I have turkey and stuffing and cranberry sauce to serve, damn it.

Over thirty volunteers packed the Arbor Community Food Pantry. Together we served roasted turkey with gravy, mashed potatoes, sweet potatoes, stuffing, green bean casserole, cranberry sauce, dinner rolls, and pumpkin pie to more than five hundred people throughout the afternoon and into the evening. Local musicians entertained everyone throughout the day. And when our guests had had their fill, we sent them off with blankets, bags of grocery staples, and gift cards (a donation from Alexander). Mayor Riddle and Mother Hildegard both declared the entire Thanksgiving project a great success. As far as the Witches of Arbor and the Manor Arts were concerned, we couldn't have done more to promote goodwill in the community.

It had been a fulfilling day, and even the familiars were all in good spirits when we returned to the manor just after seven o'clock. Somehow, Gregory and his kitchen crew had managed to not only prepare all the food we served at the pantry, but a gourmet meal for us to enjoy upon our return.

Gregory stood before the dining room table dressed in jeans that fit just right and a simple black T-shirt that hugged his muscular arms and wide chest. He winked at me before addressing the table. For some reason, my heart did a little flutter thing usually reserved for Alexander or Celeste.

What the hell was that?

"I figured we'd all be sick of turkey by now, so thankfully, that is not on the menu this evening. We're going to get things started with a winter salad of radicchio and endive with walnuts, goat cheese, dried cranberries, oranges, and a red wine vinaigrette. We'll move on to a choice of two entrees. First, we have locally raised, braised beef short ribs with Portobello mushroom and parmesan risotto, aside maple-glazed Brussel sprouts and caramelized apples. For our vegan option, we have grilled beets with roasted oyster mushrooms and cauliflower, topped with crispy onions and a tarragon oil and balsamic reduction, aside roasted fingerling potatoes. We have a Chilean Cabernet to pair with the short ribs. It's full-bodied with flavors of black currant, berries, chocolate, and graphite. Next, we have a Sancerre from the Loire Valley to accompany both the winter salad and the vegan dish. It's vibrant with citrus aromas and an edge of minerality. For dessert, we have a ginger molasses cake with a vanilla cream filling and dark chocolate icing. To go along with our cake, there is a Canadian Riesling ice wine, a sweet wine with a sharp acidity and hints of raisin and honey.

"Elliot will be coming around to fill your glasses, and Killian will take your order. Enjoy!" Gregory moved around the table and took the last empty seat.

After Elliot poured the wine, and everyone placed their orders, I got to my feet.

"It's been a tremendous day, and I couldn't be more grateful for the people at this table." I turned from one beloved face to the next, a solemnity washing over me. "Maggie would be proud of us." I choked up. "She and Ayo should be at this table. Nicolae, off scouring the state of California for them, should be at this table. Let's keep them in our hearts as we share this meal today.

"Blessed are the seeds that grow the vegetation. Blessed are those who plant, tend, and harvest. Blessed are the wind, the sun, the rain, and the earth that nourish. Through these elements, those around this table are sustained and enriched. We share this meal in gratitude and hope. Blessed Be."

And they all replied, "Blessed be," as a pounding on the manor's front doors, and impatient cries of, "Hello! Will somebody let me in," reverberated into the dining room.

"I've got this." Killian hustled out to answer the door.

A moment later, a disheveled and agitated Mayor Riddle barreled into the dining room.

"Do none of you people answer a damn phone? You made me waste time we don't have trekking up here." Riddle leveled me with piercing eyes. "You've got to come. Now. Chief Harrison had another heart attack. He's on his death bed, at his house. The damned fool refuses to go to the hospital. He's got a DNR—a do not resuscitate—and I don't know how long he has—hours, minutes? He's asking for you."

"Me?" I squeaked. "Why does he want me?" I looked nervously around the room for help but found only startled faces.

"Oh, jeez, I don't know, maybe because you're supposed to be his friend and a witch," Riddle blurted.

There was a collective inhale of breath.

"But I..."

Rocky tapped me on the hand with his beak.

Go to him. Give him comfort in his final hours.

But I...

I felt stuck. I wanted to help. If I could have helped anyone in this whole damn town, it would have been Chief Harrison. But I couldn't do what they wanted me to do. I couldn't *fix* the chief's damaged heart. I simply didn't have that power. I was a witch, not a miracle worker and not a great healer like Maggie.

"Honestly, I don't know if there's anything I can do... But yes, of course. I'll go see him. Right away. I'll do whatever I can to make him comfortable." I took in the faces around the table. "We all will." I could see ideas blooming in their minds, each witch blessed with unique powers capable of aiding Chief Harrison in their own way.

"We'll do everything we can, Riddle,"— Alexander scrunched up his brow—"but let's be straight here. None of us has the ability to heal the chief. I refuse to have whatever happens to him rebound legally on us. We'll go as it's his expressed wish, but we'll be there to offer...let's call them *prayers* only. You need to understand that."

"Fine, great, whatever. I'll meet you there." Riddle took off as quickly as he'd come in.

Alexander, Celeste, Mia, the boys, and I hurried to gather whatever we could that might aid us in our magical tasks ahead. Our caravan trucked down the winding descent of Red Hill within ten minutes of Riddle crashing our dinner party.

We arrived at the modest, craftsman-style Harrison home and knocked on the front door.

The Witches of Arbor are making house calls. Dear Goddess.

A haggard and irritated Mayor Riddle answered the door, grumbling something under his breath that sounded suspiciously like, "About fucking time," and led us through a crowd of grief-stricken loved ones. A rustle of hushed whispers spread as we entered. I scanned the crowd— the chief's family, friends from the Arbor PD, neighbors, and, yup, there they were, the Harcourts. This was apparently the place to be tonight. Mother Hildegard ducked out of the kitchen to greet us, and she leveled me with a knowing look.

"Evangeline, I hoped you'd come. I know you've had a long day," she said kindly.

"We all have," I answered. The woman had been up before dawn to prepare for Thanksgiving at the pantry, and no doubt she had had little rest in the weeks leading up to it.

I saw wisdom in the cracks and crevices of the habited nun's care-worn face as she stepped in close and spoke in swift whispers. "I'll be blunt. He's not going to make it through the night. He refuses to go to the hospital. He sent away the doctor. And he's got a DNR. He let them keep the monitor on, but he won't take any meds or allow any treatment. The coroner is on call."

I heaved a sigh and scanned the hushed and huddled crowd in the Harrison living room. They chanced expectant glances at me and the coven, and the hope I saw in their eyes scared the hell out of me.

"Forgive me, Mother Hildegard, but what do these people want from me? From us?" I motioned to the coven.

"A miracle."

Dear Goddess. What are we going to do?

Her haggard face pinched as she whispered, "And when they don't get their miracle, the Harcourts will make sure folks remember your failure." She upped her volume. "The chief will be thrilled to see you. I'm not sure anything can be done at this stage, but if you can give him solace in his final hours..." Her voice trailed off as she patted my hand.

With the stealth of a seasoned pickpocket, Mother Hildegard tucked rosary beads into my clasped fist. I considered the stringed circlet. There were five groupings of ten small pieces of black stone with a larger single bead between each group, each bead worn dull with regular attention. An additional string of one large and three small beads jutted from the circle with a medal at the base and a crucifix on the end.

Energy emanated from the rosaries. They were magic. A talisman.

"Thank you. But what's this for?"

"Your miracle. You're going to need all the help you can get."

"No offense, but if you expect me to perform miracles, I'll need more than beads. Out of curiosity, has a priest visited the chief? Shouldn't someone be here to perform the last rites of your faith?" If the Harrisons were Catholic, it made more sense to call a priest than a witch.

"He didn't want a priest here either. His sister regularly attends mass at our convent chapel, but the chief hasn't been there in years."

"Still, I'm sure a priest would be better for someone who shares the faith—"

"Eva," she said sharply. "Chief Harrison wanted no one but you."

"Well, that's not exactly accurate, Mother," Mayor Riddle piped up out of nowhere. "He actually asked for 'Miss Eva and her witches.'"

Excellent. No pressure.

I regarded the grieving family and friends, the Harcourts tucked into the corner of the room, and the six badass witches behind me, none of whom possessed the ability to cure the chief. If he died, the mourners could easily turn their grief into anger at us. They could blame us for his death. It wouldn't be the first time witches were accused in this way.

"The Witches of Arbor are here to ease a man's suffering, not perform miracles," I said loud enough for the room to hear. I handed Mother Hildegard her rosaries. "Thank you, but you should keep these. Their magic will work better in your hands." I turned to the mayor. "Take us to the chief."

Riddle showed us into a small, stuffy bedroom lit only by a bedside lamp and a cluster of religious candles. The stench of sickness and cheap incense muddied the air. The chief's king- sized bed and the heart monitoring equipment, resounding the steady *beep, beep, beep,* of the chief's life, took up the bulk of the room. The coven, the mayor, and the chief's sister took up the remaining space.

He looks so small and frail on that large, sparse white bed.

Ms. Harrison sat hunched at her brother's bedside, her beleaguered face crumpled in sorrow. Despite the fact that we hovered over her shoulder, she didn't seem to realize we were there. Her eyes remained fixed on the handkerchief she clutched in her lap. She only raised her head when the mayor tapped her gently on the shoulder.

"Evangeline's here," he whispered. "And she brought friends."

She showed neither surprise nor relief at seeing me, nor hope that my arrival meant the end of her brother's worries. Her lack of faith in my abilities gave me the confidence to proceed. I didn't want to let her down. And if her expectation had been the chief's recovery, I most definitely would have.

I took a small step forward and spoke softly. "Ms. Harrison. They said your brother asked for me. And my friends." When she didn't reply, I continued. "As I've explained before, I'm not a healer. So, I'm not here to offer you a miracle."

"Why bother coming?" she snapped.

A small, firm touch pressed against my wrist, and I turned to find Mia standing at my side. Leaning on her viper cane, Mia hobbled over to

Ms. Harrison. She placed a reassuring hand on the troubled woman's back.

"Good evening, Ms. Harrison, my name is Mia," she said in her thick Italian accent. "We came here bearing peace, for you and your brother."

Just then, a croak sounded from the direction of the chief's bed. We all turned to him and leaned slightly forward so as not to miss a word.

"Miss Eva," the chief wheezed. Small slits appeared where his eyes should be. He reached out a skeletal hand.

I leaned over the side of his large bed and took his hand in mine. I concealed my shudder at the frail, papery grasp by lifting it to my lips.

"You came," he rasped and attempted to lift gaunt, sallow cheeks that had once been so pink and plump.

"Of course I did." I managed to lift my lips into something resembling a smile in return and wiped an errant tear off my cheek.

"You're a good girl," the chief mumbled before closing his eyes again.

The steady *beep, beep, beep* from the heart monitor reassured me he slept.

"Fine. Fine," Ms. Harrison blurted. "Do whatever you want. You want to throw out the doctor but let a bunch of witches work their magic on ya, fine." She turned to me. "He was stubborn all his life. He can take his stubbornness to the grave."

Mia reached into the large bag she carried over her shoulder and rummaged around until she pulled out a small glass jar. "Mayor, be a good boy and take Ms. Harrison into the kitchen. Ask Mother Hildegard to make her this tea." She handed the jar to Riddle, leaned down, and spoke to the weary woman. "It will ease your spirit, and for a while, at least, it will bring you peace. I promise. Now, you go." She scooted the mayor and the old woman out of the room with her viper cane.

"Let's get to work." Alexander turned to shut the bedroom door.

"No, not yet." I got to my feet and laid Chief Harrison's hand carefully on the bed. "We have to sweep the room first. Keep the door open and open the windows."

Fresh, brisk autumn air wafted in and cleared the thick pong of sickness from the room.

Each member of the coven took ahold of their besom brooms and swept the room clean of negative energy. Gregory poured a thin line of black salt across the threshold of the door and windowsills to protect against invading negativity. To purify the space, I lit several white candles around the room while Mia burned white sage. Celeste took out a satin satchel from which she drew crystals and stones. She named each one as she placed them on the bed around the chief.

"Rose quartz, emerald, green aventurine, red jasper, pearl, kunzite, jade, peridot..."

Luca stepped to the bedside, and with a touch of his hand, he searched for Chief Harrison's truth. Luca closed his eyes for a moment, and when they reopened, I saw fear and sadness and pain swirl within them, followed by resignation.

"He needs comfort." Luca turned to Ethan. "Give him joyful visions," he said. And to Gregory, "Let him *feel* that joy."

The boys nodded, raised their powerful arms, and projected their magical mirage over Chief Harrison. At least the boys could take away his suffering even if we weren't able to heal him.

Don't be such a defeatist, Evangeline Clarion. Don't give up hope.

I raised my hands and spoke my incantation with intention.

"Through fire, water, earth, and air—

Fertile soil and trumpets blare,

Rapid rivers and scorching heat—

Strengthen this heart; strengthen its beat.

We call upon the Southern powers,

Hear us in our darkest hours.

We call on powers of the East,

Heal this heart, this pain release.

We call on powers of the North,

Remove disease, good health bring forth.

We call on powers of the West,

Cure what ails within this chest.

As above, so too below.

Within, without, does spirit flow.

Ever mindful of the law of three,

As I will it, so mote it be."

For a few moments, a flicker of hope burned within me; maybe we could help him. Maybe one of us had the precise type of magical energy flowing through us that could change the molecular structure of a diseased human heart to prevent him from dying.

Then the heart monitor let out one, continuous, baleful beep. The chief flatlined.

"Get Ms. Harrison," I screamed. "Now!"

Celeste took off to get help, and Alexander bolted to Chief Harrison's bedside. He spread his hands out wide and pressed them firmly over the chief's heart. Sparks jolted from Alexander's hands, the chief gasped, and the machine *beep, beep, beeped* again. Just then, Mayor Riddle charged in with authority. Ms. Harrison shuffled behind him. Over her shoulder stood Vivian and Eris Harcourt.

What are they doing here?

Before I got the chance to find out, the chief flatlined again. The high pitched, sorrowful wail tore through the cramped room.

Riddle looked to Ms. Harrison. "The DNR..."

"I know." She hung her head and sobbed.

"This can't be it," I muttered.

I looked to Alexander. His fists and jaw clenched as he fought the impulse to throw out his hands and jump-start the chief's heart again. But he couldn't display that kind of power in front of Ms. Harrison or the mayor, for that matter. That level of exposure was too dangerous, and Alexander knew it. His face glowed red with restrained magic.

Every face in the room shared some degree of desolate agony at their inability to help this good man. Every face except for Vivian's. All I saw in hers was apathy.

"Do something!" I yelled foolishly.

Apparently, I don't care about exposing their powers.

Everyone gawked at me, some in confusion, others in horror.

I charged up to Vivian. "Seriously, please, fucking do something."

She stared at me like I'd lost my mind. Which seemed to be the consensus.

I faced the room, glaring past the coven and Ms. Harrison to the mayor. "They have the power to resurrect him, Riddle. They can do this. They can bring him back."

He turned to Vivian with an unreadable expression. "Do what you can..."

Vivian and Eris stared me down, and I knew that by outing them in this way, I'd violated our agreement. But I accepted the repercussions in the hope that the chief might live.

With a snarl and a wave of her hand, Vivian parted the crowd. She and Eris moved to the sides of the chief's bed. They threw their hands out over his body and chanted.

"*Aquas ab aquilone, et veniet ad me. Aquas ab austro veniet ad me. Aquas orientalem, veniunt ad me. Occidens aquas, venerunt ad me.*"

As they chanted, water flowed from their outstretched hands. It swirled in a whirlwind around them and the chief, as it had when they healed the bank lady and her husband on Samhain. The mini typhoon spun so fast around the bed, it obscured them from view. And like before, we waited. No one spoke. Until at last, the spinning slowed. And when the water disappeared, a bright cheeked Chief Harrison sat up in bed with a jolly grin, as if he'd awoken from a sweet dream.

Flinging Vivian aside, Ms. Harrison lunged at the chief. "Oh my dear, sweet brother. It's a miracle!"

The chief patted his sister kindly. "Yes, yes. I'm here. It's all right now. Thanks to our Miss Eva, of course." He looked up at me over his sister's shoulder. "You did it. You saved me. I knew you would."

"It wasn't me," I admitted. "I'm over the moon that you're awake and looking so revived. But"—I gestured to Vivian and Eris—"they're your heroines."

Chief Harrison squinted suspicious eyes from me to the Harcourts and back to me. He took in the scene of the room around him as if seeing it for the first time. A switch flipped within his gaze as he shifted into cop mode. No one in the room spoke as he scanned his surroundings, looking for clues, evidence of what had happened while he'd been incapacitated, and formed a hypothesis.

He lifted his cheeks again. "You pulled out all the stops, didn't ya? Brought the whole crew." The chief nodded to the coven, his smile widening at the sight of Mia. "You've got brooms and candles, crystals and herbs." Chief Harrison's expression soured. "They may have saved me, but I'm damn sure they only did it because of you. I'm alive because of you, Miss Eva. Unfortunately," he eyeballed Vivian and Eris. "I'm also wet. And my bed is wet. This is your doing."

"Yes, sir," Vivian said in a clipped tone, clearly perturbed by his lack of gratitude.

"I guess you think a thank-you is in order," the chief remarked begrudgingly, reminding me of my own similar comments to the Harcourts on Samhain. He was feisty for someone who'd just been subjected to the business end of death.

Harrison sees right through them. That cop doesn't miss a beat.

"We're happy to help." Vivian tried to appear humble.

"Well, it is a miracle, that's what it is." Ms. Harrison beamed.

The mayor sidled up to the chief's bed and checked his vitals. "Your color's returned, and your heart rate's steady. You're not merely healed; you look like a million bucks." Riddle turned an accusatory eye to the Harcourts but said nothing more.

"Guess you don't need to hire anyone to replace him now," Alexander said.

"Excellent, glad I'm alive enough to work," the chief quipped. "Now, if ya don't mind, I'd like to change out of these wet clothes and grab a bite to eat. I'm sure Hildegard will make me a plate." Chief Harrison looked around the room. When no one moved, he bellowed, "I'm not dead yet. And I don't plan on dyin' tonight. So, you can all get the hell out now."

I do love this man. I gave the chief a nice, long hug. "I'm happy you're still with us."

"You're a good girl. Thanks for having my back."

"Anytime, Chief." I kissed his cheek. "Ms. Harrison, should you ever be in need, our doors are always open." I nodded to the mayor, ignored Vivian and Eris, and turned to the coven. "We've done all we can. It's time to fly."

Chapter Eleven

We drove home in silence, each lost in our own thoughts. Mia, in particular, seemed effected by the events at the Harrison house. When we stopped at the cottage to drop her off, she kissed Alexander on the cheek and hobbled inside on her viper cane without a word. Elliot must have been given a heads-up about our imminent return to the manor because he and the entire staff—including the extra crew Elliot hired for the holidays—waited in the entry to greet us. They were desperate for an explanation, but I had none to give. That woeful task fell on Alexander, who briefed them and gave them their orders for the rest of the night.

Celeste fixed my cimaruta necklace—the Italian Stregheria talisman I never removed—placing the clasp at the nape of my neck; a tender, intimate gesture. She kissed my cheek and put her arm around my shoulder, and together we followed the boys into the dining room. She ushered me to my seat before settling herself into the chair at my right. The boys filled in around the table, except for Gregory, who ran into the kitchen to check on dinner. We were a far less lively group than we'd been at this table a couple hours before. I'd lost my appetite. But Gregory and the kitchen crew had worked so hard on the meal, I hated to think of it going to waste.

Alexander pressed a warm, strong hand on my back, and I leaned into his familiar touch. He crouched down beside my chair and turned me to face him.

"Here's how this is going to go. I'm going to ask if you're okay. You're going to tell me you're fine. But I'm going to know you're being brave or gallant or some such nonsense. So why don't we skip all that, and you can tell me how you're really feeling."

How am I feeling? Now *he wants me to spell it out? Isn't it obvious? Or does he need to dip into my head to understand me?*

"I'm fucking pissed," I screeched. "I can't stand Vivian and Eris Harcourt. They had no intention of saving the chief. They would have watched him die if I hadn't said something."

"They can't exactly go around bringing *everyone* who dies back from the dead," Celeste added as Alexander settled into his seat beside me.

His voice was tentative when he spoke. "I didn't try to jumpstart his heart again in front of everyone. I'm sure that didn't escape your notice. Do you hate me too?"

I huffed. "No, of course not. At least you tried. Your instinct was to save him."

"The Harcourts have to be pissed that you forced their hand, that you outed them," Celeste's face pinched as she fiddled with one of the stones at her neck, a green one with white veins.

Jasper maybe? I absentmindedly drank in the milky pale skin of Celeste's neck beneath the stones.

"They're going to become an even bigger problem," she continued with a nervous warning note, disregarding the focus of my gaze. "Saving the chief must have created a trillion karmic ripples."

I shrugged. "It was worth it. The chief's life was worth it."

The food came out, offering us all a distraction. Gregory's meal was delicious, of course, but as soon as I cleaned my plate, I decided to call it a day. I returned to my room—alone—after saying goodnight to everyone and ignoring the disappointed looks from Celeste and Alexander.

I luxuriated in a long shower, then threw on boxers and a tank and hopped into bed. A good sleep would go a long way in helping me process the evening. But as soon as my head hit the pillow, a feverish tapping at my window forced me to my feet again. I hoisted the window high, and in flapped a flustered Rocky.

Oh, my dearest witch. Such things I must tell you! You will never believe the scene I witnessed at Adelaide's apartment.

"Lovely. What have the Harcourts done now?" I said aloud, too exhausted to communicate with Rocky in our typical mental manner.

Well, they saved Chief Harrison, of course.

"I'm aware. And?"

Afterward, the Harcourts invited everyone to their place for drinks to celebrate the chief's recovery. I do believe half the town showed up! It was far worse than their typical debauched soirée. This spilled out of Adelaide's apartment and overtook Parson Street. I perched in a tree on the sidewalk, and what I saw shocked me to my core. Supposedly devout churchgoers engaged in such salacious behavior, it would have made Adelaide blush.

"What kind of salacious behavior?" Curious but unconcerned, I plopped down on the bed.

As you're well aware, Arbor has shed its notorious Norman Rockwell propriety, its zealous righteousness, and has descended into depravity over these last few weeks. But what I witnessed tonight was appalling. Surrounding the poker game in the living room, they poured wine and whiskey down their gullets, they snorted cocaine from women's breasts and smoked opium from a three-foot-tall hookah. My eyes were subjected to more vulgar public displays of affection than I care to recount—including a completely nude couple having intercourse on the steps of the apartment. Before I left, I caught that crabby old bat who used to run the flower shop sitting naked on Vivian Harcourt's lap. Naked!

"That must have been a horrendous sight. But you know what, Rocky, I'm not the morality police. And I am sick of worrying about the Harcourts' antics, at least for tonight." I yawned. "It's Thanksgiving, and I think the tryptophan has kicked in."

Evangeline, they're calling the Harcourt women miracle workers. These Arbor nitwits are head over heels for these sashaying timebombs. You know how malleable their minds are. You know more than anyone. Mayor Crandall and Reverend Cudlow warped and manipulated this community. The Harcourts are doing that now.

I yawned again. "You're right. Arbor is filled with beleaguered folks who've been manipulated by their religious and political leaders. With the town's prejudices exposed to the world, and the foundations of their community literally in rubble, these poor bastards are left to pick up the pieces. And in sashay the Harcourt women. They offer a sense of optimism and make the down-and-out folks of Arbor feel invigorated."

And the woman who caused their downfall reigns in a castle high upon a hill, Rocky snarked.

"Huh. Yeh, I guess so."

Your empathy is positively Magdalena-like.

I shot him a sharp side-eye. "Maggie would say it's important to walk a mile in another's shoes. I say know your enemy."

Do you think Arbor is your enemy?

I considered that before answering. "Their ignorance is dangerous."

What do you plan to do—about the Harcourts and Arbor's fascination with them?

I was out of ideas and exhausted. "Nothing tonight. I'm going to sleep on it. That's what I'm going to do."

Sleep well then, my dearest witch, sleep well. May the Goddess impart her wisdom, so you may see all that must be seen and take the actions that must be taken. Rocky nuzzled me with his beak and took off into an ominous sky.

Reluctantly, I hopped out of bed to close and latch the window. I took in the view of downtown Arbor at the base of Red Hill. A great swathe of the once picturesque little village, now reduced to rubble.

It's wretched, the devastation wrought by hatred. What destruction seduction will bring remains to be seen.

With this unsettling thought, I climbed back into bed and turned off my brain for the night.

*

ARTISTS SUNDAY

I woke to the smell of coffee and bacon. A groggy-eyed inspection of the breakfast tray beside my bed also uncovered a blueberry muffin, a bowl of strawberries, orange juice, and a note. I snatched up the note and sipped my coffee as I read.

Morning, priestess. Enjoy your breakfast in bed. You've been working your fantastic fanny off with Black Friday and Small

Business Saturday, and since it's Artists Sunday, it's your time to rest. The boys are covering the gallery so you can have an Eva Day. Paint, play, commune with Nature, whatever stirs your wild soul. We've got you covered.

Gregory.

Dear Goddess, I love those men. I luxuriated over what was, quite truly, a perfectly made cup of coffee.

After an equally inspiring and disturbing Thanksgiving, I'd spent a hectic Friday and Saturday in the gallery, working open to close. I needed to get out of the manor for a bit. But I had no intention of heading into the forest to commune with Nature or to my art studio to paint. I jotted Gregory a thank-you note on the back of his message, letting him know I'd decided to take the boys up on their offer. Summoning Killian to my room, the one member of the manor's growing staff I trusted, I sent him off with the note and an impulsive kiss on the cheek.

A quick shower and one hour later, I sat on the steps of the Arbor Savings and Loan, staring down the length of Parson Street, Arbor's main drag. It was a cold, gray morning, and the air hung heavy and wet over the desolate road. The emptiness stood in stark contrast to the post-church-service hustle and bustle once typical for a Sunday morning in Arbor. Typical before the burning, anyway.

Where have they been worshipping since their church burnt down? Have they been worshiping at all?

Arbor had always prided itself on being a deeply devout community. I couldn't see them skipping Sunday services, especially during the Christmas season. They had to be attending church out of town in some local community parish.

Maybe Mother Hildegard will know more.

Soon, massive construction vehicles, backhoes, and diggers would roll down Parson Street from their parking lot around the corner—the former site of the Arbor Community Market —to continue work on the demolition and clean-up phase of the rebuild. But for now, the burnt-out shells of businesses appeared as shipwrecks from the deep. From the wreckage, I envisioned quaint storefronts and cafés and liveliness, an idyllic Arbor.

"A fantasy." I sighed.

I squinted down to the end of the block, past where the flower shop and café used to be, across from where the church once stood, across from where they burned us, where the Elder Tree memorial now stood, down toward Adelaide's apartment. I cringed at the thought of Vivian and Eris living there—throwing parties there. The Harcourts' presence sullied the space. From my vantage point, it was difficult to see more than the corner of the apartment building, yet the Harcourts' saturating energy wafted like a thick fog. The churning fire under my skin warded off the chill of their magic, but the fact that I sensed their power all the way down the street unnerved me.

And it unnerved me to think that the people of Arbor could fall for these women. It shouldn't have surprised me, but it did. Instead of calling out Vivian and Eris for being wicked witches, Arbor saw the Harcourts as beautiful, charming, successful owners of an architecture firm who promised to return their community to its former glory. Having miraculously saved the beloved chief of police skyrocketed their fame. All the booze and drugs didn't hurt either.

What kind of spin would the Sunday edition of *The Messenger* put on the story? Would they skewer the Harcourts for being agents of the devil? "For how could one produce healing water from one's hands? It must be witchcraft!" I could imagine them saying. More likely, the paper would rave about the heroic actions of Arbor's newest residents—these captivating women who'd come to renovate, revive, and revitalize Arbor.

I eyed the left side of Parson Street, the side of the street left mostly unscathed by the fire. Constructed with durable, eighteenth-century brick, Arbor's township buildings lined the sidewalk largely unmarred. The fire station and police department came first, followed by the post office, municipal building, and courthouse. I caught sight of one of those metal newsstands down near the municipal building, so I headed that way.

And there it was. The story rated the front page, top of the fold.

HARCOURTS HEAL HARRISON'S HEART

"Hell of a Herculean headline," I muttered. "A bit on the nose."

The article detailed the grim and grief-stricken scene at Chief Harrison's home. It described the chief's brush with death in startling detail, suggesting the piece was sourced from someone in the room that night. The article reported that the Harcourts produced miraculous water to revive him. It did not explain *how* they produced water from their hands that could heal a heart and retrieve a man from the dark side of death. But *The Messenger* wasn't one to quibble over particulars, not that any logical explanation was available to them. In the photo of the chief, he was propped up in his favorite armchair, wearing pajamas. Vivian and Eris crouched on either side of the sweet old man, flashing come-hither gazes and mountains of cleavage.

These hags are seriously twisted. And they are pissing me off.

I flipped the newspaper over and read under the fold as I continued strolling on down the sidewalk. Two articles occupied the paper's lower half. One warned of a severe impending storm barreling down from the northwest. They predicted we'd get hit with frigid temperatures, high winds, and over eighteen inches of snow—complete blizzard conditions— to begin sometime Monday night or Tuesday morning. A state of emergency could be declared.

Just what I need during the holiday shopping season.

Beside that article was a local politics piece about the town council's quarrel with Mayor Riddle. Apparently, serious disagreements existed between them regarding the rebuild. The largest point of conflict appeared to be the council's objection to Harcourt Architecture's proposal to turn the Arbor Community Market location into a retail pad site for a big-box store. They accused the mayor of trying to ram the plan through. This article also had a corresponding photo. A semicircle of middle-aged white folks in their Sunday best, scowling down at a cowering Mayor Riddle.

Hmm...guess not everyone is a fan of the Harcourts' plans after all.

I looked up from the newspaper to find I'd walked further than I'd intended. Much further. While distracted by the day's news, I'd taken the bend in the sidewalk, continued past where Parson Street turned into Cascade Road, and ended up at Falls Bridge. The centuries-old, stone bridge spanned the narrow, waterfall-laced section of the AuSable River. The pedestrian path across Falls Bridge offered breathtaking views, but I never got the opportunity to admire them.

Before stepping onto the bridge, a peculiar sight caught my attention downriver. I tucked myself out of view behind a stony railing and peeked out.

Nestled between the river, a rocky ledged waterfall, and a thick forest sat a ramshackle, storm-swept Victorian; four stories tall, if you included the precariously balanced turret lookout. The painted-lady-style home had faded from what had once been a blue-hued palette, to a dull and dingy gray. It seemed a haunted place, especially when the wind caught the spray from the waterfall and cast the mist like ghostly plumes across the house.

Standing like a sentry at the front door was the white horse with the dripping wet mane Luna had tormented on Samhain, the horse that had sauntered off with the Harcourts. And here they were, together again.

In front of the house, down on the riverbank, stood a dozen Arbor residents in a circle with their arms raised high to the heavens. In the center of the circle, Vivian and Eris Harcourt held long, black candles aloft.

Fuck. They're using mundanes in their rituals now. The rumors were true.

I searched the skies and tree line for their raven familiars, but if they were there, they were well hidden.

I wish Rocky were here. He'd track those ravens in an instant.

I called out to Rocky mentally and pleaded for his help.

Returning my focus to the center of the circle, I strained to listen in as Vivian and Eris sang out, and the Arbor folks chanted a reply. I stood too far away to make out their words. Curiosity spurred me to tuck my newspaper under my arm and find closer cover. I dashed as quietly as I could and hid within a cluster of trees embedded within a dense thicket of undergrowth about half the distance away from the ritual circle. From that nest in the brambles, I watched as the Harcourts enchanted my neighbors.

And it changed everything.

The naiad witches sang in an indecipherable, almost elvish language, enthralling the circle with their song. The tempo increased and whipped the circle into a frenzy, sending them dancing in wild, mindless, writhing gyrations. And then they undressed.

Dear Goddess, no.

I closed my eyes and hung my head in my hands. When I braved a peek through my fingers, everyone—including the Harcourts—was skyclad, bare-assed naked for all the world to see. Under different circumstances, I would have marveled over the intricate tattoos that covered Eris's body. Unfortunately, the Harcourts' malevolence overshadowed their beauty. With their voices and bare arms raised high, they enchanted their oblivious prey. Their victims danced with abandon, all manner of appendages flailing in the crisp autumn air. But they didn't seem to mind the nudity or the cold. They didn't seem to notice anything at all.

When the Harcourts stopped singing, the dancing stopped too, and the mundanes fell limp like marionettes without a puppeteer. They collapsed on the damp, sandy ground with their eyes wide open. Those eyes would haunt my sleep—large and round and black as beetles at midnight.

Vivian and Eris walked over to one of the twelve in the circle, a middle-aged white woman I'd often seen gossiping with former Mayor Crandall back in the day. She was a real estate agent, however at the moment, she was nothing more than a rag doll on the riverbank. The Harcourts took her hands, helped her to her feet, and led her into the frigid waters of the AuSable River.

"What secret wish hides deepest in your soul?" Eris coaxed the woman deeper into the water. "A wish so dark, you struggle to confess it even to yourself."

"Tell us what you hide," Vivian hissed in the woman's ear as she followed close behind her.

"I want to kill my husband's mistress," the woman answered in a cold, dead voice. "I want to wrap my hands around her throat and watch as her life slips away. Then I want to dump her body in the river where it can be eaten by piranha. And I want to get away with it."

Vivian sneered, her lips thinning over large, white teeth. Eris had the good sense to appear revolted.

"You've spoken your darkest wish aloud. By the power within, the power without, and the power of the raging river, it shall be done. Kneel," Vivian commanded.

The woman knelt in the river, the cold water lapping at her heavy, naked breasts, and she raised her head in zombified supplication. Eris regarded her with derision. Vivian stood behind the woman with her left hand resting on her shoulder.

I watched in horror as Vivian raised a long-bladed athame in her right hand. A scream froze in my throat. The athame sliced deftly across the woman's ear, just deep enough to leave a scar. Blood spilled down the woman's neck and chest and into the water.

Dear Goddess, they're using her as a blood sacrifice to the river. And that sacrifice is made all the more potent by the waterfalls. The river's a torrent of life and power, and they're using this woman to siphon it. And if they're allowed to continue, they will repeat this another eleven times.

Vivian and Eris dipped their hands in the river and poured the water that pooled in their palms over the woman's eyes and ear. The bleeding stopped. The black in her eyes faded away. The real estate agent rose to her feet, blinking feverishly. Then she returned to her spot in the circle, dressed, and walked away toward town.

What am I supposed to do?

If I did nothing, this scene would repeat as, one by one, these poor pawns would kneel in frigid waters, divulge their darkest desires to Vivian and Eris Harcourt, and shed their blood in the AuSable River. Could I watch that happen to these people? Yet as I debated intervention, every scenario that ran through my head involved the possibility of someone getting hurt. Frequently me. It was two against one, after all. I had more than a few tricks up my sleeve, but I didn't know the extent of the Harcourts' powers. It would be foolish to fly out there, guns a blazin', and try to drown the bitches. And it wasn't as if any of the people in this circle stepped up to help me or Adelaide off our burning pyre. Adelaide lost her life for their complicit inaction.

These fools need only sacrifice a bit of blood.

And dark secrets. Rocky's panicked voice within my mind startled me. *And the serious repercussions that will occur if these secret wishes are acted upon. This is terrible, monumentally terrible.* Rocky perched in a high branch above, shaking me out of my mental stalling tactics. Thankfully, this cluster of trees still held a thick collage of autumn leaves, and they camouflaged the stately hawk. He couldn't hide his agitation, however. His mien betrayed his distress.

Where have you been? I snapped at him harshly and immediately regretted it.

Rocky smoothed out his ruffled feathers. *I've been watching this horror show from the cliffs atop the falls and keeping an eye out for those blasted ravens. But they're either elsewhere, or masters of disguise. When that old bat raised her athame, I was ready to soar down and peck the cretin's eyes out. But then I saw you hiding down here, spying. I thought for sure you'd help. But you didn't. You did not act immediately upon witnessing these atrocities. And I am quite disappointed. I know what you're thinking. You want to walk away. And all I can say is, shame on you. Shame on you for even entertaining the notion of leaving these comatose sheeple to the mercy of those tedious beasts. You are better than that.*

Am I?

Evangeline Clarion. The stern bird used my name like a harsh scolding. *What would Magdalena say? Or Shasta? Or Adelaide?*

Adelaide would tell me to keep my twitchy witch nose out of other people's business.

Yes, well, she would say that. But my dear, these women are a menace. Look at the damage they've caused already without magic. You cannot allow this to continue.

What do you expect me to do?

Oh, bother, I don't know. You're the witch. Make magic! If you prefer not to attack, at least create a distraction of some kind. They need not know it is you intervening. But you must do something. You cannot turn your back on helpless people.

Helpless people! That woman the Harcourts just bewitched was a friend of Doreen Crandall, the architect of the Arbor frenzy and the true villain of the burning of Arbor. That woman never came to my defense. She never tried to save me or Adelaide from the flames. I folded my arms across my chest, full of stubborn surety.

So, these people should be condemned to the Harcourts' manipulation because they may have an association with the old mayor?

They should be left to this fate because they did nothing to help four months ago when the whole town went mad? You'd make yourself the arbiter of their punishment? How does that make you any better than they?

I've already saved this town once. Should I be expected to come to the rescue every time someone from Arbor gets a splinter? I'm a witch, not your friendly neighborhood superhero.

Evangeline, with or without powers, we all have a responsibility to do what is right.

I hurrumphed, reluctant to get involved. Then I recalled the request Mother Hildegard made of me on Samhain when she warned me about the Harcourts. Somehow, she'd known something like this might happen. She'd asked me to use my powers to protect the community. She believed I possessed the strength to confront the Harcourts. And she was right.

Guilt rolled over me like a wave.

The magic within me recognized a decision had been made before I was cognizant of it myself. As my power surged, I made a quick assessment of the strengths and weaknesses of my predicament. Since Rocky was with me, I could fly. I ruled out using fire, too many dry leaves. I had no doubt they could control water as well—or better—than I could, so I ceded that element to them.

Air! I'll use the wind to defend against any water attack. And Earth. The forest!

I reached out my arms and called to the trees to aid me. I whipped up a spell, but since I couldn't speak the words aloud with any gumption, given the necessity of stealth, I whispered it. I held the simple spell firm in my thoughts, and as I repeated it again and again, my connection with the trees around me intertwined, weaving together tighter and tighter.

"Leaves and branches, trunks, and roots,

Aid this witch in my pursuits.

Red spruce, hemlock, maple, beech

Do my bidding, I beseech."

The trees quivered and shook their branches in reply.

I nodded at Rocky. *Let's fly.* Breathing slow and deep, I released all that weighed me down. My toes lifted from the ground about a foot. I gazed up and evaluated the web of branches above me. As I lifted higher, I weaved as silently as I could through the crispy tangle of stubborn autumn leaves. Landing on a branch, I concealed myself behind the thick red and orange bunches and peered down at the Harcourts' circle.

Their second victim had just finished dressing. Her eyes, now free of the spell's black haze, still suggested an addled mind. She staggered on unsteady legs toward town.

Two down, ten to go. I must stop this before they choose another victim.

I enveloped myself in the power of the forest, and the trees leaned and stretched their branches to support me as I flew out to confront the Harcourts.

The horse noticed me first but galloped off without acknowledging my presence. Besides a slight upward curl of her lips, Eris betrayed no reaction whatsoever. Vivian was another story. A tumult of astonishment and anger rolled over her face as she saw me coasting in above them on an unseen wind. I could feel Vivian's anxiety increase when she realized who—or rather, *what*—had my back.

Every witch knows not to mess with trees.

Fear crept across her face, yet it took her only a moment to conceal it with a look of haughty bravado.

"Well, look who joined the party. What brings you down to the river, Evangeline Clarion?" Her tone was slick, but I caught the quiver in her voice.

"It's a lovely autumn day. I thought I'd take in the scenery." I hovered about thirty feet above the Harcourts' heads. "As the Head-Witch-In-Charge around these parts, I'd ask why you didn't invite me to this little ritual circle you've got going on here, but I see it's a mundane-only affair. You realize, of course, that what you're doing to these people nullifies our agreement." I remained calm and matter-of-fact.

Vivian narrowed her eyes. "Oh, my dear, you did that yourself when you outed us at the Harrisons'. We're making the best of it, of course; rolling with the punches, as it were. But it's you who broke our accord."

"You've been flinging your witch all over town for weeks now. What does it matter that the chief and his sister found out if it meant saving a life? And they would have kept things under wraps if you'd asked. Instead, you publicized the role you played in the chief's recovery. You made sure you were front page news. And you surrounded yourselves with those who would ply you with praise and adulation."

"Oh, please!" Eris blurted out. "Like you shrink from the limelight. You are the Queen of Praise and Adulation. Everything you do—your gallery, coven, love life—is all on display for public scrutiny. But you had no right to display our secrets too."

"The chief—" I began.

"You. Broke. Our. Agreement," Vivian cut in angrily. "Now, all bets are off, and these poor saps are fair game." She spit venom as she spoke. Yet, as she looked around the circle at the ten remaining limp marionettes plopped in the dirt, she smiled softly as if gazing upon sweet, peacefully sleeping children. The gentle turn of her aspect seemed perverse given the ease with which she manipulated others en masse.

"Their secrets and sacrifices are invaluable to our plans." Vivian spoke with deep emotion.

"What plans?" I bellowed, sounding more exasperated than I wanted to admit. "What the fuck are you trying to accomplish? I'm genuinely curious. I wish you'd lay it all out, so I'd know what the fuck I was dealing with."

"Oh yes." Eris sneered with mean-girl derision. "We'll simply spill our guts, and then we'll go make mojitos and paint each other's fingernails."

Vivian smiled cruelly. "Spelling it out would take away the fun. Though I must say, I wonder what your mother would think about your excessive use of profanity, if she were still breathing."

It took every ounce of self-control to restrain my violent impulses. "Why do you keep bringing up my mother? Did you know her, or are you just a twisted, evil bitch?"

Fury lit Vivian's face. "Oh, I knew her. She murdered my fiancé, Eris's father. Your father. He was a powerful witch. And your mother cut him down in the prime of his life."

Chapter Twelve

It was like getting kicked in the gut, hit by a truck, and flung face-first into a brick wall at lightning speed. I sensed the truth in Vivian's words – at least, the truth as she knew it. And the truth rocked me. Now burdened and weighed down, staying aloft became impossible. I fell from the sky, but the trees slowed my descent, and cradled me in their branches. The branches knitted together until they created a throne of sorts around me.

Taking advantage of my vulnerability, Vivian and Eris raised their hands, and the river surged behind them.

I called to the wind and thrust out my hands. At my direction, the air held back the river. I called out to the trees and pointed at the Harcourts.

"Get them and bring them to me."

Gnarled roots cracked through the ground around Vivian and Eris and twisted around their ankles, up their legs, cinching their waists, securing their hands—preventing them from casting spells—and tightening around their arms and shoulders. The river receded as their hands were bound. They screamed and cursed as the roots lifted them off the ground into the air and brought them to face me. They struggled in their tangled straitjackets, dangling about ten feet or so away from my throne in the trees.

"Put us down, you bitch," Eris spat.

Composed, I ignored her, and folded my hands in my lap. "So, let me see if I've got this worked out. You're here in Arbor because you think my mother killed your fiancé, Eris's father? I think it's safe to assume this gentleman wasn't merely a powerful witch, but incredibly wealthy, and his death—occurring before any "I-do's" could be spoken—denied you and Eris the prosperous life he would have provided. So, you're taking your vengeance out on me, my mother's daughter. And you're manipulating the Arbor mundane to gain control and influence in the community in order to do it."

Vivian glared viciously but didn't reply.

Eris rolled her eyes, defiant even in her precarious situation. "For the love of Hecate, Eva Clarion, not everything is about you."

I took a good, long look at her. *My supposed sister. My twisted sister.*

"You're right about that. At the moment, it's all about them." I gestured to the poor sods lying in the dirt. "Eris and Vivian Harcourt, you will not harm another one of these people. You will free them from their spells and send them on their way. You will nullify the spells you placed on the two who already left. And you will not involve another Arbor mundane in any of your *plans* again."

Eris seethed but remained mute.

"Why would we do anything you ask, you pathetic excuse for a witch?" Vivian forced out her words as she struggled against her bindings.

"I'm. Not. Asking." With a wave of my hand, the roots tightened around Vivian and Eris, squeezing the breath out of them. I waved once more, and the roots loosened just enough for the Harcourts to breathe. The trees hovered the Harcourts out in the middle of the circle. The roots reknitted themselves around the Harcourts' wrists to leave their hands free.

"Vivian and Eris Harcourt, release these people of all enchantments, release those who've left of their curses, and vow never to harm another Arbor mundane again. Only then will I release you."

"And if we don't?" Vivian snarled.

"If you think my mother was deadly, wait till you get a load of me." I snarled right back. With a wave of my hand, the trees squeezed again, harder this time, for a few extra agonizing seconds. At their feet, I placed small licks of fire, positioned close enough to singe the Harcourts' dangling toes. I whipped up a gust of wind and infused it with water and the energy of creation that flowed through me, producing a dark, undulating storm cloud which settled menacingly over the women's heads. I squeezed my fists together, and an ominous thunder rumbled from the cloud.

Fear pulsed from them in waves, and I reveled in it.

"With nothing more than the power of my will, I can inflict upon you the same horrors inflicted upon me."

The licks of fire beneath their feet swelled.

You are not evil, Evangeline. With a great sweep of both arms, I released the elements.

The mother and daughter turned to each other; their chests heaving as resignation etched into their furious faces.

"Fine," Vivian wheezed with a raised, defiant chin. "We'll fix these fools up, nice and snug. But we're not through with you."

From their hands sprang fountains of water, which they sprayed over the heads of the ten naked people laying in heaps on the ground. As the water washed over them, the black of their eyes cleared. They dressed quietly and walked off toward town.

"I've had enough of this scenery—and the company. You two enjoy the rest of your day." As the branches began to lower me to the ground, I returned my gaze to Vivian. "If you were smart, you'd leave Arbor. There is nothing for you here. And Eris, don't let her vendetta drag you down."

I thanked the trees for their aid and asked that they release the Harcourts once I'd set off.

Let's head to the cottage. I've got to talk to Mia.

Rocky ruffled his feathers and shuffled on his branch. *Please, Evangeline, let us return to the manor—where you will find comfort.*

Right now, I don't need comfort. I need answers.

*

Rocky took off to hunt as soon as we arrived on Maggie's land, a ten-acre parcel in the outlying rural area of town. A twisted grapevine arbor marked the entrance to the property. I walked alone up the long, river rock driveway, a dark, dense forest tunneling around me. I focused straight ahead to avoid the memories living in that particular stretch of wood. Eventually, the trees retreated and revealed lavender fields that lined five acres to my right and a crooked, gnarly stream to my left. The stream snaked along the perimeter of the property and wound through the woods that edged the far side of a cheerful, stuccoed, thatched-roof cottage.

I'd spent fourteen years in that cottage with Maggie, traipsing through the fields, exploring the forests, and splashing in that stream. It was magical, and it was home. Over the last few months, however, as we worked on the gallery, I remained at Morgan Manor. The time away had made me homesick. But it wasn't nostalgia that drew me back.

I inhaled deeply, savoring the ancient power permeating this swath of countryside. I tasted the magic in the air. After slipping off my shoes, power flowed through the soles of my feet. My flagging strength increased.

Maybe I do need a little comfort.

The natural energy, the spirit, that saturated the property had been amplified, generations before, by a magical boost from a witch—the first Italian la strega to cross the Atlantic. She sailed from Italy, drawn to this land. She settled here and built this cottage with her own hands and a collaboration with the elemental energy giving breath and a heartbeat to this slice of nature. It was said the witch and Nature struck a magical bond. As long as la strega of her Aradian bloodline inhabited that cottage and tended and protected the land, the elements would serve the witches who resided there. When Maggie inherited the cottage and its grounds from her grandmother, she also inherited this magical bond. But when Maggie packed up her familiar, Hanna the queen bee, and went off traveling with Ayo, it was left to her great-aunt Mia, who'd come from Italy to aid us in our time of need, to hold down the fort. With Maggie and Ayo missing, the protection afforded by Mia's la strega magic was more important than ever.

And it was Mia I'd come to see.

I raised my fist to knock on the cottage's violet-stained front door when Mia called from inside. "Puoi entrare! Come in, come in."

Mia sat hunched in an antique, Queen Anne armchair in front of the kitchen hearth, dove gray hair swept into a loose bun while her thick, black shawl warmed her shoulders. Her viper cane rested on her lap. Steaming mugs of coffee and Mia's tarot deck sat on a small table between her and an empty, waiting chair.

With a toothy, wizened grin, Mia threw her arms up in welcome.

"Buona sera, Evangeline! Sit, sit." She motioned to the armchair across from her with her cane. "I saw you coming." She tapped her tarot cards with a crooked bony finger.

I dropped into the seat with a groan. "It's been a hell of a day." Fatigue swept over me. "And it's barely noon."

"Sip your coffee." She offered an indulgent smile. "It'll perk you up. And we have much to discuss. You'll need your wits."

I followed her direction and took a precious moment to appreciate the beverage. I loved a good cup of coffee. It was a treat, a little boost, a moment of joy. I enjoyed this moment, warming my toes by the fire with a wise la strega, like we hadn't a care in all the world. As if the Harcourts weren't already hatching their retaliation for my interference.

I set down my mug and rubbed my eyes before getting to the point of my unannounced visit.

"We've got trouble, and I've got questions."

Mia leaned forward in her chair. "Is it Magdalena? Have you heard something about my niece? I know she lives, but I cannot sense more. Something blocks me."

"No, it's not Maggie. We still haven't heard anything. Nicolae is still in California following up on leads. It's...it's..." I choked up. My whole body swelled with unexpressed emotion, but I sucked it up.

"Come, priestess." She took my hands in hers. "Let me see all you have seen." She closed her eyes to capture the images from my memory. "Hmm... Le naiade streghe... Magic, taken to dark places... You wanted to choose caution over intervention. Instead, you acted to protect others... You drew on the elements for your power... You saved secrets, sacrifices, and lives... You learned disturbing histories." She opened her eyes and pierced me with her knowing gaze. "These things are true, yes?"

Her words were rich and dreamy and so deeply painful. I nodded as I fought tears.

I stifled a sob and cleared my throat. "At some point we've got to contact Mayor Riddle and give him a head's up. He has to follow up on the people in that circle and make sure everyone's ok. With Rocky's help, I should be able to identify them. I'd go to Chief Harrison, but I don't want to bother him so soon after his brush with death. Obviously, I'll explain everything to the coven later, but right now I need your guidance." My nerves sent my heartrate skittering. "The Harcourts feel I breached our agreement when I outed them to the chief and his sister. That I did it to save a life doesn't seem to matter."

"I think Ethan warned against making bargains with le naiade, no? What did you agree to?" She sat forward attentively in her chair, awaiting my answer and clutching her cane so that her wrinkled skin stretched tight across her knuckles.

"We agreed I wouldn't let the public in Arbor know about the brooms in the Harcourts' closet, and Vivian and Eris agreed not to use magic against the town. I was trying to help. I was trying to protect them." I hung my head and sipped my coffee. "But the Harcourts outmaneuvered me. They skirted around the edges of our deal by leading folks astray through temptation. And since I outed them to the chief and his sister, the Harcourts say I nullified the agreement. So, they preyed on Arbor mundane, using them—their secrets, their blood—as offerings to the spirits of the river in exchange for power." I sat up straight in my chair and set down my coffee. "But I have power of my own. I exerted it, and they retreated. I will not have random magical beings thinking they can roll up into my town and fuck with people. Pardon my French."

"That's not French." She cocked her head to the side in confusion.

I couldn't help but laugh, yet the humor faded fast. "Oh, Mia, there's so much more..." My tears welled up again. *Mother, what have you done?* "I need answers. Answers about my mother and father and their connection to the Harcourts. These women are here, exploiting, poisoning this community, and they are intertwined with my family. I need to know exactly how."

"What do you ask of me?"

"Can you *see* these things that happened in the past? Do you know a spell or charm that can show me events that occurred before I was born? I'd ask Maggie, of course, but..."

But Maggie is missing, and my heart aches, and I don't know where else to turn.

Mia planted her cane firmly on the floor, leaned forward, and patted me softly on the cheek. "Oh, priestess. The answer is simple, no? If you have questions about your momma, ask your momma."

Dear, sweet Goddess, she's right!

The answer was so simple that it struck me speechless for a moment. Why hadn't I thought of asking my mother first? I'd summoned her spirit just months before. She'd listened to my burdens and offered me guidance. Maybe she would appear to me again.

"I've got to head out to the woods." I sprung to my feet.

"Okay, okay. Hold the phone. Sit." Mia flailed her cane with the command, and I followed her orders. "First, you get cleaned up. Soap and water, clean clothes will make you feel better. Refreshed. And you are hungry, no? Of course you are. I know these things." She tapped her temple. "You need to eat. I will cook for you."

As I considered Mia's words, I tried to run my hand through my hair, but my fingers got caught in a wild nest of knots. I took in my shabby state and sighed. My hands and fingernails were dirty, my pants and bare feet were muddy, and my jacket had a rip on the sleeve – as often happens when one traipses around the woods making magic. And I reeked.

"You're not wrong. I'm a damn mess. I'm in desperate need of a shower. Or maybe a nice bubble bath." I gave a small laugh, my heart eased by her company. "But first, I wouldn't mind a drink. And then a bite to eat after I get cleaned up."

"Si, good, very good. I will start the cooking, and you get the wine." Mia emphasized her words with one hand. She gripped the viper cane in her other hand, took a deep breath, braced herself, and rocked out of the armchair onto her feet.

While Mia puttered around the kitchen, I raided the wine pantry for a couple bottles of Sangiovese. I poured out two generous glasses and passed one to Mia, which she accepted with a raised salute. Returning to my armchair by the fire, I sat and took a healthy sip.

"Now that is divine." I sighed.

The wine and the fire warmed me, and the tension in my shoulders eased a bit. I took another drink and snuggled into the chair. The instant I decided to rest my eyes, Alexander burst through the cottage door and barreled into the kitchen. As cottage kitchens go, it was a rather large space, but Alexander was a rather large specimen of a man, and his broad shoulders, wide, hard chest, and muscular arms occupied all my attention.

"For fuck's sake, woman! There you are!" Alexander roared as he charged toward me with this Kal Drogo meets Eric Northman vibe going on.

Mia rattled off a string of rapid-fire curses in Italian.

Alexander lifted me from my chair and wrapped me tight in his arms. He burrowed his scratchy bearded face in my neck. "You scared me. Don't fucking do that again. Please." His voice reverberated through my nerve endings. "I can't lose you." He spoke between kisses along my shoulder and neck and cheek. Then he clasped both sides of my face and kissed me hard and deep.

I trembled, somehow maintaining the precarious grasp I had on my glass. But I watched with agonizing, slow-motion regret as half my wine splashed onto the floor.

I was equally swept off my feet and annoyed by his aggressive masculinity. The great protector routine was getting old. But I couldn't deny he turned me on, which only annoyed me more.

He pulled back, still gripping my arms, and examined my disheveled appearance.

"You're a fucking mess."

So much for being turned on. "Gee, thanks." I wriggled out of his grip.

"I didn't mean... Are you okay?"

"Yeh, I'm fine, but you have got to take it down a notch. Seriously. You spilled my wine, and you pissed off Mia."

"Sorry," Alexander mumbled. He cleaned up the spill, then poured me the last of the Sangiovese and opened another bottle as he continued griping. "You didn't tell me you were leaving the manor. You didn't even bring your phone. I had no idea where you were."

I took a long drink. "I don't need to *check in*. I can go as I please." I was as calm as I could muster. "Plus, I sent Killian off with a note for Gregory. Gregory said the boys had the gallery covered and suggested I take an Eva day. I agreed. But as you can see—" I motioned to my crumpled state, "—it hasn't exactly been a day at the spa." I took another sip of wine. "How did you know to find me here?"

"I sent Archie out looking for you. He found Rocky hunting in the valley. Rocky told him you had a run-in with the Harcourts and then retreated to the cottage to confer with Mia. I came as soon as I heard."

I didn't retreat. I fucking won this round. I hoped, this once, that Alexander had heard my thoughts.

"And I saw it in the crystals and insisted on tagging along." Celeste appeared in the kitchen. She looked lovely as always, even as bags teetered in her arms and swung in bunches from the crook of her elbows with Luna slinking precariously around her feet. "Sorry it took me a bit to come in. I had to grab all this on my own since, unfortunately, there wasn't a gentleman around to help out." She scowled at Alexander. "Give me a few minutes to unload, and I'll say a proper hello." Celeste scooted down the hall toward my bedroom.

Great Goddess, she's a piece of work. I admired her as she walked by. When she offered me a playful wink, my heart jolted in my chest, and a pleasant shudder ran through me. I squeezed my eyes and thighs tight. *Focus, Evangeline.* I suppressed a grin as I scolded myself unconvincingly.

I returned my attention to Alexander and saw he hadn't taken his knowing eyes off me.

"Why didn't you help Celeste with all that luggage?" I challenged him.

"I told her not to bring all that shit in the first place. But she insisted I wait for her to pack your clothes and makeup and toiletries and who knows what the hell else. I don't have the foggiest fucking idea what possessed her to think you'd need any of that for a visit to the damn cottage."

"You know, I don't appreciate my things being referred to as 'shit.' I'm sure she has a good reason for bringing all that with her."

"You mean besides the fact that she's an exasperating sycophant?"

"She obviously saw something in the crystals."

"Look, can we cut the shit? Did you take on the Harcourts today?"

"Yes."

"Alone?" he growled.

"Rocky was with me. Why does it matter?"

He looked at me as if I'd lost my mind. "They're fucking dangerous!" he screamed.

"So am I," I said evenly. "And relax. I'm here; no one died, and I helped twelve people. I'm calling today a win."

"What possessed you to go after them by yourself? You fought a foe with unknown powers, alone, with only Rocky as backup. How irresponsible can you be?" He spoke as if reprimanding a child.

The insinuation that I couldn't handle things on my own seriously pissed me off, but I still found myself explaining. "There was no time. The Harcourts were about to select their third victim. I had to act quickly."

"You could have sent Rocky to us with a message," Alexander countered.

"Then I really would have been alone, *and* unable to fly." I threw up my arms in exasperation. "What do you want from me, Alexander? You didn't see what I saw. You didn't hear what I heard. I weighed the pros and cons of intervening at all. My delay, up to that point, had allowed harm to come to two people already. So, I acted. I don't need you second-guessing my decisions, or worse, thinking I'm incapable of making important decisions on my own in the first place."

"Now wait a damn minute," Alexander roared. "Don't turn this around on me. You know that's not what I meant. What you need—"

"What Eva *needs* is to cleanse away the troubles of the day." Celeste breezed back into the kitchen. "She needs to eat and drink and rest. Then she's got to talk to her mother. I saw it in the crystals." She kissed Mia on the cheek before leaning casually on the counter and pegging me with a sober, business-like expression. "I'm here to help. I brought everything, including your mother's grimoire, and I ran you a bath. By the time you're squeaky clean, Mia should have dinner ready. Then you can head to the woods."

Damn, she's good.

Mia nodded approvingly. "Celeste is right. Clean body, clean spirit, clean mind. Take your time. Everything in your room is how you left it." She stirred a giant pot, and then shooed me away with her spoon.

Alexander glowered at Celeste with a toxic blend of frustration and jealousy. And when he faced me, I found sadness in his eyes.

"Do whatever you want." He turned from me.

Oh, stop pouting, Alexander. I knew he'd hear me. *I'm just getting cleaned up. I'm not running off to fuck her.*

A sour ball rose from my belly to my throat as I turned away from him. I wanted Alexander's support. I wanted his ear and his intellect. I couldn't stand this possessive bullshit.

"Call the mayor. Invite him to dinner," I said over my shoulder.

Celeste took my hand, and I let her lead me down the hall, through my old bedroom, to the bathroom. The scent of eucalyptus enveloped me first, but once I focused in, I noticed rosemary, lavender, and frankincense in the air. Celeste lit white candles, and their warm light reflected in the crystals and stones she'd strewn on the shelf beside the claw-foot tub.

The anxiety twisting my gut eased a bit, but my pulse raced as Celeste hovered behind me.

"Let me care for you," she whispered close to my ear as she lowered my torn jacket down my shoulders.

I took a breath and gave myself over to her ministrations. Celeste removed the rest of my clothes and helped me step into the steaming bath. I shuddered as I lowered myself into the hot water, and a massive sigh escaped me. Celeste rolled up her sleeves and the cuffs of her pants and kicked off her shoes. When she turned, she busted out in laughter.

"What is it?" I asked, with a burst of self-consciousness.

"Nothing, it's just... this tub's so tiny compared to the literal cauldron you've been bathing in at the manor these last few months."

I laughed. "You're right. I could fit three of these into that behemoth. But it is a luxurious behemoth. Still—" I sighed as I glanced around my little bathroom with the claw-foot tub "—it's nice to be home. So, what are all these crystals? Let's see what you've got here... There's some pretty amethyst, jade, jasper, lots of onyx, and...rose quartz." I shot her a cheeky smile and an arched brow.

"Damn. You caught me flirting via crystals."

I flicked a splash of water at her.

"All right, you. Lean back. Relax." Celeste eased me into a reclined position against a fluffy towel folded over the side of the tub. She ran her hands through my hair, somehow flowing through without a snag, softly, gently. "Close your eyes, breathe deep."

My eyelids lowered. I breathed in through my nose and out through my mouth. I focused on the air as it brushed against my lips on an exhale. I breathed in and out. In and out.

"That's it, good. Feel the bathwater lap gently over your breasts, and between your raised knees, as your chest rises and falls."

In and out. In and out.

"Very good," she said softly.

Right as I filled my lungs, she dunked me under the water. She didn't hold me down. It was more playful than violent. But her actions had a clear message.

"Never let your guard down around water," I heard her muffled voice say. "Or those who wield it."

I got the message loud and clear.

I also had plenty of air and no reason to panic, so I figured I'd stay under the water for a bit. I gripped the sides of the tub to keep myself down. I closed my eyes, and for a few moments, peace settled over me. I stayed under for about twenty or thirty seconds before Celeste's frantic arms yanked me up, breaking through my self-imposed sensory deprivation.

"What's wrong? You okay?" I rubbed my eyes.

"Am *I* okay? What the fuck, Evangeline?" Celeste sat slumped against the bathroom wall and stretched her long legs out in front of her. "Why would you do that?"

"Why are *you* pissed? You're the one who dunked me in the first place."

"I was making a point. You didn't have to stay under." She pouted.

"I got your point. I had air. I felt like hanging out under the water for a bit."

"Well, you scared the crap out of me."

"Oh, not you too. One possessive worry-wort is enough."

"You can be a real pain in the ass, you know that?" Celeste scowled. "I'm not angry that you took off. I'm not angry that you played Wonder

Woman and battled the Harcourts by yourself to save the Arbor damsels in distress. Again. I think that's awesome. Go, you! What pisses me off is that you didn't have your phone. A smart witch always keeps her phone charged and accessible. You never know when you'll need to look up a spell or incantation or the properties of a certain kind of herb. *Or* maybe text for backup when facing off against a couple of naiad witches." She looked at me with sad, puppy dog eyes. "Maggie and Ayo are missing. What if you were next? How were we to know?"

I hung my head. *She's right. It was foolish to leave everyone in the lurch and leave myself exposed.*

"Okay, okay. Fair enough."

I leaned against the fluffy towel again and closed my eyes. I breathed in and out. In and out. In and out.

After Celeste's ministrations in the bath, she set upon my hair, braiding it shield-maiden style to make me feel even more badass. I threw on a pair of jeans, a Jane's Addiction T-shirt, and a snuggly flannel shirt I had picked out from the ungodly selection of garments Celeste brought from my closet at the manor. I ignored the bags of shoes she brought altogether, but I did snag a pair of fluffy, black-and-red striped socks. I saw no reason for makeup or jewelry—besides the cimaruta that never left my neck—so I bypassed those bags too.

Celeste had also brought along my traveling art supplies, my bag of magical sundries, and my besom broom. She'd stacked them all up neatly in the corner of the room beside my mother's grimoire. My stomach knotted up, and a chill ran across my skin.

What the hell is going on? Why was it so important to bring all this here for a Sunday visit to the cottage? It doesn't look like I'm leaving tonight. Looks like I might not return to the manor for some time, and that is out of the question. I have a gallery to run. The question is why. What did Celeste see?

I added this to the list of unanswered questions that haunted me. The day dwindled. Time for explanations waned. No doubt the Harcourts were plotting their revenge for my confrontation. And though I didn't have Celeste's gifts, I knew the Harcourts were going to be dangerous when the sun went down.

And night came early this time of year.

Chapter Thirteen

Celeste and I headed to the kitchen. A cacophony of male voices greeted us. I should have known the boys would show up for a homecooked Sunday meal with Mia. The happy crone had Gregory, Ethan, and Luca in aprons, acting as her sous chefs. Alexander huddled with Mayor Riddle around the dining table. The moment they saw me, their heads shot up. Then, as if choreographed, Gregory, Luca, and Ethan launched themselves at me, and squished me in a bear hug between them.

If only Nicolae were with us. And Maggie. And Ayo.

"Okay, okay," I said with a wheezing laugh. "I love you too. Now let me go."

They ignored me, of course, and instead of releasing me, they showered me with kisses. I'd nearly run out of breath when Mia called out, "Dinner's ready! Boys, take these to the table."

Releasing me, they hopped to attention, and brought over platters of chicken parmesan, bowls of antipasto and garlic bread, and a few more bottles of wine.

"It's nice to see you, Mayor." I addressed the outsider in the room.

"Yes, well, hello Ms. Clarion." Riddle sounded stiffer than usual. An Arbor PD bomber jacket hung on the back of his chair, and he leaned on the dining table with the sleeves of his button-down shirt rolled up to his elbows. "I hear you have a doozy of a story to tell."

"That's the truth."

"'Scuse me, everybody." Mia carefully lowered herself into her spot at the table. "Evangeline...Priestess," she said.

She didn't need to elaborate. The coven had gathered, and I had my role. I raised my arms and led them in a blessing over the meal.

The coven responded, "Blessed Be."

"Now, mangia! Everybody eat. After, we will listen to the priestess tell how she took on le naiade streghe."

"No pressure or anything," Alexander teased with a wink to ease me as the hoard around the table dove into the meal.

He pisses me off, but sweet Goddess, he is a beautiful man. Inside and out.

I knew Alexander heard my private thoughts. I caught the shadow of a smile, and it melted me a little. I knew he loved me, and it was in his nature to be protective, part of his magical DNA. I thought about all that had happened earlier in the day. Alexander's gifts could have helped. I looked around the table. All their gifts could have helped.

As I was about to apologize, Alexander laid his hand gently on mine and stilled my words. Then he projected his thoughts to me.

It's okay. He swallowed hard. *I'm in awe of you. Your bravery, and yes, your power. I'd never want to control you, Evangeline. I just want to protect you. I know I can be...too much sometimes. And I should leave your thoughts alone. I'm sorry. I love you.*

I heaved a sigh. "I love you too," I said aloud and kissed him on the cheek.

We ate and drank, and it was nice to pretend everything was all right for a while. But I'd delayed long enough. I cleared my throat.

"Mayor Riddle, I am glad you came by. I'm sorry for not getting right down to things, but honestly, it's been a long day already, and I was getting hangry. Now that I have my wits about me, let me get to the point. It's now unequivocal that the Harcourts are a direct threat—to me, to this coven, and to the entire community; a greater threat than I imagined. I'm not sure how to move forward after what I've seen. And what I've done."

After a centering breath, I rehashed everything I'd witnessed on the bank of the AuSable River. I described the creepy Victorian building and the white horse. I told them about the twelve, black-eyed Arbor residents mindlessly chanting, writhing, and disrobing to the Harcourts' mesmerizing naiad song. I explained how the Harcourts enraptured two women into divulging their darkest wishes, and how they spilled their blood as a sacrifice to the river spirits.

"Rocky wanted me to intervene the instant Vivian raised her athame, but I hedged. He was pissed, of course, disappointed in me. The thing was, I knew Vivian and Eris were going to keep extracting more wishes, more secrets, more blood from the zombified men and women around that dark circle, but I didn't want to get involved. I wasn't scared to take them on by myself. I'm arrogant enough to believe that I can destroy them. Easily. Rather, I didn't think intervening on Arbor's behalf was worth the risk. Why stick my neck out for people who'd cheered while I burned? But I remembered Mother Hildegard's counsel from Samhain. We share different beliefs, but she has faith in me. And Rocky offered his own counsel, of course." I passed my eyes over the coven. "Magic or no, we all have a responsibility to do what's right. It may sound banal, but it's the truth. The Harcourts turned people into puppets, and that's just fucking creepy. They weaseled powerful secrets out of folks, promising to fulfill their darkest wishes, and offered their blood in exchange for power. Again, seriously fucked up. The last thing we need is those two getting more powerful. So, I acted."

Immersed in my story, the coven crowded in closer. Riddle sat back in his chair, his arms crossed, his eyes intent upon me.

"What did you do?" Celeste asked with whispered excitement.

The scene played out in my head like a movie, but I struggled to describe it.

"I called on the elements, on air and earth, on the trees. And they answered. With Rocky beside me, and the trees gathered at my back, I flew above the Harcourts and challenged them. They were...unapologetic, defiant. They delight in causing chaos. But, when all was said and done, I persuaded them to stand down. They released the twelve in the circle from their enchantments."

I sipped my wine, steeped in memories.

"How, precisely, did you persuade them to do that?" Gregory's cool baritone commanded the table. "They're not exactly what one might call 'amenable.'"

"The trees." I offered a wolfish grin, enjoying the memory of the roots cracking through the riverbank and curling around the Harcourts' legs. "The roots, to be specific. They wrapped Vivian and Eris up like smudge sticks and lifted them up until they were level with me, thirty feet or so in the air. And then I reminded them of what Arbor was capable of.

I gave them a taste of what it's like when Arbor avenges itself on witches. Incapacitation, asphyxiation, fire at their feet, and a concentrated, roiling thunderstorm groaning above them. They agreed to back down."

"Seriously?" Ethan blurted with a skeptical eye.

"Can you be more specific with your derision?" I grinned.

"I can't see a naiad giving in that easily. No offense, but why would they think you'd actually kill them? Aren't you the good guy?"

All eyes around the table waited anxiously for my reply. The mayor visibly struggled to suppress his anxiety; sweat beaded his forehead, his temples pulsed, and he held his lips tight in a line.

Any semblance of humor faded. "I'm not a good guy or a bad guy. I'm Eva Clarion. I trust the power within me, and I endeavor to use it wisely. I'm a witch. As was my mother...and my father, apparently, before my mother killed him. Or so says Vivian. Seems she knew them both. It seems, she believed if my mother could kill, so could I."

Besides the fact that I'd accused my mother of being a murderer, I never spoke of my father. I didn't know him and never cared to. So, while the mayor's eyes only narrowed with this information, shock and chatter spread across the rest of the room. Alexander and Celeste turned to each other in alarm. The boys, who'd known me all my life, were particularly shaken.

"And Eris is my half sister," I said as an afterthought.

My declaration stifled the rumble of conversation around the table for a full minute before a riot of exclamations, questions, and reprimands for not having mentioned this right away, blasted me from every direction. I didn't know whether to laugh or cry or scream, so I sipped my wine until they settled down enough for me to explain.

"According to Vivian, my mother killed my father; a powerful witch who happened to be Vivian's fiancé and Eris's father." I looked over the stunned faces and continued. "So, either they're lying and simply trying to mess with me, or they're telling the truth. In which case, I have a million questions. A large one being—"

"Did Vivian Harcourt kill your mother?" Luca cut to the heart of the matter.

"Do you think the Harcourts are in Arbor to finish you off too?" Celeste asked before anyone could consider Luca's query.

"Now wait a doggone minute!" Riddle grasped the edge of the table tight and got to his feet. "I hate to break up this festival of wild speculation you have going on here, but let's return to reality. Harcourt Architecture won the downtown rebuild contract with Arbor, beating out several other firms by a mile. They weren't only the most economical choice. Their work was excellent. *That* is why they're here. Now, I like you folks." He eased up a bit. "I've tried to work with you. But I could have you arrested. You asked me here tonight, knowing doggone well that I'm the mayor, and confessed to a series of serious crimes—over dinner— as you passed wine around the table!" Red-faced, he pounded the table.

We were all stunned. And speechless.

"Ms. Clarion," Riddle went on, "you've admitted to trespassing on the Harcourts' private property, spying on them, interrupting their religious service—whose participants were there voluntarily, by the way. I've spoken to them myself. You've admitted to physically assaulting the Harcourts and threatening not only their professional livelihoods, but their very lives. As if that's not enough, you accuse them of murder! You should be ashamed of yourselves, all of you. I would have thought you, of all people, would be welcoming and tolerant to these bright, successful witches who've come to rebuild the town you all destroyed." Riddle pointed a finger at Alexander. He rounded on me. "I've got a prediction for ya. There's gonna be a warrant for your arrest in your future, Evangeline Clarion, if you don't watch your step around the Harcourts." The mayor looked away to compose himself, and turned with a kinder, gentler aspect, one that struck me as a mask. "Take this as a warning, not a threat. As I said, I like you folks and want to work with you. I understood there'd be risks bringing more magic into Arbor when I hired the Harcourts, but I believed you all would help smooth things over. Not make things more difficult."

Breaking through my astonishment, I stood. "Mayor, the Harcourts are dangerous. I don't think you understand what they've done—"

"No." He grabbed his jacket off the back of his chair. "You don't seem to understand what *you* have done. But here's where I agree with you. Vivian and Eris Harcourt are dangerous women. They will likely retaliate in one way or another. Now, I will not waste precious, finite Arbor PD resources on this. But I'd be more than happy to caution the Harcourts against retaliation on your behalf. And I could keep an eye on things here myself." He somewhat dreamily took in the cottage around him.

Luca sat up straight in his chair and looked around the table. "Yeh, you know, that's not necessary, Mayor. We're used to providing our own security."

"What, like booby-trap spells around the perimeter." Riddle snorted derisively.

"Cameras, Riddle. Lots and lots of cameras. Among many other fun security features. Set 'em up myself." Luca leaned forward. "Seeing what's really there, finding the truth, that's kind of my thing. And the cameras help me do that." He shrugged and reclined in his chair.

Turning away from Luca without reply, Riddle threw on his jacket and faced me.

"Be careful, Ms. Clarion. Your attempts at good will in the community only go so far. The gallery's great, so is your work with the nuns and the pantry. But the people wonder why you weren't the one to help Chief Harrison. And some are angry you interrupted their service by the river this morning. They think it's hypocritical. So, I'd say, you have more than the Harcourts to worry about. If I were you, I'd stay away from town altogether." With that, Riddle nodded to Mia and left.

Sure as hell sounds like a threat to me.

"That didn't go as expected," Gregory quipped.

"Oh, shut the fuck up," Alexander snapped.

Gregory gritted his teeth but held his tongue.

"This isn't a goddamn joke," Alexander ranted. "Riddle's right. Evangeline's under legal threat now, on top of everything else. And Ayo's not here to tackle it." Alexander looked down at me sharply. "I know you're going to hate this, but you need more protection now than ever. You will always have a home at the manor, but I think you need to stay here."

"Get the hell out of here." I scoffed at the suggestion. "I remember a time, not too long ago, when you insisted I go to the manor for protection, to stay safe behind your walls. Now, when I have a gallery to run and Yule festivities to plan *at the manor*, you insist I stay here. It makes no sense." I turned to the table, hoping for backup, and found none.

"The power here will amplify your magic. The land will aid you," Mia said simply.

Luca came around the table and took my hands. "Magdalena and Ayo are missing. The Harcourts are going to want revenge on you for what happened today at the river—whether magically or legally or both. And not like you've ever been real popular with the locals, but apparently, the public has new reasons to trash you. Be smart. Stay here. Between magic and tech, we'll keep you safe."

"And you can still work, just...remotely," Ethan chimed in. "We'll keep an eye on the gallery and organize Yule. And Celeste will make sure we implement your vision and follow your instructions."

"With everything going on, can't we cancel this Yule bullshit?" Alexander growled.

Celeste rolled her eyes. "I'll act as an intermediary between the cottage and the manor. Whatever you direct, I'll make sure it gets done. And I'll get you all set up here. I already brought everything you'll need." Her face filled with pity for me and pride that she'd anticipated my needs.

I hated every word. Every even-toned placation. And I hated the fear below it all. I wasn't afraid. I was pissed off.

"After everything...and *I'm* the one who has to hide away? This is such crap."

I hung my head in frustration. But when I closed my eyes, I saw Maggie's face, and guilt flooded my chest. Maggie and Ayo were missing, and I was bitching and complaining about staying home and staying safe.

You can be a real asshole sometimes, Eva Clarion.

"Fine. I'll stay here on the cottage property. But right now, I'm heading to the woods. I need answers."

Chapter Fourteen

I threw on a pair of boots, gathered up my bag of magical sundries and a walking staff, and trudged past the fallen oak tree. I headed down a well-trodden path into the forest that edged the cottage grounds. A fifteen-minute hike took me to a wide clearing. Months ago, before our Midsummer celebration, when the weight of the world drove me to reach out through the veil to my mother, Shasta the great black bear had erected a ring of boulders within the forest clearing, each three to four feet high. In the center of the ring, she'd positioned a flat stone altar. At this altar, I'd cast the spell that brought my mother into the plane of the living.

And there I was, months later, seeking out my mother's wisdom once again.

I placed a fat, white candle on the stone altar, and lit it. Then I lit white sage and cast my circle.

With my arms wide and my voice clear, I chanted.

"Earth, my body.

Water, my blood.

Air, my breath.

Fire, my spirit."

I grasped my long, wooden staff. With it, I tapped the ground three times and called out, "Hear me, spirits of the north—spirits of patience and strength." I turned, tapped the staff three times again and said, "Hear me, spirits of the east—spirits of wisdom and ancient knowledge." I turned and tapped the staff three more times. "Hear me, spirits of the south—spirits of fire and commitment." I turned and tapped three final times. "Hear me, spirits of the west—spirits of compassion."

With the grace of the Goddess and the power within me to aid my magic, I voiced my intention.

"Earthen bone and winged beat,

Let my mother come to me,

Waves that crash and fire's heat,

Allow for now her spirit free,

I call her forth from time and space,

Permit me now to see her face,

When my queries are at an end,

Take her spirit home again."

I repeated my request twice more before my mother's familiars, a deer and a crane, appeared before me. The familiars bowed low as my mother materialized, in corporal form, between them. She walked toward me, draped in the same kind of long, burgundy dress she wore in life. With each step, more animals, great and small, gathered around her.

"Hello, sweetheart." She had a sad, kind smile. "Well, aren't we in a pickle? I suppose I have some explaining to do."

"Mother," I said like a prayer and fell to my knees before her. "You know? What's been going on, I mean."

"Yes, I know. I've seen all you have seen." She joined me, cross-legged, on the forest floor. "There's no need to rehash your troubles. You need answers, and I have much to say. It's time to tell my story."

"Yes, please, start at the beginning. I need to know everything if I'm going to take on the Harcourts with my eyes wide open."

My mother reached out and gently stroked my cheek. "My brave, brave girl." She sighed. "Someday, my love, we'll have that talk, the one where I tell of the generations of witches whose magic courses through your veins. Someday I'll start at the beginning. It's important today, however, that I begin a bit later on."

I pulled out a bottle of wine I'd tucked into my bag of magical sundries and uncorked it. After a few healthy swigs, I wiped my mouth on the back of my sleeve. "Tell me."

And then, fourteen years after her death, this inexplicably corporal spirit of my mother offered me fragments of her life story as we sat on the ground in the woods where she died.

"Magdalena and I grew up together in the coven. We were thick as thieves, positively inseparable. But by our mid to late teens, our intimacy grew into a more romantic relationship. Privately, we were a couple; publicly, merely the best of friends. It was a different time then. People weren't as accepting, even among those in the liberal-minded witch community. The world at large had no idea Magdalena and I were *together*. And we had every intention of keeping it that way."

I had heard as much from Maggie over the years.

"We were beauties, if I do say so myself, made more striking by our contrast to each other—me, a petite, emerald-eyed brunette with curves for days, and Magdalena, the waif with the icy eyes and the lion's mane. Needless to say, we turned many heads. Not unlike you and Celeste. Young men hovered around us like gnats on juicy bits of watermelon, but we paid them no mind.

"Until, that is, I caught the eye of an important figure in the coven community. Maximus Waterhouse." My mother paused at the name, and its importance hit me like a brick.

My father.

"Once he set his sights on me, we were all anyone talked about. Lavinia and Maximus—we were roundly viewed as an excellent match. The coven considered me a highly accomplished witch, and my beauty and poise overcame my modest means. And Maximus, the only son of our high priestess, Circe, had a considerable magical pedigree, fine, regal looks, and money. The coven had us married before we'd gone on a single date."

People suck.

"So, when Maximus sought me out—with the approval and encouragement of both of our mothers—I was expected to reciprocate his advances. Naturally, I was devastated. I couldn't stand the idea of pretending to be attracted to this man. And what if he wanted an actual relationship—which was obviously everyone's hope—what then? How far was I expected to take this farce?

"But Magdalena set my mind at ease. 'One night can't hurt,' she assured me. 'Have a nice dinner and a movie, and then explain that you didn't hit it off.' My poor, beloved Magdalena...how she regretted this advice."

Poor Magdalena, is right. Sweet Goddess, do I tell her Maggie's missing? Does she already know?

My mother gazed deep into the woods—seeing, but not seeing.

Something told me whatever she said next would be hard to hear, and I steeled my spine.

"One evening, in late August, I conceded and agreed to go out with Maximus. Things went along swimmingly until he made advances. I wanted nothing to do with that sort of thing, of course, but my rejection threw him into a fury. Maximus berated me and admitted that he'd seen me and Magdalena together. He threatened to expose us if I didn't submit. But I told him I refused to be blackmailed."

I don't want to hear this.

"Being the spoiled narcissist that he was, Maximus refused to take no for an answer. Being the accomplished witch that he was, he had no need of fists to force me into submission. He wasn't the kind of guy that got his hands dirty if he could help it. Not when he had magic. He was a telekinetic, like his mother, but he also happened to be exceedingly adept at sleeping charms."

"'I will have you,' he said, and his cold, calm voice chilled me. 'And if you breathe a word, I'll spill your dirty secret. But I'm merciful. I'll let you sleep while I...'

"Anyway, you get the point. Maximus performed a series of hand gestures and whispered words I didn't understand. And just like that, I was out. The next thing I knew, I'd awoken alone on the side of the road by the edge of a forest. I ached all over, and my head swam. I called on my familiars, but Maximus's spell had weakened them as well. Thankfully, as you know, I've always had a way with all animals." She motioned around us to the assembled creatures of the woods. "Well, the animals of the forest came to my aid that night, surrounding me with their energy and fueling the magic within me. With their help, I astral projected to Magdalena and told her where to find my body."

Dear Goddess, no.

"I'd never seen her so furious. But she cleaned me up and took me home to my mother, your grandmother, Esmeralda. I told her everything. I confessed my relationship with Magdalena. I explained that Maximus threatened to scandalize me by spreading his knowledge of this relationship to the public unless I gave myself to him. And I described the sleeping charm he'd used to take advantage of me.

"Unfortunately, my mother did not offer me the comfort I desperately sought. Instead, she belittled me. She accused me of ruining my chances of happiness and prosperity. She accused me of ruining our good name. And then she kicked me out."

"No wonder you barely mentioned your mom when I was young. Sounds like Granny Esmeralda was a bitch," I said bluntly.

"She could be." She chuckled sadly. "For the next few weeks, I stayed with Magdalena and her parents. Mind you, everybody lived in the same coven community, the same community where you and I lived when you were a girl." Her wistful memory evaporated with the furrow of her brow. "To avoid the sight of Maximus's smug face, and because a lingering lethargy and nausea plagued me, I became somewhat of a recluse during this time. I rarely left the confines of my room. Even my familiars couldn't draw me into the fresh air with them. They knew something was off. But it was Maggie who first sensed the life growing inside me. When she broke this momentous news, she confessed she worried that I'd be angry, sad, scared. But that couldn't have been further from the truth. I felt possessive, protective, fierce. I was no longer maiden, but mother with a primal, all-consuming instinct to care for my child.

"I reached out to Maximus, but he dodged my calls and left my letters unanswered. Due to his unresponsiveness, Maggie's parents insisted I inform Circe of her son's actions. I hated this plan. Confronting Maximus was one thing, but despite my newfound maternal badassery, the thought of divulging these things to his mother, the most powerful witch in our coven, truly scared me. Still, I knew the Marammas were right; Circe needed to know what kind of son she'd raised."

My mother stood and once more gazed off into the darkness of the forest around us. Many minutes passed before she returned to her tale, and in the intervening silence, I waited anxiously for my mother to continue baring her soul.

"Maggie and I went to the Waterhouse mansion to approach Maximus and his mother with the news, but we didn't expect them to be entertaining company. You see, by that time, Maximus had moved on. He'd turned his attentions to another stunning and powerful witch from the coven, Vivian Harcourt. And he'd gotten her pregnant too. The difference was, she welcomed his advances, as far as I could tell. He'd asked Vivian to marry him, and she'd enthusiastically said yes. Vivian and Maximus had just announced their engagement to a large gathering of their friends and families when Maggie and I arrived.

"They stopped me at the front door, the three of them, Maximus, his mother, and his pregnant fiancé. I asked to speak to Maximus alone first, asked for only a moment of his time, but Circe and Vivian wouldn't have it. They insisted I say my peace, then and there, and get the hell out. So, I told them what Maximus had done to me, and I told them I was pregnant with his child."

"I assume they weren't thrilled."

"You assume correctly. Maximus stared blankly at the wall. Apparently, knocking up two women in the span of a few weeks, and being outed as a rapist to your mother and fiancé at your engagement party, can rattle a guy. As you can imagine, Circe and Vivian were irate, but not at Maximus. Circe considered me little better than a mosquito, a blood-sucking, trouble-making pest, interfering with her precious son's future. She wanted rid of me. She told me so right before she swatted me off her front step. Using her telekinetic powers, Circe flung me through the air, over their sprawling, manicured lawn, into the street. I skidded out on my ass and tumbled before scraping my hands and cheek on the asphalt. But I didn't care about that. My only thoughts were of the life inside me. And it scared me to death that my impact with the road may have hurt you. I called out to the Goddess to protect you."

My mother spoke these heartfelt, meaningful words with the faintest of expressions as if she only held the memories of feelings.

"Vivian was angry too, of course. I never meant to hurt her. She was a beautiful, clever witch about to marry the man everyone considered the catch of the coven, and I'd ruined her engagement dinner. She had every right to be pissed at me." My mother shook her head. "Deep down, I'd hoped she'd see the kind of man Maximus was and let him have it. But that was not to be. Instead, Vivian charged up and attacked me with torrents of water, a water cannon from each hand. But I repelled her attack with a spell that changed her water's elemental structure from super-soakers aimed at my head, to a heavy, damp humidity that saturated the air and ultimately left me unharmed.

"That's when Maximus broke out of his stupor. There I was, sitting in the middle of the street, soaking wet, clutching my stomach, when Maximus burst from the mansion. He was a fearsome sight. Anger warped his handsome face into that of a seething monster." She paused here again, lowered her eyes, and spoke with a tone of serene resignation. "Halfway down the lawn, Maximus raised his arms. A car parked nearby lifted into the air. He launched the car at me, and in the split second I had to react, I used a rebounding spell. The car halted in midair, reversed course, and crushed him. I didn't mean to kill him."

I wasn't sure what I was supposed to feel in that moment. I wasn't sure what I felt at all. I didn't know this man, and from what I'd heard thus far, he was a prick. But he was my father, and he died in a gruesome fashion. By my mother's hand.

I looked at my mother, the witch Lavinia Clarion, standing before me appearing as flesh and blood, yet only spirit. I thanked the Goddess for the powers with which I'd been blessed; powers that allowed me to reach through the veil between worlds and pull someone back, albeit temporarily; powers that returned my mother to me, however briefly.

"How did you get away from the Waterhouse mansion? Where did you go? To Maggie's parents? Why weren't you arrested for killing Maximus? Did the coven go after you? Was this why you were killed—revenge for his death? Do you know who killed you? Was it Circe or Vivian?" I blurted the questions, rapid-fire, hoping my mother would excuse my indelicacy.

She did, of course, and answered indulgently. "I don't know who killed me, and I don't know why, but I do know this. It wasn't Circe or Vivian. It was a man."

Well damn.

"But that happened years later." My mother strolled around the circle of stones and continued her tale. "With Maximus trapped under the car, Circe in tears, clutching her chest, and Vivian screaming like a banshee, my familiars evacuated me and Maggie from the...*situation* at the Waterhouse mansion. We couldn't go to the Maramma's house or the cottage, or we'd bring the wrath of the coven down on their heads. I was in danger. There'd be retaliation. I needed to hide. But more than that, I needed a safe place to have my baby—you, my powerhouse of a daughter.

So, I headed for Saint Francis Roman Catholic Convent, and the Mother Superior offered me refuge."

The convent? Looks like they've been helping us witches for a long time.

"Thanks to the coven's influence, the authorities ruled Maximus's death a tragic car accident. The necessity of keeping magic hidden overruled Circe's desire to see me destroyed. Yet I remained hidden, under the protection of the nuns at the convent for about a year, and only left when Circe passed away. Many said she died from the heartache of losing her son, her only child. The high priest who replaced her had been Circe's fiercest rival, and he eagerly welcomed me back into the fold.

"My own mother visited only once after I'd given birth, and even then, I saw the signs of illness. She never told me what ailed her, and she passed away not long after. I inherited her home in the coven community, the home where you and I spent a magical eight years together, surrounded by our witchy little family. And, well, you know the rest."

"All sunshine and roses until someone killed you," I said bluntly.

"Yes, that's right. Until someone killed me. But I died here, on cottage grounds, not among the coven."

"And all you know is that it was a man? Who killed you, I mean?"

"Yes. He approached from behind. But I saw his shadow and heard a male voice muttering right before the oak tree crushed me."

"A male witch." The scene spun around in my head.

"Oh, my daughter, you take on such burdens. Focus. Think. Learn all you can. And never be afraid to act. But take care of yourself. We are all made of energy, and we must recharge. Take heart, my love, you're a magnificent witch like your mother." Her smile grew wide and proud. "You are capable of absolutely everything, so long as you're willing to work for it. Only mind where you aim your talents. You have such power within you as to shake the whole world."

I sat for a few minutes digesting it all. "Why have you told me this—about Maximus and Vivian and the convent?"

"You deserve to know who your father was, that you have a sister, and why Vivian Harcourt harbors such animosity toward you. Remember to keep your friends close. And a witch's fiercest allies can be found in the unlikeliest of places, my darling, in both castles and convents." Her lips lifted softly. "And now, I must go."

"Oh, please wait. I have so many more questions." I fumbled around my brain for something else to ask before I lost her. "Did you know Jonathan Riddle when you were alive?" I rattled off before she could vanish.

She tilted her head to the side. "You mean that lump of a boy who used to trail after Maggie? He wasn't a fan of mine, but I think he may have loved Maggie almost as much as I do." She faded as she spoke. "Be well, my Evangeline. I love you."

My mother was gone. Her familiars had vanished. The animals that had flocked to her scampered off. I was alone with this story of life, death and my descent, and the darkness of the woods.

Chapter Fifteen

Steeped in a state of numbed astonishment, I packed up my candles and wine. As I traipsed through the woods, sure footed despite my distracted mind, I fretted over my mother's story—my story. Her staggering revelations had followed one after another, each more difficult to digest than the last.

I made a mental summary of my new information: Both of my grandmothers, Circe and Esmeralda, were, for lack of a more apt term, bitches. My father was a rapist. My mother killed my father, albeit in self-defense. And she'd given birth to me at the convent. Riddle not only knew Maggie but loved her—a fact he'd withheld. And I now understood the source of Vivian's anger, an anger even my mother sympathized with.

Of course, the Harcourts blamed me for my mother's offenses. My very existence deprived Vivian and Eris of a prosperous life. If I never existed, if I'd never been conceived, all would be right with their world. Vivian would have married the handsome, powerful Maximus Waterhouse, and they'd be living it up in their McMansion. Eris would be married off to some rich high priest of a coven far, far away.

Yet here I am.

The air, crisp and still, chilled my ears and nose as I trudged through the darkening woods. Instead of warming myself with the fire within, I welcomed the cold. It distracted my turbulent mind. I arrived at the fallen oak that marked the entrance to the main footpath through the forest, the oak tree that had killed my mother. Why the hell hadn't Maggie chopped the thing down years ago and removed it stump and root?

A searing pain lanced my side, and then another, and another, along my sides and back, like javelins plunging through my flesh, like giant birds skewering me with their sharpened beaks. But there was no blood, no flayed flesh. Only pain. I wailed, and collapsed flat on my face onto the lawn.

After an excruciating decade, year, day, hour, that was probably no more than a minute, the coven rushed out of the cottage. They circled around me. Alexander and Celeste fell to their knees by my side.

"Oh Eva." Alexander pulled me into his arms.

But the pain surged through me. I flung myself out of his embrace, onto my hands and knees, and retched.

"What is it, streghetta mia?" Alexander asked as he ran his hands over my body in a frantic search for the source of my agony. "There's no blood. There isn't a scratch."

"It's Rocky," Celeste said in a quiet, even voice with only the faintest hint of a quiver. She wiped my hair away from my face. "He's hurt—badly. Eva's feeling his pain."

While they spoke, the pain slashed me again and again. Stabbing, clawing. I screamed, and my throat shredded raw. When the assault ended abruptly, my cries died in my throat. The attack was over, but the torturous pain remained. The pain made coherent speech, and any semblance of rational thought, elusive.

"Waterfall house at river-fall bridge," I mumbled as unconsciousness beckoned, and I fought the temptation to drift away. "Rocky and ravens and riddles."

And then the pain conquered me, and I slipped into oblivion.

*

CYBER MONDAY

When I awoke, I kept my eyes closed, and surveyed my environment using my other senses. I felt no pain, so that was a good start. I laid against a cushion of pillows with a warm comforter over me. A hot, heavy weight pressed against my right side. I heard a deep, rumbling inhale, followed by an exhaled hush, and the steady rise and fall of a body brushed against me. I caught a familiar scent: musky, onions and garlic with an undercurrent of marijuana.

Why's Gregory snuggled up to me?

I focused in and caught the unmistakable tingling of his magic seeping into me.

Ah, shit. He's manipulating my senses. I must still be experiencing Rocky's pain, but Gregory's blocking me from feeling it.

I knew exactly who attacked Rocky—Abramelin and Reginald, doubtless on the Harcourts' orders. I'd felt the unyielding clutch of claws on my arms, and the skewering of a merciless, lacerating beak along my sides and back. I'd experienced all the pain of the attack on Rocky with none of the physical ramifications he experienced. From what I could tell, he was lucky to be alive.

I could kill those fucking ravens. And the naiad witches. A cold sweat broke out across my skin, coating my face and arms and legs. My stomach roiled. *No. No. I'm not evil. Do I have the power to kill them? Yes. It would be easy. Easier than anyone realizes. I keep trying to explain to Alexander, but I don't think he gets it. If he did, he'd be trying to protect others from me, not the other way around. But I'm not a killer. I'm not evil.*

After a few deep breaths, I peered out through my lashes. The sun streamed in through my bedroom bay window, and a clear, crystal blue washed across the sky beyond. I'd slept through the night. Peeking under the blanket, I searched my body, and found no bandages or blemish. It was clear Celeste had tended to me. Only she would have taken the time to brush my hair out and dress me in a pair of fuzzy socks, my favorite snuggly sweatpants, and a black tank top with 100% That Witch emblazoned across the bust. Though I was comfy, my heart was still yo-yoing out of my chest, my stomach splish-splashed around, and beads of sweat raced down my temples.

The movement of the blankets woke Gregory. Groggily, he sat up on the bed, grumbled, and scratched himself all over before turning to look down on me.

"Well, hey there, Priestess," he said lazily. "Glad you're up. But ya look green around the gills. Can I make you feel good?"

There were many ways to interpret his words, especially while in a bed, but at that moment, all I cared about was not puking or having a coronary.

"Please." I practically panted for relief.

Gregory lowered my blanket and swept his hands slowly over my body. He didn't touch me at first, but then, with the gentlest feathered fingertips, he grazed my face, shoulders, arms, chest, belly, thighs, calves, and feet. My pulse slowed, my cold sweats faded, and a warm, cozy feeling soaked into my skin like a mug of hot cocoa for the spirit.

But the thought of those savage, sadistic ravens torturing my hawk jolted me again.

"They have Rocky! I have to save him. We have to rescue him. I mean, seriously, what the fuck are we doing laying here?"

I tried to move but couldn't budge an inch. With nothing more than a gentle swipe of his hand across my chest, Gregory held me immobile by making me feel nothing at all. Feeling nothing, I could move nothing.

"Calm yourself, woman," he said, always a stupid thing to say to a woman.

My anger and frustration grew, and as it did, an acute pain along my back and sides grew stronger, soaking into my skin like poison.

Gregory stroked my cheek, a steady look in his eyes.

"Shh...easy. Now, I'm going to give you some straight talk, and you're going to listen. I am the only thing standing between you and a world of pain, sweetheart. They must have done a number on Rocky something fierce cause his pain's shooting through you like an electrical current. Now, I can hold it in check, but ya have to stop fighting me."

He eased up on the restraints, and I tested my arms and legs for mobility. I scooted up in bed and gestured for Gregory to continue speaking.

"Alexander and Ethan have been working on rescuing Rocky since last night. They checked in for breakfast and a nap before dawn but headed back out a couple hours ago. Nicolae is still searching for Maggie and Ayo, but he called late last night to say he was following a lead. Mia and Celeste have been trying to *see* as much as they can to help the boys in their searches. Now, Mia's at the manor consulting with Mr. Blomgren on Yule decorations, and Celeste is running the gallery with Luca. Luca, by the way, has warded the property tighter than Fort Knox. There's so much magical padding around this place, you can practically see the wards jiggle like Jell-O. And while I've been here with you, keeping the pain at bay, I've been coordinating with my crew at the manor on holiday catering and Yule prep." He gestured to his laptop and the stack of files and paperwork on the chair beside the bed. "You caught me napping. The important thing is, we're taking care of business. So, chill the fuck out, okay?"

"Sorry." I hung my head, chastised. "Thanks for everything, especially for being my personal pain killer." I smirked and peeked out of the corner of my eye.

"It's what I do. I cook food and provide pleasure."

"You should put that on a bumper sticker. So, we don't have to remain physically connected to keep the pain away, do we? Cause that would make for some seriously awkward bathroom situations."

"No, we don't have to touch, but we need to be near each other. The closer the better." Gregory winked. But then his face grew pensive, and he stroked my cheek tenderly. "It's only until Rocky's pain subsides. As Rocky heals, so will you."

"He'd heal much faster here with me." I took a breath and centered my thoughts as my stomach and heart eased. "Alexander and Ethan are looking for him?"

"Yeh, they followed your clues to the Harcourt's Victorian mansion by Falls Bridge. I expect to hear something from them soon." He checked his phone for updates. "Mmm, missed lunch," he grumbled to himself.

"Alexander and Ethan are powerful enough, in their own ways, but unless Alexander plans to destroy the place with lightning, they are outmatched." I wrung my hands anxiously. "There's going to be trouble. They need more backup."

"Now you know what Alexander went through when *you* took them on by yourself." Gregory narrowed his eyes.

"Hmm..." I folded my arms across my chest. He wasn't wrong.

"Try not to worry. They'll be careful. And I'm sure they'll check in soon."

It was pointless to press the issue, so I moved on. "You said Celeste is at the gallery?"

The corner of Gregory's mouth lifted. "Yeh. Your dutiful sidekick tended to you all night, even when I was right here with you. She spent the morning huddled with Mia, consulting every conceivable divining implement. Then she headed off with Luca to run the gallery."

"Celeste takes good care of me. I don't think I remember how to get dressed without her help." The nugget of truth in those words was larger than I cared to admit. I'd become reliant on Celeste, and I wasn't sure if that was a good or bad thing.

"Besides an apron or a chef coat, I don't see the need for clothes." Gregory teased me with a naughty twinkle in his eyes.

Damn, he's a sexy man.

I cleared my throat and changed the subject. "Has anyone told Riddle that the Harcourts have Rocky?"

"There was some discussion about whether or not to bring it up with him. Riddle has sway with the Harcourts which could be helpful, but his harsh take on your encounter at the river made it obvious that he wasn't the ally we hoped he'd be. We didn't think he'd appreciate us accusing the Harcourts of abducting and torturing your pet after we casually accused them of murdering your mother over dinner. Well, Vivian, anyway. And Luca seemed to feel that, not only was Riddle hiding something—said he couldn't get a solid read on him—but that Riddle seemed to be looking for something, here at the cottage. Your warning was the cherry on top. So, to answer your question, no, we haven't spoken a word to Riddle. We haven't said a thing to anyone outside the coven."

"What do you mean, *my warning*? And earlier you mentioned *my clues.*"

"You don't remember? Makes sense, I guess. You were in pain." He shrugged his muscled shoulders. "Well, before you passed out, you said, 'Waterfall house at river-fall bridge. Rocky and ravens and riddles.' You pointed us in the right direction."

"Oh, Riddle's definitely involved with the Harcourts. I'm just not sure how deeply." I shook my head, dejected. "I can't believe I have to deal with another pain in the ass mayor of Arbor. I hate to say this, the last thing I want to do is bother him, but I think we need Harrison."

"You're not wrong. I don't know what game Riddle's playing here, but with Ayo missing, the chief is the only one I trust to find out. He'll have a unique insight."

Gregory stopped speaking to swipe an errant lock of hair away from my face. He traced the line of my jaw with his calloused thumb as his stormy blue eyes lowered to my mouth. "And speaking of insight,"— his voice was like the rustling of feathers—"did your mother show up last night? In the woods. Did you talk to Lavinia?"

"Yes. I spoke to my mother." I shook my head to free myself of his disarming allure. "Well, she did most of the talking."

Although anxious about Rocky, I was eager to unburden my heart. Gregory and I hashed out all my mother had to say and the repercussions of her revelations. Nothing could change the horrors of the past, but I'd hoped I could use the information my mother imparted to solve some of today's problems. Unfortunately, every answer seemed to create more questions. My mother's comments on Riddle, for example, left me most puzzled. She'd given me the impression Riddle's affections for Maggie were deep, though harmless, puppy-dog in nature. Yet, an uneasy feeling settled in my stomach. He'd admitted knowing Maggie, of course. They'd both lived in Arbor for years, so it made sense that they'd be acquainted. But he'd never dropped a hint of a deeper connection. He clearly knew my mother and apparently wasn't a fan. Yet I couldn't recall him ever mentioning knowing her.

Cause that's not suspicious or anything.

Gregory and I ruminated over Riddle's feelings toward Maggie and my mother. Did he resent that Maggie loved a woman instead of him? It must have hurt his feelings, his ego, his pride, to have his love go unreciprocated. Prior to his severe reaction at dinner, Riddle had never been outwardly hostile in any way. He'd seemed an easygoing, hodunk yokel, a gee-golly-gosh sort of guy. And yet, the mayor invited Vivian and Eris Harcourt into Arbor in the first place. He must have known of their connection to my mother, to me. This, again, he never mentioned. Riddle spent his days vociferously advocating for the Harcourt Architecture agenda with the town council and the planning board while ignoring Vivian and Eris's debauched seduction of those same bureaucrats when the sun went down.

Why? What is his angle?

For the millionth time, I wished I knew where Maggie was. I chose to believe she and Ayo were simply too busy helping wayward witches to check in with us, that they'd pop up none-the-worse-for-wear any time now. I clung to this belief because the alternative was inconceivable. It would break me.

What would Maggie do if she were with me now? She would listen. She'd have wisdom and knowledge to offer—about Rocky, the Harcourts, Riddle. Her history with these people meant that, in an instant, Maggie could clear up much of my uncertainty. And her presence would ease and center me. I'd felt so in-the-wind as of late, and wherever Maggie was, was home to me.

A sense of nostalgia swept over me as I took in the snug space around me—the queen bed with pillows stacked high, my shabby chic décor, the bay window with the cushioned seat overlooking the lawn and the stream that wound its way into the woods. I'd spent so much of my life in this room at the cottage looking at that view. And although I'd only been away at the manor for a few months, it seemed like eons since I'd slept in my own bed. I hadn't appreciated the depth of my homesickness until it lifted.

Alexander, of course, wanted me to think of the manor as my home now. But it wasn't, and it wouldn't be. With all its grandeur, the manor was more hotel than home. The cottage—a place synonymous with Maggie—was a refuge at the end of the day, the warm hug in times of struggle, a place of both solace and inspiration. I'd never be of Aradian la strega descent, but my blood, the blood of my familiar, and of my own mother, soaked these grounds. My roots descended deep. The magic that resided in every stone of the cottage, every tree and blade of grass of this land, fueled and strengthened me. My sustained absence from this magic had depleted my power. My return meant rejuvenation.

And yet, the thought of remaining here on indefinite lockdown was a big *no*. The location of my confinement didn't matter. I couldn't stand being told to stay put. Of course, I understood the arguments and rationales. None of it made me feel any better. The impotency of my situation infuriated me. Rocky was being tortured. I knew where he was. And yet, instead of assisting in his rescue, I was confined to the cottage. I sat powerless, forced to rely on Alexander and Ethan to play heroes, while beholden to Gregory for every pain-free moment.

He had a million things he should have been doing—running a kitchen was no joke, especially smack in the middle of the holiday season.

But Gregory stood with me regardless. He'd do anything for me. That was a simple, undeniable fact.

I cocked my head to the side and regarded my old friend as an idea bloomed.

"So, I had a thought... Hear me out," I said cautiously, as the scheme rolled and wriggled its way around my head and into being. "The magic of this land bolsters the powers of the witches who inhabit it. It increases my strength and accelerates my healing. Why not Rocky's strength?" I paused and fiddled with my cuticles, reluctant to meet his eyes. "And you," I said finally, finding the courage to lift my chin. "You might not be able to physically heal, but you make the pain go away. Why not Rocky's pain? He and I are connected, aren't we? Witch and familiar. I should be able to send him the power I receive. At the end of the day, we only need Rocky feeling well enough to escape."

Gregory stared at me, hard. "It may be possible. Where are you going with this?"

"If we don't hear anything from Alexander and Ethan soon, we've got to be able to help Rocky ourselves." I flopped onto the pillows behind me and stared up at the ceiling. "Believe me, I'd love to stay in bed all day."

A wicked glimmer lit Gregory's eyes. "Sounds like a plan to me."

"But I can't do that. Don't you see? I can't abandon Rocky." My heart seized. I swallowed a lump in my throat.

"So, what do you propose we do?" Gregory had a lopsided grin.

The idea gained shape and clarity in my mind, but it wasn't going to be easy to verbalize. I took a deep breath. "If I can tap into your powers of pain mitigation and amplify them with the restorative power that resides within this land, maybe I can send this strength to Rocky through my connection with him."

"And how exactly do you suggest tapping into my magic, dear Priestess?" He eyed me shrewdly.

I held his gaze. "We'll go to the forest clearing. To Shasta's stone circle... and the altar. And we'll perform a ritual, linking us, and magnifying our connection in a communion with nature and the elements."

"Linking us? Our connection?" His smile fell, but his eyes remained locked on mine.

"Yes. You said to keep the pain away, I needed to be near you—the closer the better."

"I did say that."

"And is it true?"

"It is."

"Well then?"

"Eva..." His voice hoarse, he leaned across the bed, hovering over me. He cupped my cheek in his large, calloused palm and shook his head slowly.

"Gregory, it wouldn't be sex for lusts' sake; it's a ritual, a rite. I am your high priestess. I need your Druid badassery, and your...*expertise* in the field of sex magic." I took his hand from my cheek and held it to my heart. "Help me help Rocky. You're my friend, and I love you. And I know you love me. Please, Gregory."

My plea lit a spark in Gregory's eyes. He leaned in closer, slowly, inch by inch, and I could taste his masculine scent permeating the air.

"You've got to understand,"—he grazed a finger along my bottom lip—"with sex magic, it *is* about lust. It *is* about passion. It's about sweat and saliva and cum and screaming orgasms. Because that is what provides the energy. That is where the magic lies." Gregory leaned in further, so that his lips were a breath away from mine. "If we do this, you will enjoy it. You will feel pleasure like you never have before. I'm not trying to knock your lovers. I'm stating facts. Giving pleasure is my gift. I will make your eyes roll, your legs quiver, your muscles seize. I will make your body quake and convulse until you scream my name to the Goddess as you shatter. I understand that this is exactly the kind of power you're looking to harness. But you've got to understand, if we did this, Eva, we would never look at each other the same way again."

He was so close. *How have I never noticed the flecks of silver in his stormy blue eyes?*

"I understand, Gregory. Please."

Once more, my plea affected him, eliciting a groan deep in his throat. "I just... Alexander and Celeste... they're gonna kill me." His voice was low.

Feeling the desperation pulse through me in waves, he conceded. "Very well." He pressed his lips, not to mine, but tenderly to the center of my forehead, my third eye. Gregory knelt before me and looked up with eyes filled with reverence. He took my hands and kissed the backs of each before placing them over his heart. "Yes, Priestess."

An aching spread through my muscles, and a hollow wanting settled low in my stomach.

"Thank you," I said on a breath, before blinking to break the static between us. I cleared my throat. "I believe the Goddess will aid our endeavors."

"She's gonna need to aid you when you break the news to your lovelies." He stood. "You've got to tell Alexander and Celeste before we do anything. I don't want them coming after me for this."

Telling Alexander and Celeste that I was performing a sex magic ritual with Gregory to save Rocky sounded like a fucking horrible idea. Celeste would be crushed, and Alexander would be apoplectic. Despite Gregory's warnings and his obvious talents in the arena, it wasn't about the sex for me. It was about giving Rocky the strength he needed to fight the pain and escape. I could perform a ritual with Alexander or Celeste, but it would lack Gregory's innate power to manipulate the senses. That was the key. I would do absolutely anything to save Rocky, but I dreaded explaining my plan to Alexander and Celeste.

"Fine."

"Well, okay then, priestess." Gregory headed for the bedroom door. "But first, we need to hit the kitchen."

"Oh, okay. You have to gather things for the ritual?"

"No. I haven't had lunch. And I never fuck on an empty stomach." He closed the door behind him.

My calls and texts to Alexander went unanswered, but Celeste picked up the phone on the first ring. It went downhill from there.

"Are you fucking kidding me?" she shrieked after I explained my plan. "I love you, take care of you, help you organize your batshit complicated life, and bust my ass at your gallery. I stand by and watch while Alexander plays Mr. Darcy, and you're going to run off with the sexy Druid?"

"Oh stop. I'm not running off with Gregory, and you know it. If I merely wanted to fuck him, I would have done it by now. He's been one of my best friends my whole life. He's seen me skyclad more times than I can count. I could have had him any time I wanted. I love you, and I love Alexander. This has nothing to do with any of that. This is about saving Rocky."

"Right. Okay. Well then, consider me informed." Her voice was full of pain and passive aggression. "Good luck explaining this to Alex. He's fine, by the way. He texted. Said he and Ethan are still staking out the Harcourt place by the river. He'll touch base when he's got news."

I checked my phone, but I had no messages from him. "Why didn't he text me?"

"Hell if I know. Didn't want to disturb you, I guess. Probably figured you were still convalescing. Maybe he's still pissed he couldn't get in touch with you when you ran off to fight the Harcourts by yourself. Truthfully, I couldn't give two shits about Alexander's heart right now." I heard her seething through the phone. "Anyway, I'm covering the gallery with Luca until seven. I'll stop by the cottage after I close up and see if your *efforts* with Gregory were successful."

She hung up. Her icy words stung my heart.

"Just got a text from Alexander." Gregory blurted as he popped his head in the room.

"Yeh, he's fine. I know."

"Good. Figured he'd text you first."

"No, I talked to Celeste. He texted her. Alexander hasn't returned any of my messages."

Gregory sat beside me in bed and patted my knee. "We don't have to do this. I've got your back either way."

"We do have to do this. But thank you."

"Eva, we don't. There are a lot of things we have to do. Yes, we have to save Rocky. Shit, we can go down to the river and handle things ourselves if you want to. We need to find Maggie and Ayo. We've got to let Chief Harrison know what the hell's been going on. We have to take care of the gallery and plan a badass Yule. We do not, however, have to do *this*. On this land filled with magic, with your connection to the elements, and my manipulation of the senses, the sex would be explosive, creating untold power. The kind of power that could conceivably help Rocky. But you shouldn't always do something simply because you can—even with the purest intentions."

"Are you chickening out on me?"

Gregory rumbled a laugh. "No. I told you, I'll always have your back. Even when you're about to do something stupid."

"Fuck you."

"Or not to fuck me. That is the question."

Chapter Sixteen

My better judgement ultimately answered the question, to my libido's regret. I'd never been prudish a day in my life, and my flirtations often got me into trouble. I thought of Siobhan Quinn's emerald eyes and Killian's stormy grays. But my love life was confusing enough already. I loved Alexander and Celeste. Although they'd both given me reason to walk away at one point or another, they'd also stood beside me during the most challenging times in my life. My inability to choose between them hurt them. I knew it did. I'd have to decide soon. With this frantic cacophony of emotions, the last thing we all needed was another lover in the mix, especially one so skilled.

Instead of curling myself around Gregory, I curled myself up in Maggie's favorite armchair beside the blazing yule log with a cup of coffee and my mother's grimoire. I flipped through the pages, each crammed with tiny, neat handwriting, in a desperate, albeit distracted, search for guidance. While I combed the book, Gregory indulged in his second passion, cooking. After wrapping his dreads up on top of his head, he threw on Mia's floral apron, turned on some Lizzo, and danced around the kitchen as he whipped us up a late lunch.

He's going to make someone incandescently happy one of these days.

As pleasant as Gregory made our afternoon at the cottage, I worried for my friends outside the perimeter of the property. Celeste and Luca tackled the holiday traffic at the gallery. Nicolae worked his leads in the search for Maggie and Ayo. Alexander and Ethan prowled the Harcourts' riverside Victorian to rescue Rocky.

And here I dither.

"Did you mean it?" I asked Gregory as we tucked into grilled cheese sandwiches and tomato soup. "That we can go down to the river and tackle things ourselves?"

"Well..." It was his turn to dither.

"I'd assumed we were confined to cottage grounds. But if I don't have to stay holed up here, then I can rescue Rocky myself. With your help, of course. You'll have to stick close."

Gregory hemmed and hawed, taking a bite of his lunch to stall. He spoke with a mouth half full of food. "We need to keep you safe. You should stay here where the magic amplifies your power and where security is tight. Plus, you heard Riddle. You've got some legal liability for your last visit to the Harcourts. He turned a blind eye once; I don't think he'll do it again. So sure, technically, we *could* go down to the river, but I don't think we *should*."

"At full strength, I'm the most powerful weapon we have against the Harcourts. If we can leave these grounds without me buckling over in pain, what the hell are we waiting for?"

"Alexander and Ethan. We're waiting for them. They're already down there, surveilling the area. They've got a plan. They're being cautious. Give them a chance. And I'm sorry to break it to you, Priestess, but you're not at full strength."

Gregory must have withdrawn his magical morphine because pain sliced along my back and sides.

I refused to scream out. "Fine," I gritted through my teeth.

Immediately, the pain subsided.

"What am I supposed to do in the meantime?"

A wicked look crossed Gregory's face.

"First, you eat. Next, you can pick from one of the hundred other things you've got on your plate right now."

I huffed and returned to my humble but comforting lunch, still pissy about having to forgo both the sex magic ritual *and* a daring riverside rescue.

Aren't I supposed to be the high priestess? My word on issues of magical import should hold weight. Yet, I'm inconsequential. No one needs me. They need me out of the way.

After I ate, much of my grumpiness ebbed. Figuring it would distract me from my worries, I decided to get some work done. I helped Gregory clean up from lunch, and we set up our laptops on the dining table. While he settled in to review his menus and catering schedules, I got down to Manor Arts business. We worked together in companionable silence.

I confirmed three special acts for Yule: the Gay Men's Choir of Central New York who sang lively holiday tunes, Siobhan Quinn, the enchanting Irish voice who'd captivated me on Samhain before getting drunk with Vivian Harcourt—a fact I was strangely compelled to overlook—and a local singer-songwriter, simply known as Ash, whose video application I'd watched twenty times already. His voice was sultry and gritty, and he cradled his guitar like a lover. Soft gray eyes, tousled salt-and-peppered hair, shirt sleeves rolled up over bulging forearms, dirty blue jeans, and steel-tipped boots, all conspired to create the quintessential working-class hero. He was the real deal. I couldn't wait to see him play in person.

The next task on my to-do list was to review and approve the new batch of artists who would be exhibiting at the gallery in the new year. The level of talent made it difficult to whittle the list down, but in the end, the artists I selected represented a diverse vision for the future. Then, I analyzed the data from the gallery's Black Friday, Small Business Saturday, and Artists Sunday. The foot traffic had seemed steady, and the solid preliminary sales figures supported this.

And the pictures from the Manor Arts' kick-off to the holiday season were magical. I grinned with pride at my decision to forgo modern décor, instead embracing a natural, elemental Yule. Flocked in magically induced snow—a trick I was particularly proud of—and sprinkled with ice sculptures, the grounds of Morgan Manor sparkled. On the lawn, to the right of the massive, iron front doors strewn with evergreen boughs, sat the pilings for a grand bonfire – symbolizing the coming light after the darkness of winter – waiting to be lit on the solstice. On the lawn to the left of the doors, Mr. Blomgren had arranged a Solstice Spiral to my exact specifications. The spiral walking path made of white beeswax candles, apples, and evergreen boughs wound inward with a meditation bench at the center. Inside the manor, lush evergreen garland, holly berries, pinecones, and mistletoe donned every possible doorway and arch. Candlelight and greenery adorned the mantles and shelves. A magnificent wreathe—representing the Wheel of the Year—and decorated with berries, pinecones, and ribbon, hung above the fireplace in the grand foyer. Solstice trees, each adorned with its own magical theme, resided in the gallery, dining room, music room, and library. But the enormous, fragile, blown-glass snowflakes and icicles that dangled precariously from the arches and vaulted ceilings were the most magnificent. We'd transformed Morgan Manor into a witch's winter wonderland.

Pleased with this small measure of contentment, I packed up my files and paperwork. The team had the Manor Arts well under control, a relief in at least one aspect of my life.

Tires crunching up the river rock driveway drew me and Gregory to our feet. We raced to the front window to see not one, but three vehicles, and headed out to greet the caravan. Alexander's black Bentley led the way, followed by Luca's electric-blue El Camino, and a Cadillac driven by Jasper, the manor's chauffeur, brought up the rear.

And then my entire life stepped out of those cars. Time slowed to a crawl, which saved my sanity since it gave me an opportunity to process what I was seeing.

First, Luca helped Mia out of the passenger side of the El Camino, and Celeste stepped down from the back seat.

Damn, she's scowling. She's still pissed.

Next, Jasper and Nicolae got out of the Cadillac.

How the hell did Nicolae fly east so fast? Why is he back? What the hell's going on?

I thanked the Goddess when Alexander and Ethan hopped out of the Bentley, looking tattered and weary but in one piece. But when they opened the Bentley's back doors, and Ayo, Maggie, and Rocky got out, I fell to my knees.

Am I hallucinating? How is this even real? Sweet Goddess above, it's a Yuletide miracle!

Rocky swooped down, out of Maggie's arms, and landed on the slate patio before me. He appeared flawless, every feather in place.

"How is this possible?" I said aloud, unable to settle my mind enough to communicate in our typical mental manner. "What is this? I don't understand. You look amazing, Rocky, but I know you suffered. I felt it. But you're here, and you're fine. Oh, it's so good to see you! Welcome home."

Overcome with relief, I squeezed him tight, and he ruffled his feathers to wriggle away.

Ease yourself, my beloved witch. Did I suffer? Yes, and greatly. It pains me further that you shared my suffering. Yet I live, and I am well. Although I could eat a whole family of rabbits, I'm so famished. He squawked. *And don't look at me like that, Miss Witch. All will be explained to you in time. And I know you've been up to things yourself. You've uncovered romances and revelations, and not just regarding your mother. You have a free nature, but not all share it. I suggest you examine how easily your eyes wonder.* Rocky squawked again and fluffed his feathers. *Now, visit with your Goddess-mother. She misses you desperately. And she is the reason I still breathe. One of them, anyway.* He nuzzled his head against my hand. *I am happy to be home, Evangeline. We all are. Now, I must hunt and roost, but I'll remain on the grounds. Call on me at any time.*

Rocky lifted off and soared into a cold, darkening sky.

Still kneeling on the patio, I breathed deeply and took a mental inventory of my senses. Not an ache or pain to be had. I turned to Gregory, and he simply nodded.

Of course I feel better. Maggie healed Rocky, and Rocky healed me.

"My sweet girl," Maggie said softly.

Hopping to my feet, I launched myself into her arms.

"Where have you been? Are you okay? I can't believe you're here. How did you get here? You had me worried sick. I've missed you so much." I burrowed my face into the crook of her neck; her wild, golden hair tickled my nose. "And Ayo!" I lifted my head to the statuesque woman, standing strong despite the ordeal she and Maggie must have endured. I caught the weariness in her eyes. "It's so good to see you. Where have you two been?"

"It is a great pleasure to see you, too, Evangeline," Ayo said kindly in her melodic Yoruban accent. "You have many questions. We will try to answer them."

Maggie patted my hands. "But let's get inside first. It's freezing out here."

Incandescently happy, yet still befuddled and off-kilter by everyone's sudden arrival, I followed Maggie and Ayo inside the cottage. The others had already gone in, so I closed the door behind me, but Maggie called over her shoulder.

"Leave that unlocked, if you don't mind, Eva. Eris will be here any second."

"I'm sorry, what the fuck did you say?"

"Watch your mouth, Evangeline Clarion," Maggie scolded sharply, but softened. "Eris is an ally. She helped us. I know what you must be thinking, but I'm telling you, we would not be standing here without her. And she's your sister, your blood, after all. You can't imagine we'd leave her behind?"

Maggie gave my hand a squeeze and left to join Ayo and the others.

Steeped in a hazy cloud of shock, I didn't move from my position at the door. I peered into the dining room where a magical strategy session had broken out: laptops, grimoires, crystals, tarot cards, and a scrying mirror spilled out across the dining table.

A moment later, Eris Harcourt stepped across the cottage threshold. She looked like shit. Dirt and mud caked her tattered clothes, her hair was a wild mess, tears stained her grimy cheeks, and her eyes flamed red. She paused at the sight of me. "Hey. Mind if I come in?"

Apparently, I'm supposed to be nice.

"By all means." I swept my arm toward the gathering in the dining room. "It seems they're expecting you."

She muttered a thank-you and made to move on into the kitchen, but I grabbed her arm as she passed.

"I don't know what you did to convince Maggie you're one of the good guys, but I'm not buying it. You targeted Celeste for conquest the moment you showed up. You manipulated a vulnerable population, whipped them up into sex and drug fueled frenzies, extracted their darkest secrets, and used their blood as a sacrifice in exchange for power. Your familiar tortured mine...for hours. And I may not bear the scars, but his beak and claws flayed my skin," I hissed in a whispered growl.

"That was not Abramelin," she spat. "That was my mother's nasty old crow. I only went after Celeste to fuck with you. And one person's sins are another's magic. Don't judge." Yanking her arm free from my grasp, she joined the others, taking a spot at the kitchen counter beside Jasper.

I stood in the corner of the kitchen and gawked at the rough and rumpled gaggle that had overtaken the cottage. Maggie and Ayo warmed themselves in front of the yule hearth; my goddess-mother with her grandmother's grimoire on her lap. The coven occupied the dining table, leaving one chair empty for me, should I happen to crack through my anxiety and shock-ridden paralysis and deign to sit with them.

For a second, I struggled to repress manic laughter, yet the next moment, I fought tears. Instead, I poured a glass of wine, took a few healthy sips, topped my glass off again, and looked over at Eris.

Somehow, through the grace of the Goddess, everyone I love is here, together...and they're working with the enemy.

"She's not the enemy," Alexander's voice resounded over the din of cross-conversation.

The room hushed.

Yet again, listening to my thoughts. And now defending a Harcourt?

"Is that so?" I popped a hip and sipped my wine.

"It is," he said simply. "We couldn't have rescued anyone without Eris's help. And Maggie and Ayo wouldn't have survived without her."

I scanned the faces of my loved ones, and the earnestness I found there drew me down into the last chair at the dining table—between Alexander and Celeste, neither of whom appeared particularly happy with me.

"Let's hear it." I drank some more. "Somebody, please tell me what the hell happened. Maggie, where have you and Ayo been? And where's Hanna?"

Maggie's pale face turned an ashen gray. Her mouth opened and closed without a word, and she turned to Ayo as if to save her. But Ayo remained silent as well and only held her lover's eyes as if her gaze was a safety net guarding Maggie from some unforeseen danger.

"Not to be rude, but you better get her up to speed quick. The mayor and mommy dearest are going to lose their shit when they find out you're all gone," Eris warned. "I'm sure Reginald is whispering in mother's ear as we speak."

"Vivian doesn't know yet? Shit, someone give me the bullet points." I tried to remain calm. "Wait, did you say, the mayor? What does he have to do with this?"

After receiving nothing but blank stares, I turned to the man who crossed the country to be there.

"What about you, Nicolae? What do you have to say?"

Nicolae looked at the hesitant faces around the room and leaned back in his chair.

"I got a tip from a witch in LA," Nicolae said, his voice silky smooth as he clutched his glass of whiskey and stared into its depths. "It led me to a storage unit owned by Riddle. I *persuaded* the manager of the facility to let me inspect the unit. The contents were...let's say, disturbing." He shuddered and sipped his whiskey. "When I found one of Ayo's scarves in the storage unit, I knew I'd finally caught a solid lead and inspected further. That's when I found –" Nicolae's throat caught, and after a glance at Maggie, he cleared it and continued. "That's when I found Hanna, squished on the cement floor."

Oh, sweet Goddess above. Maggie's familiar is dead.

"Hanna," I breathed out and turned to offer my goddess-mother support and comfort, but Ayo held her rapt attention, keeping her distracted from the sordid tale of her familiar's demise.

Riddle's connection to their disappearance was confirmed." Nicolae continued. "I did some digging online. Low and behold, in early November, Riddle had a shipping crate from the unit delivered to the address of Vivian's riverside Victorian. I told Alexander first thing and hopped his private jet home."

A shipping crate! Is he saying they were shipped across the country in a box? In November? But that would mean...

"They were here in Arbor the entire time?" I fumed. "And you reached out to *Alexander* about Maggie, about *my* goddess-mother, but not me? We have known each other all our lives. You are my friend. I am your high priestess. And you didn't think *I* should hear about this first?"

Nicolae looked up from his glass, stung by my rebuke. "You were unconscious." He downed the rest of his whiskey and slammed it on the table.

"Oh. I'm sorry." I felt chastised and hot around the collar. "Thank you for tracking them down. It sucks you had to travel across the country to find them in our backyard."

"You're forgiven." He shot me one of his debonair grins, though with far less than his usual enthusiasm. "And very welcome, of course."

"No apology for me though, huh? Or a thank you?" Alexander groused. Anger and pain pulsed from him in waves.

"For what, exactly? I still have no idea what you did."

Alexander flinched as if I'd slapped him. His face turned a frightening shade of mottled red and purple. "I need some air." With barely constrained emotion, and all eyes on him, he stormed out of the cottage.

The room went quiet for a moment, but for the popping of the Yule log in the fireplace. And then a mighty *crack, boom* of lightning shook and rattled the cottage, and everything and everyone in it.

A collective shriek resounded.

At the end of my tether, I rounded on Luca. "Tell me the truth."

Luca rose from his chair and came around the table to kneel before me as he'd done before when dispensing hard realities. He took my hands.

"The simple, ghastly truth, as I have seen it, is that Riddle had Maggie and Ayo kidnapped, placed in crates—"

"Kidnapped... crates?" I groaned, scanning around the room until my eyes settled on my goddess-mother, her face buried in her hands.

Luca squeezed my hands, regaining my attention. "Yes, Eva. He had them loaded into crates and shipped to Vivian's place where they were imprisoned and tortured by Octavius and where Riddle siphoned their magic. Vivian encouraged Riddle's sadistic behavior and celebrated the fact that Maggie's disappearance pained you. After your altercation by the river, she was even more eager to punish you. Which she did by—"

"Abducting Rocky and having her familiar, Reginald, torture him," I said somberly.

"Yes. But Abramelin, Eris's raven, helped Rocky, kept him fed and loosened his restraints," Luca continued, getting to his feet and returning to his chair. "Thereby helping you. Your pain would have been even worse without Eris's intervention."

"Damn," Gregory muttered.

"And Eris helped us." Alexander strode back into the kitchen, his temper under control. "She betrayed her mother, deceived Riddle, and physically took on Octavius so we could rescue Maggie and Ayo."

"While Riddle held us captive, Eris brought food and water and tended to our wounds," Ayo found her voice. "We would not have survived without her."

"I should have done more," Eris said, her voice strained. "How long had you been there before I found you? I should have released you, repercussions be damned."

"Don't beat yourself up, child," Ayo said kindly. "You made the best out of the choices you had." Ayo took Maggie's hand lovingly. "We're home now, and that's what matters."

I looked at Eris again but couldn't see her face. Her raven hair had fallen across her pale cheeks as she slumped over the kitchen counter. She fiddled with her cuticles, whether out of boredom or as a defense mechanism, I couldn't tell.

I don't know this woman—my sister—at all.

"I have so many questions." I drank more wine to dull the chaos festering underneath my skin.

"Vivian is vindictive." Maggie spoke softly, and the whole room leaned forward to catch her words. "She is full of rage and resentment, hell-bent on vengeance for her grievances with Lavinia—and Evangeline." Maggie met my eyes, hers swimming with compassion. "Your existence denied Vivian the life she dreamed of. And since she can't enact her revenge on Lavinia, her daughter's the perfect alternative. She covets your beauty and talent and success. She came to Arbor to destroy you, and strip you of all you've attained; whether it be your power, influence, money, or love."

"I gathered as much. I spoke to my mother in the woods last night. She told me about Maximus. And Vivian, and Circe, and Esmeralda."

Maggie looked stunned. "Oh, my sweet girl. How you must be hurting. Yet now at least, you understand."

"She said Riddle loved you but didn't think very highly of her."

"Riddle does not love me. He never loved me, not really. He's only ever loved the power he thought he could siphon from me, from this cottage, this property. Even now. Vivian has only ever been a convenient distraction, the means to an end."

"My mother made a deal with Riddle to bring Harcourt Architecture to Arbor." Eris looked up, wiping away tears.

Her vulnerability floored me.

"This would insinuate us into the community and allow my mother to enact her plans of destruction with impunity. But Riddle had his own motives for bringing us to Arbor. Like Maggie said, we were the perfect distraction. He knew our families' connection. And he knew the chaos two naiads would inevitably cause in town. He banked on it to keep you occupied. He didn't care about the damage. He only cared about one thing. Her." Eris motioned to Maggie.

"No, that's not right. I don't believe it's me he covets, but la strega magic," Maggie corrected. "All he cares about is power."

"He manipulated my mother's obsession with you Clarion witches." Eris spoke directly to me. "He didn't need to pressure or convince my mother to allow him to use our place by the river for his exploits. All he did was ask. After all, it would hurt you. My mother jumped at the chance. Greedy for any edge against you, my mother not only facilitated Maggie and Ayo's captivity but orchestrated Rocky's capture and subsequent torture.

"Look, I had no problem screwing with you." She went on. "It kept my mother off my back. It sounds twisted now, I guess. But I had nothing to do with the kidnappings or any of Riddle's shit. You have to believe me," Eris pleaded.

To my amazement, I did believe her. I gave a sharp nod of assent.

But none of this makes sense.

"What does Riddle know about la strega magic? And what do you all mean Riddle siphoned their power?" I asked hesitantly.

Ethan answered. "That's what kelpies do." He shrugged.

"I'm sorry, what the fuck did you say?" I blurted.

"Riddle's a kelpie, sis, keep up." Eris offered a sardonic grin.

"What the hell do you mean, Riddle's a kelpie?" I asked Ethan. "You mean like the freshwater shifters who can transform from a human to a horse?"

"More or less," Ethan said.

I slumped in my chair and drank a hearty swig of wine.

"I never sensed a shred of magic from Riddle," I said completely off-kilter.

"That's because he has none of his own. Riddle's like a great sucking void," Ethan explained. "That's why Luca and Alex couldn't get a read on him. He's fucking empty. What makes a kelpie so dangerous to fae and witches alike is that it derives its power from siphoning the magic from other sources. Did you notice when in his horse form, his mane always appears dripping wet? Kelpie's tails are said to be so strong, one smack on a lake or river could cause a clap of thunder and a tidal wave so large it could swallow up a house."

"So, the horse that was at the manor on Samhain, and at the Harcourt house by the river, was Riddle transformed into his kelpie form?" I asked, although every time I received answers, the situation only became more confusing and dangerous.

Maggie replied, "Yes, and no."

Of course.

"You see," Maggie went on, "Riddle can manifest his horse form while still remaining a human. It merely weakens the host body. It's like having a familiar that lives inside you, and you can bring it out whenever you'd like. Bayard, his horse, is more than familiar to him. Riddle is Bayard, and Bayard is Riddle. But in order to maintain this magical symbiosis, Riddle must steal the life force from other magical beings. That's where Octavius comes in."

Maggie went ashen once more and averted her eyes.

Ayo continued. "Octavius is Riddle's vessel, the straw by which he sucked us dry. You see, like an octopus, Riddle is slick, able to maneuver through impossibly tight spots. He's a master manipulator. He baits unsuspecting victims with his nonthreatening looks and pleasant demeanor. But he could never lure Magdalena, and that angered him. She saw the truth of him. She knew he sought only the power she guarded here. But your goddess-mother's empathetic nature is boundless. Magdalena pitied Riddle and never confronted him about what she knew to be his ultimate goal—possessing the power of her land."

"Riddle thought if I submitted to him, if he possessed me—" Maggie cleared her throat. "—he'd have free access to the magic here. I've always known it. I knew it all those years ago when he would show up at the cottage the moment Lavinia drove away. Her presence was an obstacle to his plans. Just as you are." Shame and anguish filled her face. "But I saw good in him. I saw his pain and weakness. And I thought I could help him." Her head fell into her hands, and she wept. "I was wrong. So, so wrong."

Ayo comforted Maggie as one fact crystallized in my mind. *It was Riddle all along. He killed my mother.*

I got to my feet and downed the last of my wine. "I'm going to fucking kill him."

"Eva!" Maggie scolded. "You are not evil."

How can she be so blinded by empathy after all he's done to her?

"You'll get your chance with Riddle. The question is whether you'll take it," Celeste said. She'd pulled out her large crystal ball and placed it in the center of a scattering of smaller stones and crystals. She hovered her hands above them, moving slowly over the stones.

She sat just to my right, as always, so I examined her rocks up close. To anyone not possessed with the power of lithomancy, or stone divination, they appeared as nothing more than agate, obsidian, jade, onyx, tiger's eye, and the like. To Celeste, they were glimpses of a story, one she must tumble and arrange into proper order to comprehend the complete tale.

"They won't come tonight." Celeste's voice was a dull monotone, her hands moving faster over the stones. "They'll send an emissary with a message first. A familiar. We won't have long to respond." Her hands halted over the crystal ball and lingered there. "They will arrive at dawn."

"*They?*" I said anxiously.

"Vivian and Riddle." Celeste lifted her eyes from the stones. I saw a frightening array of emotions within them. "I can't tell if they're coming to arrest you, kill you, or burn the whole damn cottage to the ground. I'm pretty sure I can rule out their arriving with a pie and asking for forgiveness."

Celeste turned to Mia, who sat to my left on the other side of Alexander, flipping her tarot cards feverishly. "What do you see?"

"Snow. Water," Mia croaked as she grabbed another deck and continued to flip. "Danger for those with electricity." Mia looked from Ayo to Alexander—both witches who could produce this type of power—and shook her head. "You must not be here when they come. You must go."

"Everyone should go," Maggie said. "It's not safe. Everyone should head up to the manor. I'm staying with the cottage. Its magic will protect me."

"Magdalena, no," Ayo said with pleading eyes.

"Yes, my love. We must heed Mia's warning. Your energy makes it too dangerous for you and Alexander to be here. But this is my land, my stand."

"I agree about Alexander and Ayo, but I'm not going anywhere." I folded my arms resolutely across my chest. "I need to take Riddle out."

Celeste rolled her eyes, but I ignored her.

That fucker killed my mother.

I wasn't sure why I hadn't shared my conclusion with the group, except that, with everything else going on, I didn't know if Maggie could take it.

"Bullshit," Alexander grumbled.

"Excuse me?"

"You heard me. I said *bullshit.*"

"Would you care to elaborate?"

"*We,*" he slammed his fist on the table, "*We* are defending against Vivian and Riddle together."

"*You* are going to stay at the manor with Ayo where it's *safe,*" I spat. "Right now, your powers are a liability."

"But they can tackle other issues from the manor," Gregory piped up diplomatically before Alexander had a chance to bite my head off; as was clearly his intention evidenced by his gaping mouth and sharp, snarling teeth. "And we've got a room full of powerful fucking witches right here." He bravely slapped Alexander on the back. "So, Alexander's right. You're not doing this on your own. And you, Priestess, are not killing the mayor. You are a lethal force of nature, capable of inflicting untold carnage. You could take Riddle out in an instant if you wished it. But you would have to live with that for the rest of your life."

"He's right. You can pull off almost anything, but orange jumpers are not your best look," Nicolae added without his suave wink or a hint of humor.

Why don't I just tell them? Tell them Riddle killed my mother.

I took in the faces of those around me, each roiling with emotion, and I thought I might lose my bearings.

Celeste placed a reassuring hand atop mine. "We've got this."

A sorrowful blend of regret and determination filled Maggie's face. As an empath, Maggie felt my turmoil, yet her tall, straight-backed stance told me she was in fighting mode. "We are in this together, sweetheart. We've got to hunker down. It's all about defense. But we can do this. Together, we'll protect the property, the cottage, and each other. Together, we will protect magic."

"Together," I echoed.

Together, we will face off against a human firehose with a grudge, an attitude, and loose morals, and a magic-sucking, tsunami-making, horse-spawning murderer. Awesome.

Chapter Seventeen

Trusting in the accuracy of Mia and Celeste's sight, the Witches of Arbor made plans and got organized. Jasper would drive Ayo to the manor where she and Alexander would contact Chief Harrison and get the law involved. They'd try to clear up any bogus legal liability I may have had for trespassing on Harcourt property at the river and interrupting a religious ceremony. And Ayo intended to press charges against Riddle.

Kidnapping, false imprisonment, torture, impersonating a decent human being; the list is endless.

Luca and his security equipment would team up with Mia and Celeste to *see* our inevitable attackers, anticipate their advances, and get the jump on their approach. Nicolae, Ethan, and Gregory would head to the perimeter of the property to surround the area in their protective wards and illusions. That left me, Maggie, and Eris.

This ought to be interesting.

We were tasked with checking the grimoires to search for enchantments to place around the cottage itself and spells to counter Vivian and Riddle's unique magic.

We had questions, and the grimoires would help us answer them. We hoped. How would Vivian and Riddle attack? How would we respond? Would we use offensive spells? When all hell broke loose, Maggie's first instinct was to check her grandmother's grimoire whether or not it made rational sense to do so. In this instance, I had no doubt the grimoire held the keys to defending the cottage and land Maggie's grandmother spent her life safeguarding. My mother's grimoire likely contained the spell she used, all those many years ago, to turn Vivian's water canon attack into a misty humid day; an elemental restructuring spell would come in handy for those without innate elemental magic. I had the gist of it. I'd turned the water from the fountain at the manor into an orb of ice and encapsulated Octavius. But that water hadn't shot at me like a firehose.

Before we put our plans into action, we gathered outside beneath a clear expanse of deep blue sky sprayed with stars. The wind whipped so crisp it stung the nose and fingers.

There's a storm brewing. I can taste it. Snow.

We cast a circle with sage and salt, and held white candles aloft.

"We gather tonight amid nature, the elements, the Goddess's blessings—the stream streaked with slender spider webs of ice, the frost-tipped fields, the lush evergreens nestled among bare nests of oaks and maple, and we are as one being with the elements. The same energy that animates the seed and the sparrow animates us. And that energy, that power, that magic is amplified here on this land. It is this power that draws our enemies to us. It is this power we protect. And it is this power that we call upon to aid us in our fight. We call upon the blessings of the Goddess. We call upon the guidance of our ancestors. We call upon the power within. We call upon each other. When we stand together"—I looked with purpose to Eris—"we win.

"So do I will it. So mote it be."

"So mote it be," they all replied—including Eris.

After closing the circle, everyone grouped up and readied themselves for the tasks ahead. Nicolae, Gregory, and Ethan all kissed me on the cheek and headed out to the farthest points of the property to set up their wards and illusions. Luca and Mia headed inside the cottage. Celeste moved to join them but paused long enough to kiss me deeply and level me with a purposeful glare that spoke of both forgiveness and reproach.

The touch of her lips stunned me as powerfully as any hex. I watched her retreat into the cottage, waves of recognition flooding over me. With this recognition came tremendous guilt. I'd failed her...again. I'd taken everything she had to give and left her with the scraps of my attention and affections that remained after the gallery, the coven, and Alexander had siphoned me dry. She deserved better.

How could I have let this happen?

I sent a silent petition to the Goddess that Celeste would forgive me and, one day, appreciate the depth of my love for her. I vowed to make amends. I wanted to spend the rest of my life showering her with the same love and devotion she so selflessly gave to me.

I'd made the decision without intending to, but once resolved upon, it flamed within my chest. First, I had to settle things with Alexander. I groaned, dreading what lay ahead. But in my heart, I knew my time with Alexander had reached its end.

While Ayo said her goodbyes to Maggie, I caught Alexander as he made his way to meet Jasper at the cars.

"You weren't going to leave without saying goodbye, were you?" I used as pleasant a tone as I could muster under the circumstances.

"I wasn't sure you cared."

"Stop pouting." I stepped in close, so I could look up into his eyes. "Of course I care."

And I did care about him. I loved him. But I'd lost my patience with him and his morose, irritable, domineering attitude.

"Were you seriously considering a sex magic ritual with Gregory?"

"Yes, I was. I wanted to save Rocky. I'd do anything for him."

Alexander's shoulders slumped. "How could you do that to me? It would have been bad enough if it were Celeste; at least I knew she was a rival for your affections. But Gregory? Seriously?"

"Alexander, I'm sorry I hurt you." *And I'm sorry I'm going to hurt you again.* "It had nothing to do with affection, nothing to do with sex. Gregory's powers of sensory manipulation masked my agonizing pain. He was like magical morphine. With a ritual, we could have amplified that magic and sent it to Rocky. He would have been strong enough to escape on his own."

"Sounds pretty fucking far-fetched to me." Alexander's head hung low.

"Yeh, well, I didn't have a ton of options, barred from leaving the cottage or the grounds, and on the knife's edge of a hell of a lot of pain. I've already lost one familiar. I was not going to lose another."

He grunted. "When this blows over, we're having a serious fucking discussion about our relationship."

"No, we're having one now."

"We don't have time for this, Eva—"

"We don't know what's going to happen come morning, Alexander, so I'm sorry, but I have to say this now." I took a steadying breath. "I will always love you, but I have to end things between us."

Alexander gritted his teeth, and his face reddened. "What?"

"I wish I could articulate my struggles, but there are no words beyond I'm sorry... I'm in love with Celeste."

He vibrated a dark rage.

"God damn it, Eva. You just told me you were going to fuck Gregory—but I shouldn't take offense because it wasn't about affection, and now—" He cut himself off midsentence and scrubbed his face with his hands. When he looked to me again, resignation and deep sorrow had settled over him. "No." He seemed to resolve something within himself. "You've been honest about your feelings for Celeste. You've never hidden your struggles from me. And she's been nothing but loving and loyal to you, which I respect the fuck out of, though it pains me to say it. If this is what you want, then... I wish you the best."

He dropped one last kiss to the top of my head and slid into his Bentley. He rolled down the window.

"You're an evil woman, Eva Clarion. But I love you. I'll always love you." His eyes were hard, his voice thick with emotion.

"I love you too." I had a solid lump in my throat and a gnawing pain in my heart as I watched the car back out of the driveway.

I waved goodbye to Ayo before returning to the cottage. Luca and Mia sat in the armchairs before the fireplace hearth—he with his laptop, and she with her tarot. Celeste sat cross-legged on the floor beside them, poring over her crystal ball and scattered stones. Eris had cleaned herself up, dressing in a pair of my black leggings and my favorite Phish hoodie, and had made herself comfortable at the dining table with a glass of wine and my mother's grimoire.

"Hey. I thought I'd get started. Your mom was a hell of a witch by the look of these spells." Eris glanced up from her reading. "Sweet Hecate, you look like hell."

"Thanks." I pulled a face. "You look comfy. And yes, she was." My voice cracked as I spoke, uncomfortable with speaking to her about my mother.

"What's wrong?" Celeste asked, her eyes sharp and wary. "You've got this crazy energy swirling around you. Did you—" She stopped as acknowledgement bloomed. Her eyes popped open wide. "Oh, sweetheart," she began.

I shot her a warning look. "I'm fine. Really." The last thing I wanted to discuss with the group at large was my breakup with Alexander. Thankfully, Celeste got the message, and shot me a small, reassuring smile.

I moved around the table and sat beside Eris. I ran my fingers along the pages of the heavy book, crisp and new compared to Maggie's centuries-old tome.

"My mother began writing in it when she was six years old. She was a child prodigy, revered in the coven for her magic. Whip smart, too, with a canny knack for spellwork. But it was the animals who followed her everywhere that made the most startling impression." My smile fell as I took in the details of my sister's face, a face so strikingly like my own, yet with angular features where mine were soft.

"My mother never meant to hurt yours," I said without thinking. "She understands why your mother would be angry, but it was never her intention to cause anyone harm."

"How would you know that?" she recoiled.

"I spoke to her, last night. Shortly before your mother's raven began torturing my hawk. And subsequently me."

"Yeh, sorry about that. Like I said, I had nothing to do with it."

"I know. Just as I had nothing to do with what happened over twenty years ago between our parents. And neither did you. Maximus Waterhouse used magic to force himself on my mother, which resulted in my conception. He went on to seduce your mother, who seems to have genuinely cared for him." *Or at least his fortune and power.* "Hence, you. My mother called and sent repeated messages to Maximus to tell him she was pregnant, but he ignored her and refused to reply. Eventually, my mother went directly to the Waterhouse home to confront him in person. My mother hadn't known that Maximus and Vivian were announcing their engagement that afternoon, hosted by Maximus's mother, the high priestess, Circe. When my mother told them of her pregnancy, and the nature of Maximus's behavior toward her, they physically threw her out.

They attacked her in the street. First Circe, then Vivian, then Maximus himself. Maximus died when my mother's rebounding spell caused the car he'd hurled at her to crush him instead." The words tumbled out. I sighed deeply. "My mother never meant to burst in on Vivian's engagement party and kill her fiancé, our father. It was self-defense. And I hold no responsibility for anything that happened back then, any more than you do. We were innocents."

Everyone in the room stared at me.

"Well fuck." Eris dropped her eyes to the grimoire and squinted in thought. "You said my mom attacked Lavinia. How? And how did she defend herself? That spell would be handy."

"That's exactly what I thought." I looked at her out of the corner of my eye. "And her rebounding spell too."

We stared for a long moment; sizing each other up, taking the measure of one another. Without a word, we resolved to work together. We were on the same side now.

A slamming front door heralded Maggie's return. She stormed into the kitchen, her wild, lion's mane flaming, her face contorted with seething anger. Typically, a sweet, exceedingly empathetic witch, when Maggie's fury flared up, it was explosive. Clearly, having to send Ayo away when they'd just returned, was one step too far.

"This is all my fault," she said, her jaw and fists clenched tight.

"What? No!" I said, getting to my feet.

"If I hadn't been so weak, so blind, so quick to justify and excuse Riddle's obsessive behavior, none of this would be happening. The people I love have been hurt and remain in danger. The cottage and its magic are under threat. I've let my grandmother down. I've let you and Lavinia and Ayo down."

"Okay, seriously, shut the fuck up." I wrapped my arms around her. "Your empathy is your greatest gift. You are not responsible for Riddle's actions any more than I'm responsible for Vivian's." I stood on tiptoe and kissed her cheek. "But you're right that we're in danger, and the cottage is under threat. So, let's figure out how to protect ourselves."

As Maggie's fevered pitch cooled, she smiled serenely. "Yes. You're right. Of course. See, that's why you're the high priestess." She cleared her throat, and sitting down across the table, pulled her grandmother's grimoire toward her. "I'll just get started then."

So, while Luca, Mia, and Celeste consulted their unique methods in search of sight, I hunkered down over the grimoires with Maggie and Eris, collecting spells to aid our defense. Not only did we find the rebounding spell that killed Maximus and the spell my mother used to turn Vivian's high-powered jets of water into vapor, we also found multiple protection spells for the property and cottage in Maggie's grandmother's grimoire. Along with those, we found a vanquishing charm, a spell to deprive enemies of their strength, and instructions for multiple talismans. We gathered the tools, mixed the potions, wove the charms, and cast the spells. The plan—throw everything at the wall and see what sticks.

"We got action," Luca called out from behind his laptop as he straightened up from his hunched position in the armchair. His gaze never left the screen, however, and his fingers continued to tap away on the keyboard.

Just then, Rocky reached out to me mentally. *We have company. I'm handling it.*

What the hell do you mean, you're handling it?

It's Reginald, that sadistic fowl. I'm going after him. I'll talk to you soon, my precious witch.

And then, radio silence.

Rocky! You tune in right now, you crazy freaking bird.

Rocky didn't reply.

"I've got the raven." Luca stared at the screen. "He and Rocky are headed straight for each other."

"Fuck." I took off out the door. Outside on the lawn, I stared up at the sky, spread my arms wide, and called out. "Habrock"—I used Rocky's proper name—"you will not engage. You will return to me. You are my familiar, I am your witch, and I command you to return to the cottage!"

"He made a bee-line." Luca's voice sounded from just over my left shoulder, startling me. With his laptop in his hands, and his eyes locked on his screen, he monitored the security cameras he'd installed as they transmitted the birds' movements in real-time. "Pretty sick aerial maneuver. Rocky dodged a head-on collision with the raven. They're both heading back here."

"The raven is the messenger." Celeste arrived at my right.

"Reginald is old and stubborn but savvy. Abe can communicate with him if need be," Eris said. My sister, with her albino raven familiar Abramelin perched on her shoulder, stood alongside Maggie and Mia. All three witches wore determined expressions and had their feet planted firm.

"Thank you. That may be helpful." I returned my attention to the skies.

I wished Alexander had been there to listen in as the birds spoke. My heart clenched. But when Celeste gave my hand a small squeeze, my whole body sighed.

A moment later, I caught sight of the birds. Rocky soared at top speed with his wings at full extension and landed with a skid before me.

I must have revenge, Evangeline.

A moment later, the raven landed deftly on the lawn twenty feet or so away.

This isn't the time for revenge. Yet. First, let's hear what he has to say.

Abe hopped off Eris's shoulder and stood between the two fowl foes.

A black raven, a white raven, and a red-tailed hawk.

The birds' communications remained silent to me. I looked around at my fellow witches to see if any of them could hear, but they all appeared equally ignorant. We were going to have to wait patiently, and let the familiars sort it out.

They want us gone. Rocky explained, and I repeated to everyone. *All but Maggie. They expect her to stay. They want us to vacate, abandon the cottage and property to them. Well, to Riddle.*

"What the hell would make them think we'd just hand Maggie and the magic over to them?" I asked aloud, incredulous.

Riddle says he'll devour us all if we don't.

I relayed Rocky's warning to the group as the fire beneath my skin sizzled.

"And he'll make that shit look like an act of God." Eris gazed up at the sky. "It's snowing."

Good thing we've got the Goddess on our side.

"I think I speak for everyone when I say, *fuck that bullshit*." Luca said. "Tell Reginald we're not going anywhere. They can't have the cottage, and they can't have Maggie."

The assent was unanimous.

Rocky relayed the message. Minutes later, the raven flew off, and Rocky and Abe turned to face us. Rocky remained uncharacteristically silent.

"Abe says we're fucked," Eris blurted.

"Care to elaborate?" I asked.

"These flurries are the start of a blizzard that's barreling down on us. We're going to get snowed in, and at dawn, Riddle's going to suck us up like a slushy."

"Yeh, well, I've never been a fan of slushies."

Chapter Eighteen

GIVING TUESDAY

The sun would rise at 6:56 a.m., but I rose at five. A riot of fluffy, glittering snow cascaded against the black sky beyond my bedroom's bay window. Mounds of white sat like icing atop the trees and blanketed the lawn and fields. The hushed rustling of flakes against the window was the only break in the stillness of the cottage. I breathed in the serenity of my surroundings and exhaled a shiver of anxiety. It wouldn't be long before the stillness shattered.

It's gonna be a hell of a day. But I'm going to kick today's ass. I rallied myself in a pathetically lukewarm attempt at bolstering my self-confidence.

I snuck out of bed, leaving Celeste behind to keep the covers warm for a while longer. She'd spent the night curled around me, her waiflike frame snuggled into my softness. I'd welcomed her tender affections. We loved each other. And with the future so terribly uncertain, we trusted in that truth.

I tiptoed across the cold floor into the bathroom, did my business, brushed my teeth, and took a quick shower. By the time I reentered my bedroom, Celeste was already awake and dressed with her makeup applied. Her getup made me giggle. She looked like she'd walked off the set of Hunger Games or some high fantasy series. She wore a form-fitting, utilitarian jumpsuit with straps and pockets and zippers—in pale pink!—with heavy, black, steel-tipped boots. My girl dressed for battle in style.

She handed me a steaming mug. "Good morning. Are we ready to kick today in the balls?"

"Ab-so-fucking-lutely." I sipped my coffee. I sighed with the bliss of the first sip of the morning. One of my favorite things in life. "That's good. Thank you. Anyway, I'll be ready soon. I don't suppose you packed me one of those." I smirked and motioned to her outfit. "Maybe in leather?" I wiggled my eyebrows.

Her cheeks blushed pink. "Oh, I brought you something better."

"Well, that's not ominous or anything." I laughed.

Celeste dipped into my walk-in closet and came out holding my scarlet, ceremonial high priestess gown, cleaned and pressed.

"It is perfect." I choked back the emotions that threatened to spill out. Celeste understood my nature perfectly. Despite the freezing temperatures and the piling snow, I needed no warmth or protection against the elements. She chose the vestment that suited me best, those that clothed a priestess. "I'll keep my hair down and my feet bare. It's not as if the cold bothers me. And I'd like to stay as grounded to the earth as I can, in case I need to call on it."

A naughty thought entered my head, and a foolish comment spilled from my lips. "I guess it isn't the best time to suggest doing this all skyclad?" I offered a cheeky grin.

She leveled me with a disapproving scowl and dodged my comment. "Get ready. I've got magic of my own to attend to. I'm placing a crystal-forged protection spell over the cottage using hematite, amber, onyx, and diamond at each of the outside corners." She glanced up with an almost angelic expression. "Every little bit helps, right?" She gave me a soft, sweet, lingering kiss and then flitted off to do her crystal work, leaving me to prepare for battle.

I draped the blood-red robe of the high priestess over my bare curves. The Goddess' magic surged within me. Warmth radiated below my skin. I lifted myself onto the tips of my toes with my head tilted reverently to the heavens and my arms wide, and I allowed my magic to surge freely. The forces of creation and powers of the elements swam in the fire of my blood. I reminded myself of the great responsibility such power required and why using it to protect the vulnerable against Vivian and Riddle was not only appropriate but a moral imperative.

"Because I'm not evil," I said to no one and everyone and myself.

Once I'd readied myself, I found Celeste—her crystal work complete—sitting with Maggie, Mia, and Eris around the dining table. The four powerful witches sipped tea and nibbled fretfully on the fruit and eggs and muffins set out family style on the table. Luca hunkered down on the sofa in the living room, scowling at his laptop, monitoring security. No one spoke. The nervous magical energy in the room thickened and swelled.

I grabbed a muffin and ate, staring at the swirling white expanse beyond the kitchen window. Icicles hung like boney claws from the eaves outside the window, curving menacingly inward toward the cottage as if drawn to the pulsating power within. I shivered.

"Incoming. Friendly fire," Luca called out.

The rumble of the boys' voices reverberated up to the cottage from outside. Nicolae, Ethan, and Gregory barreled through the door in search of some warmth and a cup of coffee. The boys huddled in the living room with Luca to keep from tracking snow through the cottage and to put their heads together in hushed rumbles over Luca's monitor. Their visit was brief. After finishing their coffee, they wished us luck, kissed my cheek, and trudged out into the blizzard to return to their posts on the perimeter.

Before Gregory made it to the door, however, I snagged his arm and slipped four silver coins and four copper pennies into his hand.

Every little bit helps. I looked to Celeste.

"Please, bury these at each direction point around the property," I whispered. "Quickly."

He didn't investigate the items in his hand or question my request. "Yes, Priestess." Gregory took off into the early morning.

I stared out of the window, unable to make out the retreating men's backs through the cottony veil of billowing snow. The dark sky grew a hazy gray at the edges, lightening ever so gradually at the horizon.

Celeste joined me at the window. "The weather worsens. Use it to your advantage and use your advantages against it."

I checked the rooster clock in the kitchen. Six forty-six. Ten minutes before sunrise.

"There's one more thing I have to do." I turned toward the door.

"No!" Came a chorus of voices.

Maggie and Mia shared a glance and stood.

"We are Aradian la strega, protectors of this land," Maggie said proudly. "We're coming with you."

"Now wait a minute. If they're going with you, I am too." Celeste stood with her hands firmly planted on her hips. "Why should they have all the fun?"

"Damn right." I beamed at her.

I looked over at a pale-faced Eris and at Luca, whose face never left his laptop. "You two hold tight here. Whatever you do, protect the cottage. And stay in touch with the boys." I headed toward the front door with my bag of magical sundries in one hand and my besom in the other.

"Quickly ladies, grab your coats and brooms."

"Riddle and my mother will be here any minute," Eris blurted. "What the hell is so important you have to go out there now?" Her brow furrowed. She seemed genuinely concerned for my welfare, which I found both disconcerting and strangely comforting.

"Magic." I smiled with more bravado than I genuinely felt. "You're welcome to join us, but we're leaving now."

Maggie, Mia, Celeste, and I trudged out to the center of the lawn, a clearing between the cottage, forest, and stream. My oldest familiar, my momma bear, my Shasta, died on this lawn. Her blood soaked into this soil. Only yards away, by the fallen oak tree at the mouth of the forest, my mother took her last breath. This was hallowed ground, a sacred space. I would not relinquish it.

A minute later, as we set up candles in the snow, Eris jogged out of the cottage, bundled in her parka, and dragging her besom broom behind her.

"Wait up." Eris was out of breath and huffing.

I gave her a smirk. "Seriously? That jog got you winded?"

"I may be skinny, but it's not from exercise." Eris finally reached us. She heaved for breath as she hunched over with her hands on her knees.

"Smoking? Cocaine? Eating disorder?" I raised an eyebrow.

"Back off, okay? I'm a woman of many talents. Physical activity is not one of them. And I fucking hate snow. But don't tell anyone, or I'll have to kill you." She teased. "So, what are we doing exactly?"

"Protection magic."

"Dream come true," she said glibly. "Well, since we're sisters, my power will amplify yours, so...let's get to work."

The night's inky sky had been replaced by a stormy gray haze. We were almost out of time. *Okay, let's do this.*

I raised my arms wide, breathed deeply, and let my power swell. The fire under my skin sizzled with unspent energy, and the magic within me filled to bursting. Maggie, Mia, Celeste, Eris, and I clasped hands and stood at the five points of a pentacle we'd created with candles and crystals in the snow.

I called out. "I summon the elements—connected to me through blood and magic and the grace of the Goddess—rise at our call! Fire, you are bound to us. Earth, you are bound to us. Air, you are bound to us. Water, you are bound to us! And I charge you to protect the magic of this land.

"We call upon the Goddess to protect the magic from falling into unworthy hands, and to protect the witches here assembled and those under our care. We call out to our ancestors, to the witches who came before me—Lavinia, Esmeralda, and Circe, and to the great grandmothers whose names I don't yet know. We call on the spirits of generations of la strega in whose wise hands this land found formative guardians. Stand with your daughters today."

"Stand with your daughters!" Maggie, Mia, Celeste, and Eris replied in one amplified voice.

"Oh, yes!" came a droll voice. "Please amass all your ancestral power together in one, sumptuous pot for me, will you? So much easier to siphon it that way." He was pleasant, even as he spewed bile.

That's what makes him so dangerous.

I turned to face my adversary, the man who so convincingly played the part of an ally.

"*Really* look at him," Celeste whispered.

She sees something. She sees who he truly is.

So, I did. I studied Riddle for the first time. He seemed like the type of man you could pass on the street, and never give a second look. I once regarded him as handsome enough in an average Joe sort of way, but there was nothing distinctive about his features. Neither his plain clothes nor mousy brown hair left an impression. He seemed an amalgamation of all men, the ultimate *every man*. He blended in through life, a devil hiding in plain sight. The only remarkable thing about Riddle had always been his down-home charm and hokey friendliness, yet all that had been an act.

Vivian stood smug beside Riddle on the lawn, dressed as always in the height of sophistication, even in a blizzard. Reginald perched on her shoulder.

"Vivian. Riddle," I addressed them without enthusiasm.

"Ms. Evangeline Clarion." Mayor Riddle greeted me with a faux-friendly smile and pretended to pick his teeth. "Thank you for the appetizer. The charms and wards and illusions you and your henchmen erected were positively scrumptious. Sucked them right up. Helps to have a chef on the payroll, I guess."

Fuck. He fed off their magic. And he wants to feed on the magic here.

"Where are the boys? What have you done to them?" Fury surged beneath my skin and melted the snow around our feet.

Just then, Rocky landed beside me, and I heard his reassuring voice in my mind. *The boys are weak but recuperating. They've called in backup—the big guns.*

The big guns?

Reinforcements are on the way, dearest witch, hold tight! Rocky lifted his noble head and took off again.

"Your lapdogs are inconsequential." Riddle answered the question I'd posed.

"So, it's been you all along?" I stalled for time.

"You could say that."

"It's been me too," Vivian shrilled.

Is she fucking serious? She can't help herself, can she?

I cocked my head to the side and did my best to *see* Vivian's truth, beyond her slick, sexy businesswoman vibe, past the bravado. Vivian had tied herself to this man because he promised her the power she'd been denied, the power she needed to get revenge on my mother through me. But Riddle never intended to share power with her. She was a useful, but ultimately disposable, tool. When would she realize it?

"Yeh, I think that's clear, Vivian." I pulled myself out of my thoughts. "You've been a valuable henchman for Mayor Riddle. You've done a masterful job of distracting me by throwing the town into a tizzy with your temptations. But manipulation wasn't all that difficult, was it? These folks just had half their downtown eviscerated. They're still reeling after having been ripped off and manipulated by their reverend and their last mayor. Arbor was easy prey, low-hanging fruit."

"You've proven more formidable than your mother." Riddle brought the focus back to his own agenda. "It may be because you've surrounded yourself with a posse, coven, whatever. Lavinia wasn't big on social interaction." He began to pace. "That left her vulnerable and easy to catch unaware on an afternoon stroll through the forest. Once she was out of the way, I thought I could simply console Magdalena, ingratiate myself into her life, and therefore, into the cottage, closer to the magic. But no. You moved in. And that batty bitch Adelaide Good lurked incessantly."

Realization dawned on Maggie's face: here stood the man who killed Lavinia. I thought she might collapse. But Maggie steeled her spine, clenched her fists and set her jaw ridged as Riddle continued his diatribe.

"But, you see, I'm patient. Over the years, I cultivated my good name in the community and my good-neighborly relationship with Maggie. In the soup kitchen and pantry and as a key ally of hers during my time on the town council, Maggie and I grew closer. She saw me as a good man. Everybody did. Doesn't that make me one then? I did those volunteer hours. I walked the walk. Does it matter that this brought me to the brink of possessing what I've been yearning for all my life? The magic here could sustain me forever. I must control it. I will."

"The fuck you will," I blurted. I'd already had one mayor of Arbor burn me at the stake. I wasn't going down like that again. "I don't know who you think you are, but you have no authority—by law, rights, or otherwise, to confiscate this property or evict anyone from it, and we aren't intimidated by the fact that you possess magic of your own. If you attack us, we will retaliate. With force. And you will lose."

Riddle folded his arms and sneered. "I'm saving you for dessert. You're going to be tasty."

I whipped out my arm to restrain Celeste from attacking Riddle, then moved closer to him one small step at a time.

"You are nothing but an incel, pissed you didn't get the girl, angrier still that she chose a woman over you. You envied my mother. You envy Maggie. You envy women with power. Their strength makes you feel weak. Because you are. You're a parasitic husk who sucks the magic from others in order to sustain your own. Maggie went to those soup kitchens and stocked those pantry shelves because she is naturally empathetic; she genuinely cares and wants to help people. You did it because the appearance of philanthropy benefited you. You're an opportunist.

"And you," I snarled at Vivian, "are being used. Played like a fiddle. Neither one of you fucking scares me."

I turned back to Riddle. "And why are you talking about Maggie as if she isn't standing right there?" I pointed fiercely at my goddess-mother.

"I mean nothing to him now," Maggie answered. "He once cared about me, in his own way. This is how he excused his pursuit of the power here. I'm sure that's how he excused killing Lavinia. But since Ayo..."

"You're fucking soiled," Riddle spat.

"And you're a racist and a murderer along with everything else," Maggie blurted before collecting her wits. "That's why you kidnapped me. I disgusted you, but you still needed me to control the immense power in this land. But you've been thinking about things all wrong."

Riddle stiffened but did not speak.

"You think you need me in order to access the magic here. But that is not the way it works. For the magic to benefit and defend you instead of rising and crushing you like the insignificant creature that you are"— Maggie's fury seethed—"you must be under the care of the specific Aradian la strega who resides in this cottage and protects this land. At the moment, that is Mia Aradia, not me. But in harming me, an Aradian la strega, former protector of this land, you've guaranteed that the power that resides here will never bend to you. Your own actions have made certain you will never control this magic."

"I will!" Riddle called out. He shimmered and swirled out of shape. The next thing I knew, a white horse, Bayard, stood beside him. It was the most bizarre thing I'd ever witnessed—and I'd seen some crazy shit.

"Fuck," more than one person said.

My brain hadn't yet wrapped around what had happened when Bayard turned and trotted off toward the stream.

"Stop him," Eris screamed. "Don't let him near the water."

It was too late. Kicking snow up in his wake, Bayard charged into the icy stream at full gallop, flicked his tail high into the air, and slapped it down onto the water. With any normal horse, this would have resulted in a playful splash. But Bayard was a kelpie, so his actions resulted in a twenty-foot tidal wave of frigid water.

Eris and I shared a quick glance, gave a nod to the witches around us, then raised our arms. Using my mother's spell and the elemental magic within us, we repelled the wave, sending it rushing toward Vivian and Riddle.

Before it reached them, Vivian froze the water, turning it into a wall of ice. Then, with a great sweep of her arms, she shattered the ice and sent the razor-sharp shards shooting at us.

This time, we didn't confer. Eris and I threw out our hands and turned the barrage of icy projectiles into mountains of soft, fluffy snow. It blanketed us, covering our heads. Eris screamed. I heated up the fire under my skin and melted the snow, letting it seep harmlessly into the ground.

Eris heaved, and leaned with her hands on her knees to catch her breath. She turned her wide, dark eyes to me. "Thanks, sis."

"Are you kidding? Up top," I said like a total dork, raising my hand for a high five.

Eris's face split into a grin, and she slapped my hand. "Fuck yeah." She laughed.

"Oh, isn't this a sweet little love fest," Vivian sneered. "You do seem quite over-confident. This isn't finished. We're just warming up."

Straightening her spine and squaring her shoulders, Eris turned her back on her mother. She crossed her arms and stared defiantly into the forest behind us. This simple move clearly injured Vivian as she looked like she'd been slapped. The self-satisfied expression slipped from Vivian's face, and a blend of pain, regret, and confusion replaced it.

"So this isn't just some game? You're really doing this?" Vivian asked Eris in a shaky, incredulous voice, exhibiting more vulnerability than I'd ever seen—more than she probably meant to show. "You'd turn your back on me? Your mother!"

"You turned your back on me when you sided with that kelpie. He's leading you off the deep end, Mother. Face it. He's a nut job." Eris kept her gaze on the forest.

"Fool. I'm trying to give you, my daughter, everything that was stolen from us. And yet you side with them!" Vivian's voice cracked. "You're an ungrateful little bitch."

I didn't see it coming. Eris glowered off into the woods with her arms folded over her chest. The next moment, she'd whipped around, strode up to her mother, and slapped her in the face.

Vivian's hand flew to cover her cheek, her jaw hung low, and she struggled to form coherent speech.

Riddle strode forward as Bayard dissipated into a misty haze and reabsorbed into him, an angry, impatient scowl contorting his face. "Enough of this female prattle." He brandished a wand.

I couldn't help it, I burst out laughing. Celeste, Mia, even Maggie joined in.

"You're joking, right?" I buckled over, slapping my knee. Tears threatened from the absurdity of his aggression. "A wand! He thinks he can take me out with a wand!"

Hilarity clearly was not the response Riddle expected. "No, I'm not joking." He charged up to me and placed the crystal tipped wand to the center of my forehead. "Do you want to test me?"

"Sure." I didn't flinch. "What do you think you're going to do with that? Shoot a laser beam of magical energy into my skull? I suppose you could impale me with it, but then again, you could do that with any old, sharpened stick."

A look of genuine confusion overtook him. "You have no idea what this is." He appeared wide-eyed and a bit crazed. "Is it possible you've never seen it? This is your mother's wand. I stole it the day I killed her. Slipped it right out of her cold, dead hands."

Despite my recent urges suggesting the contrary, I didn't believe myself to be a violent person. But at that moment, I genuinely wanted to kill him. I glanced at Celeste and her badass fantasy bitch getup and steel-tipped boots, and contented myself with kneeing Riddle in the balls.

Riddle crumpled over. His face bloomed scarlet, tears sprung to his eyes, and he clutched his groin. "Bitch. You fucking stupid bitch." His voice was hard and guttural.

Riddle dropped the wand onto the grass, and I snatched it up. The wand wasn't going to start shooting magical lasers. However, he seemed to think it could. So, I pointed it at him the same way he'd pointed it at me.

With the smallest of smirks, Riddle lifted himself to his full height, shrugged, and put his hands in his pockets. "You dumb witches haven't caught on yet. I'll ingest any magic you throw my way. Your attacks nourish me and make me stronger. Bring on the spells and elemental trickery. They're like steak and blueberry pie." He chuckled, delighted with himself. "You see, I take what I want. I stole that wand along with your mother's life. Snuffed her out when she wasn't looking. The same way I snatched up Maggie...and *that other bitch*." He scowled in disgust but then barked out a laugh as if a thought dawned on him. "I took this fucking job as mayor, practically walked right in after Crandall was arrested. Somebody needed to lead the shit show, and my non-threatening, whitebread façade appealed to the weary community. And now"—his eyes turned dark, and he moved boldly toward me again—"I'm taking control of this property. I'm going to suck up the magic here like a fucking juice pouch."

"You will not take another thing that doesn't belong to you." A great sense of relief rushed over me.

"Is that so?" he scoffed.

"Yes, it is," Chief Harrison said behind the mayor. Bundled in his navy-blue Arbor PD parka, scarf, snow hat, and thick gloves, the chief stood with Alexander, Ayo, and the boys just behind him.

Thanks to the muffled snow and his overinflated bravado, Riddle obviously hadn't heard their approach. He swung around in fear and confusion.

"Who's the dumb witch now?" I said with a twisted snicker. "Chief, you're looking well."

"I'm feeling fit-as-a-fiddle, thanks to you, Miss Eva. And I must say, you're a sight for sore eyes, Ms. Maramma." The old codger looked kindly at Maggie.

"It's good to see ya, Chief." Maggie smiled brightly despite the circumstances. "Can I offer you a cup of coffee or a brandy to warm you up?" She asked him as if we were nothing more than a gaggle of neighbors chatting about the weather.

"No, thank you kindly. Not today. Although, I will take you up on the offer another time. Mayor Riddle and I have some business to attend to downtown." He frowned as he returned his knowing gaze to Riddle. "Let's go, Mayor. You're coming with me."

"What?" Riddle asked stupidly. "Why?"

"Well, sir, cause I'm arresting you for the murder of Lavinia Clarion and the kidnapping and torture of Ayo Kehinde and Magdalena Maramma. I'm sure there's a handful of other charges we're going to throw at ya after we watch Luca's security footage. But I have your confession here on tape, so we can go ahead and get the ball rolling." The chief held up an old-fashioned, handheld tape recorder. He made his point clearer when he read Riddle his rights, handcuffed him, and escorted him into the back of his police cruiser.

What was most satisfying about Riddle's arrest was how mundane it was. The lack of magic in a jail cell would, over time, drain away every ounce of magic within him.

"Looks like we're going to be needin' another new mayor." Chief Harrison walked back to us. He shook his head and turned to Vivian. "Ms. Harcourt, I believe there's an animal cruelty charge coming your way. And you're either a witness or an accomplice to Riddle's nonsense. Point is, don't leave town."

Without another word, Vivian trudged off down the snowy driveway, stopping only once to scowl at Riddle in the back of Harrison's cruiser.

As the chief turned to leave, Mia stepped forward. "Signore Harrison." She took his hand. "This is the last time we shall meet. Now that my niece is home and her threat has passed, I must return to Italy right away." This declaration shocked us all, and I heard more than a few gasps. "Grazi, thank you, thank you for taking care of my family here. You are a good man, and you have more to do in this life."

The chief's cheeks turned rosy pink. "Well, I thank you." He lowered his eyes reverently.

"May I offer you a blessing?" the crone asked.

"That'd be kind of ya, ma'am" The sweet old codger nodded and removed his hat.

Balanced on her viper cane, Mia placed a bent, knobby hand on his forehead.

"*Nell'oscurità e nella luce,*" Mia began.

"In darkness and in light," Alexander translated.

"*In generosita e beatitudine.*"

"In bounty and bliss."

"*Nella carestia e nella fatica.*"

"In famine and toil."

"*Che la magia trovi le tue dita.*"

"May magic find your fingers."

"*Possa la gioia essere presente nei vostri piccoli momenti.*"

"May joy be present in your little moments."

"*E che tu possa vivere lunghe giornate per tutto il tempo che desideri viverle.*"

"And may you live long days for as long as you wish to live them."

She lowered her hand and kissed the chief on each cheek. "*Arrivederci*, my friend."

"I appreciate that. I wish you well, Ms. Mia. Safe travels." The chief blushed scarlet.

He grinned kindly at her before looking around at the rest of us. "I'm glad you're all safe. Ms. Maggie, we'll have that brandy soon. And the rest of you lot, stay out of trouble. I'll see you at Yule. I missed your last shindig. I'm not missing this one." He tipped his hat. "I do love Christmas."

Chapter Nineteen

WINTER SOLSTICE

"I love this time of year," I mused.

Curled up amid mountains of pillows and a twist of sheets with a steaming mug of coffee warming my hands, I stared dreamily at the light snow swirling outside my bedroom window at Morgan Manor.

"The first day of winter," I said on a contented sigh. "I think Yule may be the most magical of all Sabbats, even more than Samhain. Everything's so quiet, like Mother Nature's sleeping. Tonight is the longest night, and that gives me hope for brighter days ahead." I peered down at the enticing woman snuggled beside me. "I want to celebrate. But I also kinda want to stay in bed with you all day."

Celeste looked up from the pillow on her side of the bed with a sleepy, lopsided grin. "You're sexy when you're happy." She laughed groggily. "I get it. I love Yule too. Winter in general. Any season where it's equally appropriate to celebrate or hibernate, is all right with me. But ya know, we did all this work. We've got about two hundred people arriving in a few hours, and we wouldn't want to disappoint them."

"Oh, all right," I heaved a teasing, over-dramatic sigh, and flung myself out of bed. "Let's do this thing."

I threw on a T-shirt and was wrapping my hair up in a bun when Celeste cleared her throat.

"Have you heard anything about Riddle?" she asked haltingly, clearly worried she might set me off.

She was right to be concerned. Everything in me sizzled with hatred when I thought of him, and I didn't want to feel that today. I kept my boiling rage damned up inside and lived each day as if I hadn't just added to the list of murderers I'd put in prison. How long could I hold back the tide? Chief Harrison had Riddle locked up, but something told me this wasn't a permanent situation. Our victory was a temporary one. Trials laid ahead.

"They don't tell me much. Ayo's handling things, thank the Goddess. There's a chance he'll get bail, but she's fighting it. I mean, the chief of police heard him confess." My blood pressure spiked, so I took a few calming breaths. "Either way, we can't be complacent. They could release Riddle from prison tomorrow or five years from now. Given his penchant for lifelong grudges, he isn't likely to forgive and forget. And you know Vivian isn't going away simply because her meal ticket is behind bars. Sure, she's likely to be arrested soon. Her bird tortured Rocky, and Riddle used her home to hold Maggie and Ayo captive. But she has a score to settle, and I don't see her playing nice under a little legal pressure. And speaking of settling old scores, the Cudlows and Crandalls might be locked up, too, but who the hell knows what will happen in their cases. Plea deals, prison overcrowding. We've got to be on our guard. Always."

Celeste rolled her eyes and rolled out of bed. As she stood beside the window, the morning sun glistening off the snow bathed her slim, bare figure in radiant light. "That sounds like Alexander talking. I refuse to think that way. I won't spend my life looking over my shoulder, cowering in fear of unknown assassins. Life is dangerous, Eva, as you know all too well. Death comes for each of us in our time. Why waste a single precious moment worrying about it? We have too much to do already." She wriggled into her clothes but stopped and stared at me with a look of surprise when she caught my horrified expression.

"Eva, I'm not reckless. There is always a level of awareness you've got to have as a woman. I take precautions every day. And I will continue to do that. You should too. But you can't let these villains rule you. The authorities know what's up. Ayo's all over it. And we have a fucking party to put on." She kissed me quick. "I'm gonna head to my room and get cleaned up. I'll see you later." She tiptoed out the door.

I wondered at her thinking. It didn't sit well in my gut. Vivian and Riddle were not run-of-the-mill dangers. These were erratic, magical beings with axes to grind. Now more than ever.

The thought of Celeste getting caught up in all this made my fiery blood run as cold as the ice that clung to my windows. I resolved to keep her close but chuckled—she rarely left my right side! We'd returned to the manor after Riddle's arrest to focus on the Manor Arts and the coming Yule festival, and every morning since had been spent like this one. After long, loving nights, she'd leave my room quietly before the sun rose, so as not to rub our rekindled relationship in Alexander's nose. His room being right across the hall didn't help matters.

Our interactions with Alexander remained professional. I hoped we could stay friends. Certainly, we still cared for each other, loved each other; that didn't go away with the flick of a switch. Still, I'd made the right decision. I loved Celeste, and she loved me. I couldn't allow Alexander's grief or anger to shadow us.

It didn't take Celeste and I long to realize we couldn't work on a relationship if we continued living at Morgan Manor with Alexander. After discussing things with Maggie and Ayo, who'd resumed residence at the cottage since Mia's departure, we planned to move back to the cottage with them after Yule. From there, we'd look for an apartment to share. It felt good having something exciting to look forward to with Celeste. Despite all we'd gone through, I was happy.

Alexander, on the other hand, had become a complete bear. Besides his emotions over our breakup, and having to see me with Celeste every day, the holiday hubbub overtaking Morgan Manor irritated the hell out of him. He'd never shared the source of his disdain for the seasonal merrymaking. I'd always chalked it up to poor-little-rich-boy syndrome—a child given everything he wants, except love, affection, or genuine familial connection. When not sulking about the manor, Alexander devoted his time to the downtown rebuild efforts—with Eris. They'd salvaged the plan despite Vivian and Riddle's fall from grace. I didn't need to be clairvoyant to see that Alexander and Eris would end up together. Maybe not forever, but for a while.

Maybe it should have bothered me, but it didn't. I wanted Alexander to be happy. If a relationship with Eris, or anyone else, made him happy, so be it.

Why should I be angry? I broke it off with him this time. I'm not alone. I have Celeste. Should I fall into depression, cry and wail?

Celeste seemed to think I might, even though Alexander's departure from my romantic life benefitted her. Maggie, Ayo, and the boys seemed to believe I should be wallowing in break-up tunes and pints of ice cream. Except for Gregory, that is. He kept me stocked up on wine and chocolate, but otherwise ignored the development in my relationship. The rest hovered, waiting for my inevitable breakdown. Their lack of faith in me stung. I'd lost Alexander once before and survived. I could do it again.

I don't have time for an emotional breakdown. Not about Riddle, and not about Alexander. I have business to take care of.

With the arrival of Yule came a nasty winter snow squall. The morning flurries morphed into a walloping blizzard by the afternoon. The governor declared a state of emergency for the region. Yet folks from Arbor, nestled in the valley of the majestic Gothics Peak, had lived through their fair share of rough winters, and did not scare easily. Despite weather forecasts predicting a much stronger band of snow expected to hit later that night, we didn't receive a single cancelation for the evening's festivities. By the time the sun set, the worst of the snow had let up, and the snowplows had cleared the streets. Instead of scaring anyone off, the wintry weather made the manor appear even more magical as it glistened in ice and snow from high atop Red Hill.

Shortly before six, snow tire clad SUVs began filing up the driveway. While Jasper directed the valet parking, Elliot escorted our guests into the manor. Just inside, Killian assisted folks with their coats and hats. Celeste and I stood at the head of the reception line beside the enormous hearth decked in festive greenery and bows and greeted each guest as they arrived. Celeste wore a billowing gown in the palest ice blue with crystalline embroidery that shimmered in the candlelight, while I wore my scarlet high priestess robe atop an elegant, black velvet dress with garnet beading. Maggie and Ayo stood next wearing gowns of silver and gold respectively, and Alexander grumpily brought up the rear of the reception line in a tux and white tie. The boys scattered around the manor to ensure the night went off without a hitch.

Some of the first through the mistletoe-strewn doors were the sisters of Saint Francis Convent, with Mother Hildegard leading the way.

"Blessed Yule, Evangeline." Mother Hildegard wore a jovial smile.

"Merry Christmas, Mother, sisters." I offered the silent, habited sisters a welcoming nod. "I am so happy you're here. It means the world to me."

"It is where we're needed tonight." The old woman patted me kindly on the cheek and hustled the sisters off to the dining room.

Streams of people followed the nuns through the iron doors, all decked out in their holiday best. Artists, designers, theater folk, and restaurant types from down in the city, local volunteers from the food pantry, teachers from the public school, historians, activists, and the members of our original coven—the Masseys, Loveridges, and Finnegans, Alastair Gant, and the old Wiccans all came to join our Yule celebration.

The last guest through the door, however, had no invitation considering she'd been my nemesis when I'd sent out the invites. By the way Alexander lit up when she walked in, he'd added her to the guest list. I was surprised to find I was glad to see her too. With her serpent-green lace dress, up-swept hair dotted in emeralds, and the gems continuing on her ears and neck, she reminded me of a Slytherin princess.

"A blessed Yule to you, sis. Nice foliage." Eris simpered as she fiddled with the garland. Catching sight of the mistletoe, she clutched onto Alexander's arm, dragged him underneath it, and kissed him hard on the mouth.

A bolt of lightning flashed in Alexander's eyes. He tucked his head to Eris's ear and whispered something apparently hysterical. Eris glanced over at me, smiling like a Cheshire cat.

"The least she could do is have the decency to look humble," I hissed to Celeste.

"Don't go letting her get your knickers in a twist."

"Isn't that what sisters do? I'm being serious. I haven't the foggiest idea what sisters do. I've never had one until recently."

"Me neither. Only child, I'm afraid. But ya know, you can't blame Eris too much. I don't think she can help it. She only recently became one of us good guys."

"Oh, I'm a good guy now, am I?" I laughed.

"Don't worry, sweetheart. I know how wicked you are." She kissed me slow and curled her arm through mine. "Now, let's join the celebration."

The dining room was transformed into a magical winter forest. Round, linen covered tables adorned with candles and greenery and pops of red ribbon were scattered amid snow-tipped evergreen Yule trees. Everything in the room sparkled; from the crystal tree ornaments to the enormous, intricate, glass-blown snowflakes that magically hovered overhead.

I surveyed the dining room for anyone from our group, but the singer from Ireland captured my attention. At the far side of the room, Siobhan Quinn sang a lovely, lilting tune. She brightened when she caught my eye, and she sang the next few bars just to me. Her fiery-red hair and emerald eyes dazzled me. Heat flushed my cheeks, and I averted my gaze. Only one woman held my heart, and she stood to my right.

We wove our way between the tables until we caught sight of Gregory. He wore a black chef's coat and pants with a tall, black, chef's hat balanced atop an intricately knotted nest of dreads. His blond, bearded face split open in a wide smile. He waved us over. Celeste and I made our way to the table he'd reserved for us.

After a bear hug and a big, furry kiss on the cheek, Gregory growled low in my ear, "You look good enough to eat." Stepping back to admire my dress, he spoke louder. "Blessed Yule, Priestess. And a blessed Yule, Celeste. Please, allow me." He pulled out my chair and took my hand to assist me into it, and then he turned to help Celeste in the same fashion.

Celeste and I said quick hellos and made small talk with the table—Maggie and Ayo, Nicolae and Luca, Alexander and Eris. I treasured them all so dearly—even Eris. The warmth of family filled my grateful heart.

My stomach growled, and my mouth watered as waiters descended upon the dining room, filling the tables with bowls of nuts and dried fruit, mini charcuterie boards of cheeses, cured meat, olives, grapes, and honeyed figs along with pitchers of cider and carafes of wine and wassail.

Gregory handed me a menu proudly. I salivated as I read it over. The wild mushroom risotto, glazed parsnips and carrots with pistachios, roasted goose, venison tenderloin, and the spit-roasted pig melded old and new traditions. "This sounds delicious. A culinary masterpiece, as always."

"Let me know what you think *after* you've tasted what I have to offer. Enjoy your meal." He winked at me as he left through a side door that led to the kitchen.

"I lost one rival for your affections and gained two more," Celeste said with an easy grin, somehow without a note of jealousy. "Siobhan Quinn and Gregory both appear rather predatory tonight."

"I don't want anyone else." I took her hand and put as much emotion into my words as I could.

"But they want you. And who could blame them. You're beautiful, talented, and fierce." She peered up with such gentle sweetness, my eyes pricked with unshed tears. "I know what you're thinking. Gregory's a dear, old friend, a trusted confidant. And you don't even know Siobhan. These things are true. But nothing is so solid as a relationship built on a foundation of longtime friendship. And nothing is more exhilarating than a fling with someone new. And here I am—" Her voice cracked "—someone who's betrayed your trust. Someone who's caused you such heartache for selfish reasons. Because I wanted you. And I want you now."

"You have me," I said a bit too loudly, thankfully drowned out by Siobhan's festive song.

Maggie gave me a questioning look from across the table, and I offered her a small reassuring grin. I leaned in close to Celeste and whispered again.

"You have me. You have been by my side through the most mentally, emotionally, physically, and magically turbulent experiences anyone could imagine over these last few months. I couldn't have done any of this, I couldn't have survived and thrived, without you. I love you."

Celeste cupped my cheek in the soft palm of her hand and kissed me with such passionate tenderness that my soul sighed in contentment. "I love you too."

Siobhan's song ended, and Ethan, dressed in a dapper,'50s style charcoal suit with his silver hair slicked into shocking icicle spikes, stepped to the microphone.

"Good evening, ladies and gentlemen. Blessed Yule!" he shrieked, and the crowd chuckled.

Has he been hitting the wassail already tonight?

"The name's Ethan Massey, and I'll be your Master of Ceremonies. We've got a magical evening planned for you. First, my brother, the legendary Chef Gregory Massey, and his talented team in the Manor Arts kitchen have prepared a festive Yuletide meal, fit for the Druids and wise folks of old. During dinner, the Gay Men's Choir of Central New York will perform some rollicking holiday classics. After we eat, we'll all move over to the great hall for some dancing. Then, we're bundling up and heading outside where we'll all take a walk around the Solstice Spiral to symbolize the turning of the great wheel of the year, the ending of one cycle and beginning of a new, and the darkest night that leads inevitably toward the dawning of the sun." He droned on with a definite slur. I made a mental note to scold him. "Finally, we'll cap off the evening with a bonfire! How's that sound, folks?"

The crowd applauded.

"I said, *how's that sound, folks*?" He egged our guests on, and they responded with hoots and cheers and applause. "That's more like it. Well" —Ethan looked toward the opposite side of the dining room and beamed—"let me introduce you to my brother, Chef Gregory Massey, and tonight's main course, a big-ass roasted pig!" He laughed. "Enjoy!"

My whole table collectively groaned, but our guests enjoyed every second, especially when Gregory and three of his sous chefs carried in an enormous, charred pig on an eight-foot-wide butcher block. The oohs and aahs reverberated through the room.

Gregory's meal did not disappoint. Neither did the choir. Soon, the crowd filed out of the dining room and into the great hall to dance. Everyone from our table headed off too, but I hung back to wait while Celeste visited the ladies' room.

As I sat at the table, full, happy, and sipping wassail, I thanked the Goddess for Her many blessings, namely Celeste. These last weeks had been some of the happiest of my life, especially the hours Celeste and I spent lying in bed, dreaming about our future together. I didn't care if we lived in Arbor or the city or on a desert island. All I wanted was a long life with this incredible woman.

As if the Goddess heard my plea and wished to waste no time in replying, a blood-curdling scream sliced through the empty room and across my heart.

"Celeste!" Her name wrenched from my soul.

From the corner of my eye, I caught the shadowed figure of Vivian Harcourt outside the window, spiriting away from the manor and into the woods. I sprang to my feet, hoisted up my skirt, and took off out of the dining room toward the front door and the direction of the scream. I skidded to a stop at the sight of Celeste.

She stood in the center of the grand foyer with a six-inch shard of blown glass snowflake protruding from her chest. Violent crimson gushed in waves that surged with the beating of her heart, drenching the front of her crystalline gown, and pooling on the marble at her feet.

Sour bile rose in my throat. I wrapped my arms around myself to hold back the retching that twisted my stomach and threatened to overtake me.

So much blood. Did it hit her heart? How is she still standing? I'm going to fucking kill Vivian Harcourt.

"No, this isn't right," I said stupidly, unable to will myself to move. "The Goddess wouldn't allow it. You can't leave me yet."

"It's okay, sweetheart." Celeste glanced down at herself. "This is as it should be. I saw it coming." She gurgled out a twisted laugh, blood dribbling from the corner of her mouth. "I love you." She closed her eyes and collapsed like a ragdoll onto the marble floor.

I ran to her, gathered her limp body onto my lap, and cradled her in my arms. Her blood jetted out from around the glass impalement, splattering my chest and arms and hands.

"No, Celeste, no. Fuck, fuck, fuck. Help! Maggie! Somebody, help!" I cried out. "I've got you. I'm here." I buried my face into Celeste's neck. I breathed her in and rocked her as I murmured, "It's okay. You're okay. I love you. The Goddess loves you," again and again.

A crowd grew thick around us, yet they gave us a wide berth, not daring to step closer than fifteen feet in any direction. No one cursed or shrieked. Not a single person pulled out their phones to call for help or even to record this horror show for the gore of posterity. The crowd only stared with shock and revulsion and deep, deep sadness in their wide, transfixed eyes.

"It's okay. You're okay. I love you. The Goddess loves you," I muttered into the nest of Celeste's hair as if in a trance.

So much blood. So much fucking blood.

"Come on, stay with me. Open your eyes, sweetheart. Please, please, please stay with me."

For an instant, her eyes fluttered open. Her lips parted, and she breathed out, "Be brave." The light in her eyes dimmed, and they closed once more.

I flinched at the amazing grace of this woman. With her life pouring from her, Celeste used her breath to strengthen *me*.

"Find me...after, somehow," I said through a haze of tears.

"Don't worry," she wheezed with the faintest lift of her lips. "I promise to haunt you."

Her cheeks grew sallow and gray. The humor fled her face, replaced by a cringing wince of pain. Her body tensed and then relaxed.

I cracked. I shook Celeste violently by the shoulders, my tears washing the spray of blood from my cheeks. I wailed my grief to the heavens, begging, pleading with the Goddess. I called on the magic within me, on the elements that, up until that moment, had heeded my will. My soul implored every power in the Universe. But Celeste's eyes remained closed, and her pale lips stained in blood remained silent. I pulled her tight against my chest and rested my cheek on the top of her head.

"It's okay. You're okay. I love you. The Goddess loves you."

Eons passed before the first of my friends arrived. Nicolae and Luca pushed through the onlookers. Their angular faces twisted in grotesque fear at the sight of Celeste's life spilling out in scarlet waves. After a second of panic, Nicolae whipped out his phone and called 911. Seeing the truth of the matter as always, Luca recognized the futility of his brother's call and knelt beside us on the floor. His knees slipped in Celeste's blood as he wrapped his arms around us. Nicolae watched his younger brother as he spoke to the 911 operator, and an understanding struck him like a terrible flood. When he pocketed his phone, he too knelt in the pool of red and wrapped his arms around us.

Two by two, the Witches of Arbor arrived at this scene of horror and encircled me and Celeste with their arms. First, Gregory and Ethan ran out from the direction of the kitchen, followed by Maggie and Ayo from the ballroom, and finally Alexander and Eris, who descended onto the scene from the winding staircase. All but Eris entwined themselves in this great embrace. Each coven member sent their own unique energy, and their magic surged around us. Maggie's therapeutic, healing powers coursed so intensely, her magic shimmered silver as it encompassed Celeste.

Eris stood horrified and immobile over the huddled coven; the color washed from her cheeks.

"Do something," I screamed at her. "You're my sister, aren't you? You want to stand with me—with us? Then fucking do something. This is your mother's fault. Fix this! Save her!" My words reverberated off the vaulted foyer ceiling and rattled the chandelier dripping ruby red above us.

"I can't do the spell alone. It doesn't work without...her." Regret spilled out with Eris's words. "I'm so sorry."

"You *can* do this." I raised fierce eyes to Eris. "You don't have to be like your mother. Try. Please."

Eris wiped away the tears that streamed down her cheeks with the back of her arm, and without another word, threw her hands out over Celeste and the huddled coven enveloping us. She closed her eyes and repeated the resurrection spell as she allowed her restorative waters to stream from her hands. A mighty wind gathered and swirled around us. One by one, each witch fell back and allowed Eris's water to pour directly over Celeste's wound.

The foyer's marble floor flooded with wave after wave of blood-tainted water. This fresh horror broke the crowd's spell. They ran screaming from the manor, tracking hundreds of bloody footprints out into the frigid, snowy night.

All the while, I held Celeste tight in my arms under the gushing water and within the vortex of air churning around us, rocking her and repeating, "It's okay. You're okay. I love you. The Goddess loves you."

The water trickled to a drip from Eris's hands, and she dropped her arms, her desolate eyes falling closed.

When the cry of ambulance sirens echoed through the manor, the faces of my coven blazed with the brutal truth I already knew—Celeste was gone.

The slight flutter of her eyelids caught my attention. Her fingers gave my right hand an almost imperceptible squeeze. Frantically, I searched her face and then down at her chest that now rose and fell. The wound still gaped open wide around the clear glass projectile, but blood no longer hemorrhaged. Flickers of hope radiated through me.

Oh, dear, sweet Goddess, please.

And then Celeste's eyes blinked open. I thought my heart would burst with joy—until her gaze fell on me and darkened.

"What did you do?" Celeste bit out in a wet, garbled voice, blood dripping down her chin.

I gaped at her, dumbfounded. "Eris saved you," I blurted. Gregory snorted behind me.

Celeste flicked her fury to my sister before returning it to me.

"You made her save me." She strained to speak.

"You bet your ass I did," I roared, indignation firing me up. This was the last reaction I expected from her. Why wasn't she as fucking elated as I was that she was alive?

Her icy gaze narrowed, and a deep crevasse formed between her brows. "How could you be so foolish? You're a hypocrite, Evangeline, you know that? You decried Vivian's resurrection spell on Samhain as dark magic, then excused away its use on the chief. What you once considered dark magic, suddenly seemed perfectly reasonable when it benefitted you. So, you forced *her*"—she sneered in Eris's direction—"to do your dirty work."

"It's good to know you're alive enough to argue with me," I snapped.

"I was supposed to die! Don't you get it?" Celeste's voice grew stronger with every word.

"What the hell does that mean—supposed to die?"

"It was my time." She seethed. "I was ready to move onward. I have another lifetime waiting, and you took that from me."

Sweet Goddess, what have I done?

"All I wanted—all *we* wanted"— I motioned to the coven scattered around us—"was to save you. I won't apologize for that. I love you. There is no universe in which I don't do everything in my power to bring you back to life, to bring you back to me."

"My spirit wasn't ripped from across the veil through your power, but yes, it was done at your behest. And you deserve all the repercussions of such a command." Her voice dripped with venom. "This action will have consequences."

I reached out my hand to graze her cheek, and she recoiled from my touch. My heart splintered, my throat closed, and tears spilled across my cheeks.

Her wrathful, icy-blue eyes bore into mine as the EMTs and Arbor PD swarmed onto the scene. Our gazes never strayed from each other as they tended to her and strapped her onto a gurney. But as the medics rolled her away, Celeste turned from me. Her lilting voice reverberated through the vaulted foyer.

"You brought me back to life, but not back to you. Goodbye, Evangeline Clarion."

And then she was gone. Again. And fury filled me.

Vivian. The name crashed over me as a vengeful sense of purpose fueled the fire under my skin. *She couldn't have gotten far.*

Closing my eyes, I reached out to the elements once more—to the ground over which Vivian stepped, to the air she stirred as she fled. *Tell me where she is.*

This time the elements wasted no time in replying. My eyes snapped open. I got to my feet. Gregory took my elbow, steadying me as I slipped on the wet, bloody floor. I looked out through the manor's iron doors, across the wide, snowy yard, dotted in red footsteps, and into the forest beyond.

"She doesn't know those woods like I do." I didn't recognize the hard tone of my voice as my own.

I looked over to my grief-stricken coven now being shielded from the Arbor PD by Mother Hildegard and the Sisters of Saint Francis and back to Gregory.

"I'm going to kill Vivian."

Before Gregory could argue, I hiked up my blood-soaked dress and sprinted out the door. I took off in the direction I'd seen Vivian running, where the elements led me, across the glistening lawn, toward a path I'd traveled often. I raced into the forest and skidded to a stop only yards from the tree line as I caught Vivian's scent on the air. My fists clenched, my magic straining for release. The fire under my skin flamed red hot, melting the snow around me.

From deep within the dense, white expanse knitted with gnarled limbs, Rocky descended, his magnificent, outstretched wings blending in every shade of coffee, and his appearance just as eye-opening. He landed lithely at my feet with the body of Vivian's familiar, the black raven, Reginald, clutched in his sharp, hooked beak. He laid the limp, lifeless bird at my feet and bowed.

We have been avenged. Rocky presented himself with all the reverence of Lancelot. And then his head lifted, and he trained his piercing eyes into the forest.

I heard her before I saw her. Vivian's screeches pierced the muffling of the snow-packed wood. And then the vile, naiad witch emerged, gripped tightly by Killian and Keegan O'Shae. Celeste's loyal familiar Luna clung to Vivian's face in full lioness attack mode. I watched in manic delight as the cat shredded Vivian with her teeth and claws, spraying her clothes in pin-prick gashes of blood while the two brawny, stony-faced, redheaded guards dragged her screaming toward me through the woods.

The gruesome sight that would surely mark my memories evermore overwhelmed me with glee at that moment. I clapped like a child with a new puppy.

"Oh, aren't you all brilliant." I relished in the horror.

Killian and Keegan stopped before me.

"Miss Clarion," Killian said in a solemn, polite greeting, maintaining decorum despite standing amongst a monstrous spectacle. "My brother and I were taking a smoke break out by the maintenance shed and saw her running from the big house with the cat sprinting behind her. Keegan knows these grounds as well as anyone, so we followed them. When we found them, the cat was already doing a number on her, but I figured we'd bring her to you before letting the chief do his thing. Would you like a few words before we haul out the trash?"

"I would, yes. But first, thank you, Killian, Keegan." I stepped forward and kissed the young man, and then his silent brother, on the cheek—a precarious task avoiding the maniacal cat and hysterical witch between them.

"Vivian, you vile hag, can you hear me?" When no answer followed, I flung out my hands and commanded the water in her body to freeze, just as she had done to me on Samhain.

Vivian's cries choked in her throat, and her limbs went ridged. Luna halted her attack and hissed at me but did not retreat from her position on Vivian's head.

"How does it feel? Hmm? Do you enjoy the chill?" With a wave of my hand, she thawed, only to grow hotter, to the brink of a boil. "Or do you prefer it toasty?" Another wave of my hand and her temperature regulated.

I could kill her...right now. There are so many ways. I could rip every ounce of water from her body and leave her dried carcass to rot. I could burn her alive the way Arbor had burned Adelaide. No, she doesn't deserve that kind of honor or the relief of death.

"They're not going to give a fuck what you prefer where you're going. And you're not going to manipulate anyone ever again."

I leaned down, gripped the bloody hem of my dress, and tore off a long piece of black cloth. With the blood-soaked fabric clutched tight in my fist, I raised my arms.

Trusting that the Goddess had not abandoned me, I called out, "By air and earth, by water and fire, be you bound as I desire." I tied three sets of three knots in the strip of fabric and secured the cord around her wrists.

"No!" The single word ripped from Vivian's throat as realization dawned—a binding spell.

"By three and nine, your powers I bind. Cord go round, powers be bound. Through flood and flame, tremor and gale, the knots that bind you shall not fail. So do I will it, so mote it be."

"So mote it be," Killian replied, surprising me.

"I'm forever in your debt, and your brother's too, of course. Let me know if you need anything. For now...take her away."

Killian nodded. "As you wish, Miss Clarion."

"Just Eva."

"You aren't *just* anything."

As the O'Shae brothers marched Vivian through the woods toward the manor, Luna recommenced her biting and clawing while Vivian resumed her screams. I followed slowly behind, Rocky on my shoulder, and watched as police and EMTs converged on them. They flung Luna off Vivian and set to work on her wounds. After the medics patched her up, Killian and I gave statements to the Arbor PD—carefully avoiding the last-minute resurrection, and they read Vivian her rights. Then I had the pleasure of watching Chief Harrison, dressed to the nines in a tux and tails, throw Vivian into the back of his police cruiser.

My sadistic glee faded as I took in the fullness of the chaotic scene around me. When I found our Solstice Spiral destroyed by rampaging bloody footprints, my knees weakened, and bone-deep fatigue threatened to claim me.

There is no shame in falling, Evangeline. But now is the time to rise. Breathe deeply, my dearest witch. Then let it all go, and fly with me.

Rocky and I soared above the snowcapped treetops, swept down Red Hill, caught a gale across the valley of Gothics Peak, and followed the AuSable River until a stream split off to the east. From there, it was a quick flight along the stream to the forest on the cottage grounds. We headed for the clearing. I landed in the center of Shasta's stone circle while Rocky came to rest deftly on the altar beside me. Before exhaustion could overtake me, I fashioned a large nest of moss and ferns in the wide crook of a beech tree and made what would become my bed for the next eleven nights.

Chapter Twenty

For eleven days, I haunted the forest, staying out of sight of the cottage and venturing no closer than the stream that snaked its way through the woods. That first morning, I spent hours bathing away Celeste's blood and washing my dress and high priestess robe. I scrubbed both my body and the clothing against the stream's rocky shore, staining the water red. Each morning afterward, amid a serene vigil of trees, I waded into the cleansing, icy water and allowed my tears to flow away with the current.

I craved solitude, peace, and freedom from my rage, pain, confusion and guilt, but since I couldn't leave my brain and broken heart behind, this respite in the woods was as close as I was going to get. I required the communion with Nature, with the elements, to recharge, cleanse, and purify. And I needed time for contemplation, to wrap my brain and heart around all that had transpired. I'd lost and found and lost my love again. And she blamed me for wrenching her away from the infinite possibilities of another lifetime. Celeste's murder, resurrection, and subsequent rejection left me brittle and cracked like a peanut shell crushed under foot.

What should I do next? Did I try to get her back? Or had I done irrevocable damage? What did my life look like without her? What did it looked like without any of it—the cottage, manor, gallery, Arbor? I dreamt of leaving it all behind, not to settle down somewhere new, but to explore, to travel, to seek out new possibilities, new horizons.

Despite my clear desire for privacy, every day brought a visit from concerned loved ones. Maggie and Ayo checked on me first, the morning after Yule, baring pillows and blankets and tea. I concealed myself in a nest of brambles until they left. Eris came the following day, trudging through the woods in a vain search for me as she ranted about my childish behavior. I hid in a towering pine until she, too, left. I submerged myself in the stream, crouched behind the veined roots of a fallen tree, for an hour to avoid Ethan, Luca, and Nicolae. Gregory stopped by every morning, but always while I slept, and left a basket filled with food, a thermos of coffee, bottle of wine, and a joint.

A brief note accompanied each morning's basket, but nothing more consequential than, *Can't wait for you to try the pasta salad. Let me know what you think.* He'd provided a pen so I could reply, which I did.

Five stars, I wrote, impulsively drawing a smiley face beside it.

The following day, Gregory's note read, *Glad I can still make you smile.*

Killian O'Shae was also a surreptitious visitor, one I hadn't expected. When I'd returned from bathing in the stream on my fourth day in the forest, Christmas Eve, I spied a package wrapped in plain, brown paper sitting on the altar. I ripped off the paper and found two classic novels, both lovingly worn: *Pride and Prejudice* and *The Princess Bride*.

The handwritten tag read, *Your favorite novel and mine. So you can travel until you're ready to take that first step. So you can dream until you're ready to face your nightmares. – Ever your faithful servant, Killian.*

I rolled my eyes when I read his audacious words.

"Faithful servant, indeed," I scoffed. "Silly boy. Still, it's an incredibly sweet gesture."

That silly boy just turned twenty-one, and there is more to him than meets the eye, Rocky noted.

Mother Hildegard visited on Christmas day, but I avoided her like the others. From my nest in the beech tree, I watched as the habited nun knelt at the stone altar and recited the rosary. When she finished the prayer, she pressed the crucifix to her lips, lovingly laid the beaded circlet on the altar, and departed.

Inevitably, my pain returned, and the images that flashed behind my eyes, images of blood and Celeste's cold stare, blocked out any comforting thoughts of softly spoken prayers, novels, and picnic baskets. My heart broke all over again.

Unfortunately for Arbor, that's when I took to the skies.

Like a wintry Armageddon, my grief-induced blizzard conditions pummeled Arbor for eleven days, defying conventional explanation. High winds, sleet, hail, and stinging snow ebbed and flowed with my sleep schedule and emotional tides. Awake, the storm raged; passed out from wine and weed, and my sweet oblivion offered Arbor a reprieve.

When my mother died, I never cried, and for weeks, I never spoke. I reverted into myself, into the confines of my eight-year-old witch's mind. My goddess-mother's healing touch, the potent magic on her cottage grounds, the arrival of my first familiar, and the restorative power of art and creativity saved me, pulled me out of my own head and back into the world. When Shasta and Adelaide died, I grieved deeply, but by throwing myself into the opening of the Manor Arts, the grief didn't swallow me. I indulged in distractions—my sewing and designs, playing music, interludes with Alexander, and quiet moments with Celeste—in order to fill the void of my priestess and familiar's absences.

But this time, despite the knowledge that Celeste breathed, that blood flowed in her veins, and her heart pumped in her chest, I cried. Sometimes, only a whimper, a sniffle. Other times, I wailed her name into the ether and fell into fits of incoherent rambling interspersed with wild bouts of fury. And my grief rained down on Arbor in torrents of snow and ice.

*

NEW YEAR'S EVE

"People I love get hurt, they die. I'm fucking dangerous. I'm a liability. Why the hell am I even sticking around here? I should go." My speech was slurred. I downed the last drops of the first of two bottles of champagne Gregory had left in my New Year's Eve basket. "People I love die."

"Good thing you don't love me. Guess I'm safe."

I whipped my head around, making myself dizzy. Eris leaned against the stone altar with her arms folded across her chest.

"You look like shit, by the way. I can say that, right? Since we're sisters and all."

"Get the fuck out of here," I hollered. "No one asked you to come."

"Actually, the boys did. They're worried about you. They all are." She sounded bored.

"What, and you're not?" I took her apathy as an insult.

"No, not particularly. You watched Celeste die, and then she dumped you. That seriously sucks. Now, you're in mourning. You want to drink and smoke and wallow in your pain. I get it. Do it. I couldn't care less about your blizzard. I figure you'll cry yourself out at some point. Just run a brush through your hair every now and then, would ya? You'll be fine."

"Why are you such a bitch?"

She had the gall to laugh. "I'm trying to be nice, ya big dummy." She reached out, grabbed me by the arms, and hoisted me to my feet. "Look, it's New Year's Eve. The gang's all up at the manor for the night, but I braved the bitter snow to hang out with you. Why, you ask? Because, my poor, pathetic sister, we could both use a little music therapy. I ordered us the livestream of the Phish show tonight from Madison Square Garden." She wiggled her eyebrows. "Come on, you funky bitch, let's vibrate with love and light."

A smile threatened my lips for the first time in days. My heart clenched at the memory of Shasta, who'd been known for her love of rock quotes.

"Why are you even here? You realize I kill your mother every night in my dreams?" The alcohol and weed in my system had loosened my tongue.

She closed her eyes a moment before planting her hands resolutely on her hips. "She dug her own grave."

"What about Alexander?" I grumbled. "Why aren't you spending New Year's Eve with him?"

Eris sighed and looked sheepishly at her feet. "Well, because I got dumped too, and I'm not a fan of spending New Year's Eve pining. Not that my heart's too heavy. Alexander's a good guy, but he's got a bit too much baggage for my taste." She grinned softly. "Plus, I doubt he'll leave his study tonight. He's barely left it at all this week. He's been a mess since—"

"Since Yule," I finished for her. "Yeh, me too. Alexander was right, ya know. He tried to warn me against having a big-ass Yule shindig. He hated the whole holiday season. He never explained the reason why, but it shouldn't have mattered. I should have trusted him. I should have taken his feelings into consideration. It was his fucking house, and I took it over! Well, he can have it. I never want to step foot there again."

Emphasizing my point with a wild flourish of my arm caused me to teeter over, lose my balance, and land on my ass. Thankfully, another bottle of champagne rested in the basket beside me. I grabbed it and fumbled to open the metal cage at its neck.

"How the hell do you plan on accomplishing that since you run a gallery out of his house?" Eris ripped the bottle from my hand.

I shook my head in frustration. "How can I go back there? Every day, I'd have to walk across the foyer, over the spot where she died in my arms, where her blood pooled around me, where she returned to me, and then left all over again. How can anyone expect that of me?"

"So, you're going to turn your back on the gallery? On everything you worked for? On your dream?"

"What does it matter if you get everything you ever dreamed of, but—"

"Look, I know you've lost a hell of a lot, but you're blessed to have Maggie and Ayo, the boys, and even Alexander; people who love you. And you've got a sister who's gonna be right here to help pick your ass up. My mother will be punished. So will Riddle. So, take your time to grieve, but understand, the pain will dull with time, and love will find you again." Eris offered a sympathetic smile. Her lip piercings glinted in the shafts of sunlight streaming through the trees. "If you want to honor those you've lost, you've got to live a full life. Your mom, familiar, priestess—they can't. You've gotta do it for them."

Her words struck me. She was right. Their futures had been stolen. I owed it to them to live fully.

So much easier said than done.

"Look, I'm the one who brought Celeste back. I can't believe I pulled it off, honestly," she said with an astonished shake of her head. "But it's my fault she's pissed."

"She's alive because of you," I said sharply, but my tone softened as I caught the sorrow and regret in her face. "And I will never be able to express the depth of my gratitude. Celeste may never speak to me again, but my heart can rest easy knowing she's alive in the world, thanks to you."

"I treated you like shit," Eris admitted bluntly. "I got wrapped up in my mother's vendetta and my own jealousy. I'm sorry. Women have to lift each other up. We have to support each other. We can't let men like Riddle terrorize and manipulate and use us as pawns in their power games." She took a deep breath to settle her growing fervor. "I want to... I don't know, make amends for the pain I've caused, and any role I played in your suffering. I want to be here for you. That's what sisters do, right?"

"Thank you," I murmured around the lump rising in my throat and choked back tears, shocked by her words. "Can we really livestream Phish?" I asked sheepishly. Music had the power to heal, and there were few things in the world more life-affirming than a Phish show.

Eris laughed and threw her arm around my shoulder. "Hell yeh. Gotta live while we're young, right? But we have a couple hours before show time, and I think we need to work a little magic first. What d'ya say, sis? Wanna get witchy?"

An actual smile strained my cheeks. "Why the hell not. It's New Year's Eve, right?" I gave myself a giant stretch.

"Killer." Eris wrinkled her nose in disgust, and then she pulled out a stack of clothes, sneakers, a hairbrush, and a compact mirror from a black leather bag slung across her chest, and placed it all on the altar. "But you really do need to pull yourself together first. You're a mess, woman."

"Fuck you." I laughed and then caught myself. It seemed obscene to laugh. "Give me half an hour."

"That works." She ignored my emotional summersaults. "I'll head into the cottage, setup the livestream, and rummage around for snacks. After that, I'll meet you on the lawn."

I'd spent the majority of the last eleven days skyclad, only occasionally donning my scarlet cloak. The sensation of the jeans and hoodie against my skin were both irritating and comforting, reminding me of my new sister. As I gazed into the small mirror Eris had provided and dragged the brush through my wild tangle of hair, I barely recognized the wide-eyed, fledgling witch I once was, back when my biggest concerns were the disapproving sneers and insults of my Arbor neighbors as I walked downtown to buy art supplies and fabric. Even then, I created.

The magic within me, that had coursed through my veins since birth, that had grown and flourished as I grew and flourished, first manifested as creation with an affinity for the elements. I'd known this magic all my life, but over the last six months, my powers surged. And I thanked the Goddess they did, or I wouldn't have survived the burning of Arbor. My ability to manipulate the elements, like whipping a breeze into a gale, merged with my creativity, resulting in my ability to create the elements. This alone constituted a life-altering magical shift. Yet my greatest power surge occurred at the Midsummer Litha ceremony when the Goddess consumed me in the solstice bonfire. And from that moment on, Her mystical fire lived within me. She'd made me impervious to the flames in which my neighbors would later consume me.

I'd come far in six months. Still I'd lost so much that I wasn't sure where I stood anymore. It was difficult to look forward to anything when the past held me so firmly by the throat. I'd had such victories and desperate losses, made mistakes, and learned lessons. With all my time spent looking backward, the path ahead eluded me. I remained the director of the Manor Arts, but my break with Alexander and Celeste, and the horrific events at the manor, tainted what had once been my greatest dream fulfilled. My own gallery, the place where I felt more powerful than a queen, now only filled me with pain. My working relationship with Alexander had been rocky even when we dated. The idea of sitting through a board meeting with him at this point, especially as he seemed to be battling his own demons, did not interest me in the slightest. And how could I work in a place, day in and day out, that Celeste had been so integral in building? Her fingerprints painted the walls. Her blood stained the floors. All of it would be a constant, agonizing reminder of her absence in my life.

I can't live like that. I'm not Maggie.

My thoughts turned to my goddess-mother. Her ability to endure all she had and yet remain empathetic and hopeful, astounded me. But Ayo balanced Maggie's empathy with clear-eyed pragmatism. Maggie and Ayo shared an electrifying bond. Where Maggie and my mother had been soul mates, I suspected Ayo may be Maggie's twin flame, if such a thing truly existed. I made a mental note to look into it. I knew they'd be happy together at the cottage.

And I'll be a third wheel, not to mention a magnet for trouble.

Even the thought of subjecting myself to the minutia and tedium of an Arbor PD investigation enflamed the fire within me. The specter of all those I'd put behind bars loomed large in Arbor; not only Vivian and Riddle, but Reverend and Gladys Cudlow, their son Stuart, former mayor Doreen Crandall, and her son Jay. My former BFF Gwendolyn Reed, AKA Bunny, escaped jail time and moved down to Jersey after testifying against the Crandalls and Cudlows. But I didn't trust that she wouldn't pull something if she came back to town. I'd drawn enough danger to Maggie's doorstep. That had to stop.

I cleaned up the clearing that had been my home since Yule, making sure to leave the sacred spot as I found it, and made my way out of the woods. As I reached the fallen oak, Rocky swooped down and landed on the leaning trunk. He held an envelope in his mouth and dropped it into my outstretched hand.

It is from Mia. Her viper delivered it this afternoon. Without elaborating or waiting for instruction, he took off again into the snowy skies.

My curiosity piqued, I eagerly opened the envelope, and my hands shook as I withdrew three first class plane tickets to London.

Why London? And why three tickets? Are Maggie and Ayo coming too? Regardless of the answers to those and the million other questions swirling around my mind, Mia's gift confirmed my instincts had been correct about travelling. Except, I had no intention of limiting myself to a visit to London. I'd made up my mind. I had a lifetime of exploration ahead of me. A shiver of excitement shot up my spine. For the first time since losing Celeste, I felt genuinely excited for the future.

"I'm leaving," I confided to Eris as I trudged out to the middle of the snowy lawn to work our magic. The sun and a fair bit of blue sky peaked out between thinning clouds for the first time in eleven days. "I'm selling the gallery to Alexander, and I'm taking off. Traveling."

"Bullshit, you are not. Traveling where?" Eris squinted at me like a judgmental owl.

"I don't know yet," I answered coyly, not wanting to divulge my destination until I'd firmed up my plans. "Maybe I'll head down to the city like Rocky's been bugging me to do for years. Maybe I'll go further.

New Orleans? I have my passport. I could travel to Europe. Maybe I'll visit Mia in Italy. Maybe Ireland. Maybe I'll investigate my mother's ancestral line. The point is, my time in Arbor is over." I lifted a determined chin. "It's safer for everyone."

"What about Maggie and Ayo? You're going to leave them here all alone?" Eris challenged incredulously.

"They'll be fine, definitely safer without all the trouble I attract. And they're far from helpless. Ayo is no one to trifle with. Plus, they've got the boys, of course, and Alexander. And I'm sure they've beefed up security measures."

Eris gawked at me for a beat before responding. "You're really going to do this? Leave the cottage? Leave your home? Sell the gallery, the thing you've dreamt about all your life, and just...take off?"

I stood in the center of the cottage lawn upon the spot where Shasta bled to death from a gunshot wound to the head, fired by a best friend who'd betrayed me. I peered down the driveway where two privileged, powerful men had attacked me. I looked over to the fallen oak tree where Riddle killed my mother. I turned to the stream whose water Riddle and Vivian used as a weapon against us. I closed my eyes to hide from the horrors surrounding me, yet within my mind's eye, Celeste's blood pooled over the marble floor of the Morgan Manor entryway, beside the ever-blazing alabaster hearth and the sweeping marble staircase, under the bloodred ruby chandelier. Once a fantasy, the manor's garish opulence sickened me as much as the blood itself. A large lump formed in my throat, and my eyes watered. I fought to compose myself.

"I can't stay at the manor, and I can't stay here. I have to go."

Eris studied my face, and after some deliberation, she nodded, resigned. "When are you leaving?"

"Soon."

She took a deep breath and then shook her head as a wide grin spread across her face. "You crazy fucking witch. Okay, let's start with a spell for good fortune and safe travels, and move on from there?"

I nodded in agreement. "Let's get witchy."

With my mother's grimoire between us, Eris and I worked magic, casting spells and charms for new beginnings and safe journeys, to honor grief, and to heal mental, spiritual, and magical wounds. The ease with which we worked together demonstrated not only a deep, shared affinity for elemental magic, but a level of comfort unusual for so brief an acquaintance. A connection. A bond. Thanks to Eris, my soul began to feel some semblance of relief.

When we returned to the comforting warmth of the cottage, we hunkered down on the sofa with mugs of cocoa, an epic snack spread, and the Phish livestream. Over the course of the night, we danced and laughed and cried, and then we danced and laughed some more, allowing the music to move us like a current. Our arms and lives entwined, we counted down to the new year. Eris and I bonded in a way I'd never experienced. More than friends. More like family. Like sisters.

*

NEW YEAR'S DAY

I awoke early the next morning after only a few hours' sleep and set to work straight away. Even these few hours of REM in the comfort of my own bed offered a clarity I hadn't felt in over a week. I knew what I had to do. First, I shot Maggie a text, letting her know I'd returned from my self-imposed exile in the forest and had spent the night at the cottage with Eris. And I told her there were things I needed to say in person. She replied that she and Ayo would return from the manor in an hour.

Just enough time to get things in order.

After checking my finances and documentation, I set up reservations and wrote a series of letters—including an agonizing missive expressing my love and saying goodbye to Celeste, and one to each of the boys. After sending these off with Rocky to deliver, I packed as quickly and quietly as I could so as not to wake Eris who'd passed out on the sofa.

I walked outside into a light, crisp breeze and blue sky, pulled out my phone, and called Alexander. I paced while we spoke, as if channeling the man I would always love. But his acceptance of my decision eased my mind and heart as much as Eris's had.

"You sound like you've got your mind made up, and I know you too well to argue when you're set on something. I'll wire the funds to your account and have the lawyers email you the paperwork. You can sign electronically from wherever you land. The coven and manor staff will look after the gallery. And I promise to keep an eye on...well, everything and everybody, damn it." His gruff voice broke. "Stay safe, straghetta mia."

I could hear his sad smile through the phone.

"I love you too."

Maggie and Ayo arrived as I finished my call. I wasted no time filling them in on my plan. Once more, I was stunned by their approval, though I began to think it wasn't so surprising after all. These were my friends, my family, my coven, and they wanted what was best for me.

"I'm so proud of you," Maggie gushed.

"Really? Why? How?" I asked, flummoxed.

"First of all, you're fully clothed and quite literally out of the woods." She laughed lightly. "And I'm proud because you're taking a major and necessary step. You need to leave. Arbor is no place for you right now. There's too much sorrow here. So, go. Go, my sweet girl, my strong, capable woman. Live your life. Have adventures. Maybe you'll even find love again. But live."

Tears of gratitude flowed down my cheeks.

"Thank you, Maggie." I embraced her and held on tight. "Thank you both for everything." I let go and stepped back.

"You two wouldn't care to join me on the first leg of my trip, would you?" I asked, thinking of the two extra first-class plane tickets burning a hole in my pocket.

"Oh no," Ayo piped up. Stepping behind Maggie, she wrapped her arms around her waist and rested her chin on her shoulder. "We are home, precisely where we are meant to be."

The lovers nuzzled each other a moment or two more than was comfortable.

"I've done my travelling. I'm home now," Maggie said finally with a contentment that squeezed my heart. "This is your time for adventure, my sweet girl."

"There's one more thing," I trudged ahead before my courage could waiver. I knew Maggie never wanted the position of high priestess of the coven. Adelaide had known this too, which is why she passed the broom to me instead. But I needed Maggie to step up now. "Magdalena Maramma, I relinquish the honor of high priestess of the Witches of Arbor and bestow this trust to you. Do you accept it?"

Her gray eyes widened in surprise, then shot to Ayo and back to me before narrowing.

"If the Goddess wills it, so mote it be."

A swirling gale of snow whipped around us before settling into a triquetra symbol of the maiden, mother, and crone at our feet.

The three of us gaped down at the Goddess's message in awe.

"So mote it be," I replied.

Maggie, Ayo, and I headed into the cottage to gather up the last of the necessities for my trip. Once Rocky and I were packed, I woke a comatose Eris who glared up at me from her nest of throw blankets on the sofa.

"What the fuck, bitch, how'd you wake up looking so bright eyed and bushy tailed?" She grumbled and rubbed her eyes, smearing mascara across her face.

I chuckled lightly. "I'm leaving. I wanted to say goodbye before I headed out. And I wanted to thank you."

"Where the fuck do you think you're going?" she asked, her voice and brain still thick with sleep.

"I'll send word when I get settled in."

I could see Eris's mind clearing, and the realization of my words cutting through the fog of sleep. When she sprang to her feet, I knew she'd gotten there.

"Now? You're going *now*? I mean, you said soon, but I didn't think you meant, ya know, like, *soon*. Fuck, okay." She eyeballed Maggie and Ayo before giving me a shrug. "I think you're fucking crazy, but I kinda love you for it."

We embraced and chatted while Eris helped me pack up snacks for the road and settle Rocky begrudgingly into his travelling case. My sister gave me one last hug, and I hopped into the driver's seat of my truck.

"We'll make Arbor beautiful... and kind again. I promise," she said. "You'll see when you get back. Without my mom and Riddle's influence,

Arbor's descent has stopped. Their spells are broken. People are waking to the realization that the future is their own responsibility, but we shape it together. And I think, with a bit of planning and courage, Arbor will rise."

"Arbor is ascending, you might say." I smiled brightly. "Well, I'm glad I'm leaving the town in such capable hands. I'll see ya around, sis."

Standing beside the violet-stained front door, Maggie, Ayo, and Eris waved goodbye as Rocky and I set off down the long, forest-enclosed, river rock driveway.

"Goodbye Arbor," I said, the words a somber lament from weary lips.

As I neared the end of the darkened driveway where the woods ended and the morning sun washed down from the heavens, two hulking figures leaned on the arbor that marked the entrance of the cottage property. Large packs rested on the men's backs, and more stuffed duffle bags piled at their feet. From such a distance, I couldn't make out their faces. The shorter of the two men was by no means a slight figure with broad shoulders and a straight back, but it was his shock of red hair that sent a jolt of recognition through me. My attention shot to the other man. With his neatly clipped, dirty-blond head raised into the brilliance of the sun as if in worship, I couldn't make out the details of his cleanly shaven face.

Although confined to his cage on the passenger seat beside me, Rocky saw easily out of the windows. At the sight of the men, Rocky squawked out the hawk equivalent of a laugh.

Yes, of course! How did I not see? Why did I not think of this? Rocky mused.

Are you going to share your revelation with the class?

But Rocky didn't need to elaborate. I pulled up beside the men, rolled down the window, and a cloud of pot smoke engulfed me. When I found stormy blue eyes with flecks of silver, all became clear.

"Hey, Priestess. Got room for two more?" my old friend with a slick new look asked in his deep rumble.

"Won't they miss you guys at the manor?" I stifled a fit of giggles, barely able to contain my astonishment.

"We covered our shifts," he said, his smile even brighter without the fuzzy beard to hide it.

The sweet redhead beside him wrung a ballcap in his hands before leveling me with steel-gray eyes. "I'd like to call in that favor now... Eva."

"Get in, Druid," I said as I scooted Rocky's cage closer to me on the seat. "And Killian, hop in the back."

"As you wish," Killian said brightly, and Gregory winked.

The guys hoisted their bags into the flatbed of the truck, and Killian flung himself in afterward, slapping the truck's roof, eager for our adventure. Gregory jogged around the front of the truck and climbed in.

"Nice haircut, by the way," I teased as he settled in and put on his seat belt.

"Gotta go low-maintenance when you're on the move."

"I assumed dreads were easy to care for."

"It's a common misconception."

I pulled onto the road that led away from Arbor and sighed. "At least I know I won't starve, and I won't be in any pain." I glanced over at my old friend. "Thanks for coming."

"I told you, I'll always have your back. Even when you're about to do something stupid."

"Fuck you."

"Or not to—"

"Shut up and let me drive." I gripped the steering wheel and squeezed my lips shut to suppress a grin.

"Yes, Priestess."

About J.L. Brown

Author of the Witches of Arbor series, J.L. Brown is a writer of fantasy and lover of magic and nature. She requires copious amounts of coffee and can be bribed with wine and chocolate. When not writing, J.L. enjoys time at home in her gritty, small town in South Jersey, painting, playing chess, reading romances, listening to Phish and Suburban Sensi, watching Philly sports, raging about the politics of the day, and making killer meatballs and ziti for her rock star husband and two incredible sons.

Email
1authorjlbrown@gmail.com

Facebook
@AuthorJLBrown

Twitter
@AuthorJLBrown

Website
www.jlbrownbooks.com

Other NineStar books by this author

The Witches of Arbor Series
The Burning of Arbor
Arbor Ascending (Coming Soon)

Also from NineStar Press

To Summon Nightmares by J.K. Pendragon

Three years ago, Cohen Brandwein was a teenage media-darling, a popular author and internet celebrity. But ever since he came out as trans, public opinion has been less than golden, and these days he wants nothing more than to escape the big city and find somewhere quiet to work on his next book.

When he inherits an old house in the Irish countryside, Cohen sees it as a perfect opportunity to get away from it all. What he doesn't count on is becoming embroiled in a paranormal murder mystery, and falling for the primary suspect, a handsome but mysterious self-proclaimed witch, whose reality makes Cohen's fantasy books seem like child's play...

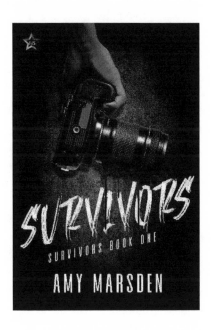

Survivors by Amy Marsden

It's Jennifer's 24th birthday and she planned to spend it having fun with her friends. Instead, she ends up running for her life through the dark streets of London.

Her world is torn apart by a new disease, the likes of which have never been seen before. The government's decision to conceal its deadly nature exacerbates the panic, and in all the confusion Jennifer is bitten by an infected person.

That's it, right? Her life over.

Wrong.

Immune to the virus's ravaging effects, Jennifer finds herself with a small group of survivors. Together they must fight to stay alive long enough for a cure to be found. Humanity won't be beaten so easily.

But madness looms large, and safety seems forever out of reach.

Connect with NineStar Press

www.ninestarpress.com

www.facebook.com/ninestarpress

www.facebook.com/groups/NineStarNiche

www.twitter.com/ninestarpress

www.instagram.com/ninestarpress

Made in the USA
Middletown, DE
09 September 2021